ADVANCE PRAISE FOR A DROP IN THE OCEAN

"Mira's story is a coming-of-age journey told through a harrowing labyrinth of mental illness, institutionalization, and plain-old hormonal adolescence in a manner that reveals a heroine who is incredibly kind, loving, fantastically romantic, and unavoidably angsty, just like the novel's author, Léa Taranto. Able to draw deeply upon her own life experience, Taranto is a new voice to watch out for. I can't wait to see what she writes next."
—JJ Lee, author of *The Measure of a Man: The Story of a Father, a Son, and a Suit*

"Léa Taranto is a bright new spark on the YA scene."
—Susin Nielsen, author of *No Fixed Address*

"A brave, beautiful novel that will speak to teens everywhere who struggle with mental health challenges. Mira is a compelling character, privy to a darkness that adults don't always see but so many teens will immediately recognize. She's also creative, romantic, funny, and kind, the literary BFF you never knew you were waiting for. This book is a gem."
—Annabel Lyon, author of *Consent*

A DROP IN THE OCEAN

A DROP IN THE OCEAN

LÉA TARANTO

A NOVEL

ARSENAL PULP PRESS
VANCOUVER

A DROP IN THE OCEAN
Copyright © 2025 by Léa Taranto

All rights reserved. No part of this book may be reproduced in any part by any means—graphic, electronic, or mechanical—without the prior written permission of the publisher, except by a reviewer, who may use brief excerpts in a review, or in the case of photocopying in Canada, a licence from Access Copyright.

ARSENAL PULP PRESS
Suite 202 – 211 East Georgia St.
Vancouver, BC V6A 1Z6
Canada
arsenalpulp.com

The publisher gratefully acknowledges the support of the Canada Council for the Arts and the British Columbia Arts Council for its publishing program and the Government of Canada and the Government of British Columbia (through the Book Publishing Tax Credit Program) for its publishing activities.

Arsenal Pulp Press acknowledges the xʷməθkʷəy̓əm (Musqueam), Sḵwx̱wú7mesh (Squamish), and səlilwətaɬ (Tsleil-Waututh) Nations, custodians of the traditional, ancestral, and unceded territories where our office is located. We pay respect to their histories, traditions, and continuous living cultures and commit to accountability, respectful relations, and friendship.

This is a work of fiction. Any resemblance of characters to persons either living or deceased is purely coincidental.

Cover and text design by Jazmin Welch
Cover art by Jazmin Welch
Edited by Catharine Chen
Proofread by Alison Strobel

Printed and bound in Canada

Library and Archives Canada Cataloguing in Publication:
Title: A drop in the ocean / Léa Taranto.
Names: Taranto, Léa, author.
Identifiers: Canadiana (print) 20240445813 | Canadiana (ebook) 20240445899 | ISBN 9781551529813 (softcover) | ISBN 9781551529820 (EPUB)
Subjects: LCGFT: Novels.
Classification: LCC PS8639.A685 D76 2025 | DDC jC813/.6—dc23

For everyone who has lived, is living, or will live in places like the Residency, especially Shaun Baggaley (1991–2021)

Shaun, I will always love you—
these words are how you live on.

For Mom, my favourite superhero

For Poh Poh, Gung Gung, Peter, Leslie, and Dr. Mathias

A Note on Romanization

The Cantonese terms in this work are transliterations based on my limited knowledge as a fourth-generation Chinese Canadian who has only learned bits of her heritage language. Rather than using a standardized romanization system or including tone numbers, family and friends helped me decide on English homophones for these words and phrases, like "poh poh," which I grew up using.

Content Warning

This work includes scenes with self-harm compulsions and wounds, suicidal ideation, disordered eating (excluding weight data), underage substance use, religious trauma, intramuscular sedation, grief, and property damage. There are also some references to racism, and conversations where characters reckon with ableist, antisemitic, and queerphobic language.

Dear reader,

I don't know your story, but I know you've got one and I know it matters. You matter. As does your well-being. That's why I wrote the above warning about potentially triggering content in *this* story, which centres institutionalized experiences of neurodivergence. Or, as Mira would say, the fucked up lives of kids in psych care.

The world and our own heads can be scary, brutal places. Books have always been my refuge. What I value most about them, though, is their ability to expand our empathy with the flip of a page. To do so, their content might challenge and inform us. But hopefully in a way that inspires us to better care for, rather than harm, others and ourselves. If you feel unsafe while reading this book, please put it down. Whether that means closing it halfway through to take a break or not reading past this paragraph, do what you must to put your mental health first. That's one of the main points of Mira's story.

Warmly yours, always,
Léa

CHAPTER ONE

The administrative building's air con makes my bare arms erupt with goosebumps as I sign paperwork for the certification and transfer to Ward 2. This one needs initials next to each reason justifying my exile to a secure ward: noncompliance, severe self-harm, aggression. My new shrink, Dr. Grant, claims it's a safety measure, not a punishment. Liar. As I pass him the form to check, Nurse Margaret comes in.

"Mira, dear, you're going to need to phone your mother and tell her to get you some new clothes."

My brow furrows. Something's up—I haven't been anyone's "dear" since my intake to Ward 1 over a month ago. "What's wrong with the clothes I've got?"

"Contamination," Margaret says, staring at my forehead before meeting my eyes. She goes on about how blood's a biohazard. "We had to throw out your other belongings too."

"What the fuck!"

I don't say any more, just run out the office building's front door to the parking lot. When my fingers stop touching the door, I stop breathing. For forty-five seconds my world narrows down to the ritual. Sprinting, airlessness, and the shortening distance between me and the dumpster where the collected trash of the Residency Adolescent Treatment Centre lives. Once I touch it, I can breathe. Completing the ritual *right* consumes me. Holds my actual ~~helplessness~~ hurt at bay. I'm so focused that I don't notice Dr. Grant until he's in my way. He reaches me after I'm heaving in my second lungful of garbage air. A rotten-things sweetness mixed with the rankness of sour milk

13

and mouldy broccoli. I'm about to climb into the bin when again, he blocks my way, gesturing for me to move back. His loafers have less grip than my sneakers and he slips, but after a few scrambles he makes it. He pulls himself over the edge, lands cushioned by giant black plastic bags full of food waste and worse. Jesus, I can't watch. When he crawls out, he's lugging a garbage bag with him. A dried banana peel flops off its side as he lands. He sets it down and even unties the damn knot before handing it over.

Kindness is weird that way, so sharp sometimes that it pierces you. It's the nicest thing a shrink has ever done for me. Eyes swimming, I snatch the bag from him, blink away tears to focus on the task ahead. Throw T-shirts, jeans, books, even Stella Bear on the ground until I get to what matters most. Its front and back cover are intact. Phew. A quick flip reveals no missing pages either. Double phew. My journal's with me, it's whole.

♦

Standard Ward 2 procedure = no family visits for five weeks, staying on unit with constant monitoring for twenty-four hours, hourly room checks, and no sharps like scissors, metal cutlery, or even pens. Ward 2 is bigger than Ward 1 and way more prisony. In case the giant chain-link fence didn't clue you in. Unlike Wards 1 and 3, Ward 2's under lockdown to make it as hard as possible for kids to go AWOL. The steel-bolted front door opens to the dining room, where a long-ass banquet table has benches, not chairs, on either side. In Ward 1 chairs are easy to throw—these heavy benches, way harder. Every window here has steel mesh, not just the one in the Quiet Room. And instead of having a stand, the TV in the living room is mounted in a corner between the ceiling and the wall, up too high to smash.

A Drop in the Ocean

At least my bedroom on the girls' wing is a clone of the one I had before. Same plastic mattress and bed frame built into the floor, a dinky two-drawer dresser on the opposite wall.

Okay, that smell. Fucking disgusting. Everything I own reeks so badly of garbage that even breathing through my mouth, I dry heave. Time to do laundry.

Laundry room usage is always monitored in case patients try to kill themselves by guzzling detergent. I tell the mental health tech, Janelle, that eating bleach isn't really my MO, and she tells me that I'll be at a higher clearance level, going on day passes, before I know it. Good, because I'll need to hit up Winners and buy myself a whole new wardrobe if this third wash doesn't do the trick. Deep-clean setting, hot water, and a cup of baking soda along with the detergent because Mom always does that for Lawrence's gym gear.

First, I transfer the warm, wet mass of my clothes and a considerably less-fluffy Stella Bear to the front-loading dryer. Add five scented fabric softener sheets to combat what's left of the smell. Next, I get out the shoebox grave where I buried my journal for two hours in baking soda and even more fabric softener sheets. Time for a sniff test. Janelle clears a bunch of mismatched socks on top of the washer to do a drum roll as I go in for a whiff. Under the fresh laundry scent there's some residual gross, but it's barely there compared to the stench from before.

"It'll do," I say, and she cheers.

Then I spritz the front and back covers three times each with Febreze for good measure.

I'm folding the last of my now-dry socks, all seven pairs, when there's a crisp knock, knock, knock on my door. It opens to Janelle, whose long beaded cornrows click as she tosses her head to peek in on me. She says the other patients are back from rec and that art therapy will be on unit this time so I don't have to miss out just because I'm under newbie lockdown. Her bubbly voice makes it sound like a good thing—art therapy, meeting other kids, lucky me.

Not.

Not when I'm why they have to come back early. It might be a small reason to resent someone—oh, this new chick's here so we can't make art in the room where all the supplies actually are—but all it takes is one bad first impression to end up a pariah. Especially when your rituals don't make you a clean freak so much as a *freak* freak. Everybody thinks OCD means that I spend hours vacuuming, that I'm some sort of germaphobe. But I'm not. It's so much weirder and sadder and more fucked up than that.

"Is it okay if I finish sorting out my stuff?" I ask, to buy some time.

"Sure," Janelle says. "You get settled in first. We'll meet you at the dining room table."

I end up refolding all my clothes just so my trembling hands have something to do. Give myself a pep talk: *You're a human being, Mira, a human freaking being. They can only bug you if you let them. Or they might actually like you. Get up, get it over with.*

There's at least eight hours until my big nighttime rituals, what Elsie, the nurse I hate most, calls my "self-harm histrionics." That's all the time I have to bond deeply enough with these kids that they decide to like me in spite of the banging and the blood. Or at least to respect me enough to mind their own business. When I first came to Ward 1, both Chelsea and Kate seemed to like me. Then I did my rituals. Chelsea, basically Regina George but meaner and prettier, went from promising to teach me some Pussycat Dolls choreo to full-blown shunning mode. In her worst moods she'd egg me on, which killed the last of my crush on her. Kate just got scared. She'd still talk to me, even shared some legends from her Squamish Nation since we both like myths, but any raised voice or sudden movement on my part and she'd peace right out. This is where BC Youth Court sends you if you're not criminally responsible, so the kids here are probably worse. Less *Mean Girls* and more *Prison Break*.

Fifteen minutes of that precious first impression time are gone by the time I make my Ward 2 debut in the dining room. Everyone looks up as I inch toward the table. They stare at me as I stare at my lap while taking a seat on the bench. Janelle introduces me to my fellow inmates and fills me in on the art prompt: draw an image of your ideal future self.

Across from me is Jorge, whose face is obscured by a ball cap—its big bubble letters literally spell out "BALLER"—slouching over a pile of pencil crayons. He uses a gold one to draw a chain, much thicker than the one he's wearing, on a much more muscled, bare-chested version of himself at a nightclub.

"Sup?" he says, nodding to me.

The guy next to him, Franco, barely lifts his buzzed head before turning back to his stick-figure drawing of himself snowboarding. He's in shorts and a T-shirt, and his large limbs are hairier than anything I've ever seen—we're talking full-on Chewbacca fur. Before I can wonder whether he doesn't like me or he's always this quiet, I'm being introduced to Dinah. Her picture is a felt-pen oceanscape with a mermaid holding a merbaby in her arms. Her hooded eyes widen with urgency as she announces, "The baby is alive." I can tell that the mermother is meant to be her and the merbaby her kid, because they both have tightly coiled curls and a sprinkling of freckles.

The last person I meet is Taryn. She bites her lip, the same metallic black as her eyeliner and the elastics on her braces, in concentration. Her neon-pink hair clashes in a good way. Beneath the netting of her mesh shrug and on either side of her neck are ginormous scars. The fresher ones stand out as red welts. Cutting is pretty common—me and Kate both have scars—but this is next-level shit. If Taryn told people she was attacked by a cougar, they'd believe her. My hands fly to my bangs, making sure their chunky layers hide my forehead. Thank God Taryn's too absorbed in her drawing to notice me ogling her arms. She's sketching herself flying a jumbo jet with a bunch of Grammys and records in the other seats.

"So, Taryn, would you rather be a singer who can fly a plane or a pilot who can sing?" I ask. Yup, my small talk's pretty pathetic.

"Don't call me that," she says. "Only old people call me that. My name's Sweets."

"Hey, I'm not that old." Janelle pretends to be hurt. "Am I?"

"No, you're not," I cut in.

Sweets says, "Don't waste your time kissing Janelle's ass, she's one of the nice ones. If you're gonna butter anyone up, go for Vikas. Dude's a stickler but his Benz is his baby. Compliment the custom rims and he's your man."

Dirt on the staff? Yes, please! I start to sketch the table that future Mira will be sitting at. The way Sweets has a stack of platinum records next to her, there'll be stacks of books in my award-winning fantasy novel series, the Archetype Chronicles, that I'm signing for fans. At the foot of the table, I'll draw the half-wolf stray I plan on rescuing from

A Drop in the Ocean   19

a shelter. "What about the therapists?" I ask, trying to sound casual. "What's that Dr. Grant guy like?"

Sweets purses her lips. She's adding clouds visible through the plane windows. "Meh. I have Dr. Park. She changes my meds around way too much. I don't work with Dr. Grant, but his giant-ass smile is the last thing I wanna see when I'm in a depressive episode. Once I looked up tragic statistics to tell him so he'd be sad like the rest of us. Shit like, twenty-two thousand kids die every day because of poverty."

"Damn." My soul slumps the way my shoulders do. Now I'm sad. "Did it work, or is he kind of insufferable?"

"It worked." After a small, awkward silence she adds, "Don't get me wrong, he seems like a nice guy. It's just anybody who's that happy for that long must be high or hiding something."

Jorge leans toward us. "I could see that dude being all about yayo, the way he's so perky and shit. Next time I'm in his office I'll do some snooping." He motions to Franco. "Yo, Hostageman, want in on this?"

Franco shakes his head no.

Sweets snorts. "Good call."

"What's that supposed to mean?" Jorge straightens up from his slouch.

"It meeaans," she says, drawing out the word, "if the doc catches you going through his stuff, and he will, the only thing you'll find is a one-way trip to juvie. Forget partying at the club, your sad ass'll be stuck trying to get a buzz from toilet wine."

Jorge grimaces, tsking. "That was too far. You know how scary my court order is, how quickly they'll ship me back. Avocado." After Jorge utters the name of this fruit (avocado's a fruit, right?), everyone at the table looks at Sweets expectantly.

A second later she cracks, throwing her hands up in surrender. "Okay, you're right, I was outta line." Reaching over, she pats Jorge on the shoulder. "Sorry." Next, she turns to me. "Avocado is my safe word. Anytime we're talking and I get too cunty, just say 'avocado' and I'll dial the sarcasm down."

Weird. "Oh, okay, cool."

◆

So I always jump after I go to the bathroom. Out in public that's nine times, and I can't touch anything, which is super hard when you're in a tiny stall. At what used to be home, or at whatever psych facility I'm living at, those nine times become twenty-one plus nine reps of the twenty-first jump because twenty-one doesn't feel *right* unless I count it like this: twenty-one, twenty-one, twenty-one … twenty-one, twenty-one, twenty-one … twenty-one, twenty-one, twenty-one. Yeah, yeah, I know I'm weird. Now everyone else does too. The staff have read my chart, they know my compulsions, but the kids have no clue until they hear my sneakers slamming down on the painted cement. By jump seven, Dinah and Sweets are pounding on the door, wondering if I'm okay.

"I'm fine, I'm fine!" I yell from the other side.

"Good, then can you stop now?" Sweets asks. "It's really annoying."

I can't. I'm only on jump fifteen. "Soon."

Dinah yells, "For fuck's sake!"

By the time I'm done, somebody has the stereo cranked up playing Akon. I wait for one full song before cracking open the door. Good, the hallway is clear. My heart pounds harder against my rib cage than the bass vibrating through the walls as I dash to my room.

At dinnertime I come out of hiding. The hairs on my arms and the back of my neck prick up from everybody's eyeballs fixed on me. They're all waiting for me to tweak more. I sit on my hands to stop them from shaking. Then I launch into the speech I've been rehearsing for the past few hours.

EXPLAINING OCD TO OTHER PATIENTS

Like a mosquito bite—the obsession. For example: "If I don't exercise enough I am lazy and slothful which make me worthless" is the bite, and it itches like a motherfucker. The scratching is the compulsion, the behaviour that makes the itch feel better for a bit, for example: jumping as a form of exercise. But then the scratching reinforces the itch, and as soon as I stop, the only way to numb the itch is to scratch again. The more I scratch, the harder it itches, which makes me scratch even more, which intensifies the itch, so I scratch, scratch, scratchscratchscratch until that's all I do for hours every day. Dr. Grant calls it a positive feedback loop.

◆

The stain on the bricks is still there, dried blood a ketchup-coloured splat with drips tendrilling to the floor. Creating it went surprisingly well. Excruciating—duh—but uninterrupted. I stayed as quiet as I could, did it all in my room so no one saw. The only person who might've heard anything is Sweets because our rooms share a wall. Good thing the cement absorbs the sound of my thuds. What sucked is that I was slow, so by bang seventy-eight, panic overflowed from my aching lungs, spilling out my throat in whimpers and shrieks. Those she heard.

She's complaining about them now to Nurse Vikas at the nurses' station med dispensing counter while he monitors Franco. From behind the half-open door where I'm crouched, I watch Franco down his pills one by one, each time opening his mouth wide with a silent "ahhh" so Vikas can put a check mark next to it: yes, safely swallowed.

Sweets goes on: "I don't know shit about OCD, other than that each obsession is like an itchy mosquito bite or whatever, but I know pain when I hear it. Those weird animal noises she made were hella freaky. There's no way I'm getting shut-eye tonight unless I take my special chill pill."

Hella freaky, sounds about right. I make sure Vikas and Sweets can't see me as they talk PRN dosage (that's fancy Latin for meds you take as needed). Kids can't access this room unless they get let in for medical reasons, like I've been. The ice pack freezing my fingers soothes my forehead, which throbs beneath a slathering of Polysporin and a dressing of medical tape and gauze. I put the ice pack down on the chair I'm supposed to be sitting on, then peel the gauze away. It's not just the tape that's sticky. The cotton fibres are soaked with blood beginning to clot. Separating the two reopens the scab. Fuck. I reattach the bandages tighter, gritting my teeth against the ooze of the open wound and the pain of the tighter pressure. What I really want is to cocoon myself in bed, lose consciousness for eight hours until the morning, when I have to make a new stain all over again. I can't though. Can't risk being seen like this by the other kids. Sweets is taking her meds while Franco … shit. Franco is walking toward the treatment room I'm in.

Vikas raises his voice. "Hey Franco, what do you want from there?" I'd like to think he's looking out for me. But really, he's worried about patients making a mad dash for the meds.

"Water. I'm thirsty." Those are the first three words I've heard from Franco all day.

"Me too," says Sweets. "You never fill the cups enough."

There's barely time to glare at the giant Canadian Springs dispenser before I have to dash out of my position or risk getting squished by the door.

Franco sees me first, entering with an empty paper cup in each hand. His expression stays flat as he takes in the wreckage of my face. He blinks, then beelines for the dispenser. Sweets is a step behind him. Her eyes widen as she focuses on my forehead, which I try to cover with my hands.

"Why are you—"

I don't let her finish, just say, "Avocado."

CHAPTER TWO

*J*esus Christ, it's all day long, echoing through the hallways and my ear holes on blast from the unit stereo. The soulful hip-hop moan of Akon's "Locked Up" is our Ward 2 anthem. Pillows and earplugs do fuck all at this point, the song's already burrowed deep in my brain. I almost shriek when I find myself humming it.

"You hate it too?" whispers Sweets, looking up at me with her pierced eyebrow raised. She looks up at everyone because she's so short. We're at the far end of the girls' wing, waiting for Dinah to finish up in the girls' bathroom. Sweets clutches hair dye and a basket of other shower stuff. I'm just waiting to take a shit. We're out of earshot of the Akon lovers but still keep our voices low, aware we are talking treason.

I hunch down a little toward her, taking care to not stare at the giant vertical scars on her arms. She ignores my forehead. It's a mutual respect thing. "How can anyone like a song that overplayed?"

"Right?" As she smiles, she does a goofy, exaggerated eye roll.

Bonding over shared hatred? I'll take it. "I bet it's what Jorge or Franco lost their virginity to or something." That's pretty snarky, an offering.

She smirks. "Yeah, in a threesome with Jessica Alba at homecoming, after scoring the winning touchdown."

◆

Memory loss. Brain damage. A deformed forehead. It will get worse unless I stop. We all know I can't since I won't risk Mom's life. So now I'm not just journal writing for other people to know what it's really

A Drop in the Ocean   25

like—my "truth," or whatever, as a singular drop in the ocean that is teens in psychiatric care—I'm writing to keep a record of whatever the fuck that truth is. At least my No Sharps status got removed. Goodbye felt markers that bleed all over my journal pages, hello black ballpoint pen with the clicky top.

♦

We hear "Locked Up" faintly through the door from our huddle outside on the basketball court. Sometimes kids have court orders that forbid them from ever going off unit, and this basketball court area is the closest they get to leaving.

"Akon wasn't even really a convict," Jorge complains. He's only fourteen but hardened from two months that he said felt like forever in Prince George Youth Custody. He takes a puff of his hand-rolled cigarette and rolls his light-brown eyes, pupils dilated. His exhale infuses the air with the skunky tang of weed. Ha, I knew it was a joint. The lengths and collabs kids go to so they can sneak in contraband are ridiculous but ingenious.

Standing on the other side of the chain-link fence are the kids from Wards 1 and 3 badass enough to risk rule breaking. "You got the stuff?" Jorge asks them.

Chelsea looks behind and to her left, where two MHTs are chatting about shift change. They're close enough to see us without seeing any details. She shoves a gel-nailed hand into her bra and fishes out a baggie of dehydrated bud more brown than green. Bras are one of the standard hiding spots—staff can't feel you up or strip search you every time you go outside, that's sexual harassment. To actually enforce the rule of no underage smoking, staff would have to restrain and confiscate cigarettes from almost every patient multiple times a day. They'll only bother with that for hard drugs. Like the time a Ward 1 kid hid Special K tabs in his socks. Sandals all day every day after that 'til he discharged. Weed is a soft drug. If you're disgustingly obvious with it you'll get caught, otherwise ... meh.

Chelsea threads the baggie through a link of the fence and gives it to Franco to roll. He takes it silently. Then Jorge mashes his face through a higher fence link so his chapped lips reach out the other side. Chelsea goes on her tippytoes to meet his mouth with hers. As more time passes, her dark-pink lip gloss smears over the lower half of his face. I pause from wondering how soft her lips are to roll my eyes. They flick down to my chest, still pancake flat, even though it's been two and half years since my feeding tube days. Yeah, yeah, I was anorexic, but even back then OCD stole the show. Boys don't like girls who don't eat. And according to Sweets, girls don't like girls who don't eat either. Despite internet Rule 34, it goes without saying that no one likes girls with gross, oozing foreheads.

CHAPTER THREE

*T*HERAPY GOALS:

1) Keep banging head in room so nobody sees me or the mess after. (Bonus, if I get too worked up, staff have to open door to reach me.)

2) Hold breath between Ward 2 to school and then to the gym, instead of Ward 2 all the way to the gym.

3) Use stepper machine not treadmill during rec—too tempting to get obsessive with treadmill speed.

That's my list of stuff to work on to make my rituals smaller, or easier, at least. Everyone in group therapy had to do a goals list. Just like how everyone has a mandatory turn to tell their life story before they can get off unit and have group outing privileges. Last week Franco went and actually talked in fullish sentences. Turns out the reason people call him Hostageman is because he held his whole class hostage with his uncle's hunting rifle. He's serving his last ten months here instead of juvie for good behavior. That's it—good behavior or not, I'm never arguing against him about watching *Beavis and Butt-Head* again.

Today the life storytelling falls to me.

I shift in my seat, an office chair that's been rolled from the nurses' station to the centre of the day room. It's the biggest room on unit, enclosed with Plexiglas so everyone can see what's going on but can't hear you. That's why shift changes, group therapy, and patient phone calls take place here. The size and partial privacy make it ideal for sharing confidential information with both small and large audiences.

My audience is sprawled on the sofas and loveseats against every wall, talking among themselves before my big sob story. At least I don't

27

have to stand up the way you're expected to when giving speeches at school. If I had to stand up, I'd be trembling. One of many bad things that makes this different from school is that I have no cue cards. Nothing I've memorized and rehearsed a million times to hide behind. Nope, this is all ad-freaking-libbed, which is supposed to make it more authentic or something.

MHT Alan, who has OCD like me (except his is mild and contamination based) clears his throat. The chatter reverberating off the Plexiglas dies down as he announces that group therapy's officially begun, so let's stay silent and respectful while Mira tells us about her life.

Everyone expects me to reveal childhood traumas that explain away my rituals. They wait for a narrative that gives them some sort of sense. News flash, I'm waiting for it too. The magical insight that helps me see beyond my fucked-up-ness to a future without it. They'll all have to settle for what I've got.

"I was born in France, which is where my dad lives, but I don't have much contact with him. Instead my mom and stepdad, Lawrence, raised me here, in Burnaby. My old hood is the Heights." That's pretty good, right? Doesn't get much more beginning than birth. The prologue to my book series starts with the moment the protagonist, Evvy, is born in Avalon, as the elven city is stormed by orcs.

Jorge's brow furrows. "What do you mean, 'old'?"

I flush. Two sentences in and I've already screwed up. "I haven't lived there for like, three years, but I'm getting to that." I flash him a grimace meant to be a smile. "Um, anyway, my childhood was decent. No siblings. I spent most of my time with adults like my poh poh—she's my hard-core Christian grandma on my mom's side. I loved school, reading, Jesus, and my family even more. That's why I was ready to die the summer I turned eleven. I was stuck in Children's

A Drop in the Ocean 29

Hospital ICU for months while the doctors tried to figure out the illness behind all my fainting, puking, and failing organs. I felt at peace, holy, even. I knew I was going to heaven because I'd done everything I could to be a good person. Then the doctors did a biopsy that showed I had Wilson's disease, a fancy way of saying I was allergic to copper. As long as I paid strict attention to everything I ate and took lots of meds, I'd be fine. As if. My whole life until then, I'd proven I was good enough by what I did: working hard at school and even harder at making friends, obeying my elders, and writing every day so I could get published in my teens, like Amelia Atwater-Rhodes and Christopher Paolini."

Nobody nods their head in recognition the way I hoped they would. I shrug and continue.

"I was nice, pushed myself, tried 110 percent at whatever I did, to earn my worth. But then it stopped working. I couldn't be good enough at things that cancelled each other out. Getting straight *A*'s meant everyone hated me and said I was screwing my teacher. The list of what made me good enough got shorter and shorter, until I started hating me too. And if I couldn't prove my worth through what I did, then did I even deserve to live? Why did I get to leave the hospital alive when so many other sick kids didn't? I decided if I could be good enough at fitness, lose some weight, maybe things would get better.

"It wasn't hard at first, especially since I was already monitoring my diet because of the disease. I cut the fat off meat and skipped lunch, drank Diet Coke instead of regular Coke, drank water instead of eating snacks. That's how my ED started. It's what motivated me to jog or do jumping jacks for an hour when I'd rather have been reading in bed. But then an hour of cardio wasn't enough, so I'd do two hours.

But then if I stopped to go to the bathroom or if I stumbled, I'd have to start over again. That was how my OCD started.

"Maybe if I'd worked really hard at resisting my compulsions when they were new, things would be different. Like maybe I'd be in Burnaby North and never even know this place existed. But when the compulsions started, with that feeling of doom, of do this one thing or else, I didn't fight them. They gave me back my good enough. Whether it was two hours that turned to four that turned to eight hours of non-stop jumping jacks, or flicking a light switch on and off, or making sure not to step on cracks while walking. I knew they didn't make sense. Things weren't *right* before I avoided that part of the floor, so why would they be *right* now that I was hobbling around it? But if I narrowed the whole world down to these tasks, these stupid, random, ridiculous tasks, and did them perfectly, then at least I could be good enough again for however long they took.

"They started taking more and more time and getting more and more complicated to do perfectly. Until there was no space left for school, or friends, or being a good person, or even my family. And when I failed at them I obviously had to punish myself. Then punishing myself became a ritual too."

"Hold up."

I jolt, startled by the fact that there are people in front of me and one of them's talking.

"Sorry"—Dinah gives me a sympathetic wince—"but what's the difference between a ritual and a compulsion?"

And now I'm back to flushing. *Stupid, Mira, stupid.* I keep interchanging terms, of course they're confused.

"Nothing, they mean the same thing," Alan says. The only other person here who gets it. Who has at least a version of this same

A Drop in the Ocean 31

fucked-up-ness in his own life. "Where were you living back then? Were you still at home, with symptoms that bad?"

Home hasn't been home for years, but bitching about that when some kids have been in the foster care system since birth or in jail would just be pathetic. Instead, I try to remember all the places I've been. "First, I went to Children's Hospital, bounced around different wards like CAPE, C1, and EDIS. Then I went to this place in Arizona called Remuda Ranch, an intensive Christian-based eating disorders facility. All I did there was gain weight and a whole bunch more obsessions after reading Dante's *Inferno*."

"Dante's what-no?" Jorge asks.

"It's a book about this Italian guy from the Middle Ages who gets a tour of hell. *Inferno* means fire, as in the fires of eternal damnation. Anyway, being surrounded by God stuff got me thinking about that question from all those years ago, whether it was a mistake that I was still alive. Since I *was* alive and God doesn't make mistakes, it must be because he wanted me to suffer, to pay for being so despicable and worthless. The book talks about the ninth circle of hell, where the worst sinners are banished. Like Mordred, who killed his own father, King Arthur."

"You mean the fairy-tale dude with all the knights and the Round Table?" This time it's Sweets who interrupts me.

"Yup."

"He got iced by his son?" Jorge grimaces and sucks his teeth. "Damn, that's twisted."

"Right? That's why it stuck in my head. Like no matter what I did, it wouldn't go away. When I went to the neuropsych hospital at UCLA, the book came with me. I couldn't stop thinking about hell, about how King Arthur still loved his son, even though he was betrayed and murdered by him. Just like how my mom still loved me. There's no one I love more than her, so there must be a parallel. The more I tried not to think about it, the more the obsessive thoughts came back: paranoia that something horrible would happen to Mom because of me, images of a man with a vicious red aura—Mordred—and knowing I somehow was him. Or had been. In my past life I killed my father, so in this life, where I love my mother more than anyone, God will punish me by killing her. Unless I prove I'm sorry. I have to show him I'm making myself suffer, or else—"

"So that's why you bang your head?" Jorge cuts me off with the most obvious of questions. His face is scrunched up, a scowling portrait of zits, pity, and disgust.

Pity for me, really? When he and Franco are the ones who went to juvie? It's not like I have rotating delusions the way Dinah does, cradling an imaginary dead baby or telling people I'm a mermaid who was raped by a shark. Or Sweets-sized gashes all over my arms and legs.

"Well, duh. When my doctor at UCLA said there were lots of head bangers in the seventies, I thought she meant like me. Not like, people who listen to heavy metal music."

Jorge snorts, and he's not the only one. Dinah's shoulders shake as she giggles. Sweets tries and fails to stifle her laughter. Even Franco joins in. My trembling hardens into tension, leaving me rigid. I want to snap, "Shut up!" the way I do whenever people slam the door or make loud banging noises. Instead, I ask, "Can I be done now?"

Alan nods.

Relief slackens my muscles. I don't so much get up as ooze out of my seat, eager to escape to my bedroom.

"Wait a sec," Sweets says.

"What?"

A Drop in the Ocean   33

"How about now? Do you still believe all that past life shit? Do you still think you're worthless?"

"I don't think," I say. "I know."

"If we're talking past lives, isn't it way more likely that you were some anonymous peasant person or like, a centipede or a blade of grass? Why do you think you'd be someone famous?"

"So maybe there's not much proof. But I'm not about to risk my mother's life on the 0.01 percent chance that I'm wrong. If that means doing punishment rituals the rest of my life, then that's what I'll do."

"Have they gotten better? Or do you … I dunno, at least feel okay about them these days?" Jorge's disgust from before has been replaced with a soft frown.

It takes me a sec to find the right words. Within that time my fingernails find their way to my mouth. "Am I good enough at them now?" I let out a bleak chuckle. "Barely. Do I hate them? Yes. But ever since I realized the truth about my past life, I know what'll happen if I don't do them. Even if I can barely force myself to say it because of how crazy it sounds, I still know." I look from face to puzzled face. How can I make it click? What pop culture reference? And then I have it, the perfect one. "It's like that bit in *Fellowship of the Ring* where Gandalf says that Gollum hates and loves the ring as he hates and loves himself. That's me and rituals."

Nobody speaks. The only sound is me chomping the rind off my index fingernail.

Then Jorge says, "Lord of the Rings, are you for real? That's for dorks."

♦

Besides the fact that it's empty, the first thing I notice about Dr. Grant's office is the chairs. There are two. His, behind a large desk, and one for a patient, across from it. They're both cushiony office recliners with arms, wheels, and the ability to adjust for height. Pretty standard stuff. What's weird about them is their sameness. Lots of times there is a discrepancy between a therapist's chair and their patients' chairs. Some make the hierarchy on-the-nose obvious, with them in an expensive leather executive chair and you in a cheap metal thing with no cush for your tush. Or them in something functional while there's a full-on array of plush seating options for you to faint on. Your craziness either makes you a subordinate or it makes you frail. Chairs of equal comfiness—now that's new.

What I notice next are the photos. On his desk is a wedding photo of him and his wife, and on the filing cabinet, one of her leaning against him as they both hold a tiny newborn.

The third is the sound of footsteps and Dr. Grant's brusque voice as he says, "Of course I remember my promise, if this was any other board meeting I'd skip it. Don't you think I know ..." And then there's the whine of the door being opened. Dr. Grant's olive-green eyes widen as he notices me waving at him. "I've got to go."

"You okay?" I ask him.

He sets his cellphone on the desk and sits down. "That's what I'm here to find out about you." He leans in toward me and rubs his hands together in a getting down to business way. "Now, I haven't read your file yet, because I want you to tell me about yourself first, everything you think is important, in your own words. I might ask some nosy follow-up questions, but that's okay, because you get to ask me nosy questions back."

A Drop in the Ocean 35

God, this guy is perkier than a cheerleader on E. He's like a dude doctor version of Mary Poppins with an almost unibrow. "I just did my life story in group therapy, guess I could rehash it for you."

"Mira Durand's origin story, I'm all for it."

"Origin story—that makes me sound like a comic book hero or villain or something."

"Hero or villain—those are pretty all or nothing, don't you think? I tend to find real life happens in the middle."

I grin lopsidedly. "All or nothing's sort of my thing." Then I give him the same speech that I gave everyone yesterday morning, except there are no interruptions or laughing. Since we have a whole hour to kill, I go into more detail. Explain how controlling things were at Remuda, where even bathroom usage was monitored. How every meal or snack was a competition. Along with how out of control things were at UCLA, where a doctor forced me to walk on cracks in the court-yard, thrusting me into *wrongness* as part of this nightmare branch of cognitive behavioural therapy called exposure therapy. Just talking about it makes my stomach heave, bile lurching up my throat. Out of everything the health care system's done to me "for my own good," that was the worst. No wonder UCLA was where my head banging started.

Dr. Grant keeps quiet while I explain the obsessions behind my head banging. As I catch him up to the present, I decide what the hell and tell him my Gollum analogy. How I hate and love rituals the way Gollum hates and loves the One Ring.

He leans in even closer. "So out of all the characters from Middle-earth and Aman, do you relate most to Gollum?"

"Hmmmm." I take a moment to pan through the rest of the entire population of Arda. "Yes."

"I'm talking the *Silmarillion* cast too, including Valar or Maiar or even Melkor."

I straighten up from my slouch on the chair. Aman. Valar. Maiar. Mentioning the lesser-known prequel to the Lord of the Rings trilogy? Dr. Grant's a nerd!

"Still Gollum, because even though I'm a bad person, I'm not boss-level evil. More pathetic henchman than primary antagonist, just like Gollum."

Mr. Cheerful has nothing to say to that. Good. But as time passes, my satisfaction shrivels. To make up for it, I ask, "So, you like Tolkien, huh? Are you into fantasy stuff?"

Dr. Grant's eyes crease as he beams. "Equal parts D&D dork and sci-fi superfan."

Sci-fi too? He's even nerdier than me. "I love fantasy. Sci-fi's kind of new territory for me, other than the Star Wars movies and *Dune*."

"*Dune* the book or *Dune* the eighties flick?"

"The movie," I admit, looking down. It's common nerd knowledge that the book is almost always better than the movie or show.

"Oh, you've gotta read the book."

"Meh." I shrug. Maybe one day. "I'm more of a Malazan Book of the Fallen, Earthsea Cycle girl. Myths are cool too, like retellings."

"If you're into retellings then check out *The Bloody Chamber and Other Stories.*"

"What's that about?"

"You'll have to read it to find out."

I roll my eyes. "How did I know you'd say that?"

"What about you, got any book recs for me?"

"There's an epic fantasy series called the Archetype Chronicles. The main character is Evvy, a half elf who's a goddess but doesn't know it.

A Drop in the Ocean   37

Her soul magic connects her with any being's soul so she can feel their life as if it were her own. She has to hide it, though, even wants to get rid of it, because there's this prophecy that it's going to make her lose in the ultimate battle between good and evil. The person she's supposed to lose to is a demon guy she falls in love with who eats pain."

"Sounds fascinating. What's the first book called?"

I have just enough self-control to hold back a fist pump. "Book one's *The Fates Unleashed*, but you won't be able to find it. I have to finish writing it first."

"You better. I'm invested in this thing. And if you follow it through to publication, I want an advance copy."

Woot, woot, my first hypothetical sale! "Well, someone's gotta test read it first before I even think about sending it out."

"Deal." He holds out his hand for me to shake, squeezing my limp fingers tight. "Is that what you want to do in the future, be a fantasy novelist?"

"Hopefully ASAP. For a little while I wanted to be a missionary, and then a doctor before I realized I wasn't good enough at math. What made you decide to be a shri—I mean a psychiatrist?"

Dr. Grant explains how he was studying corporate management at Stanford—yes, Stanford—when he got a call from home about his younger brother's death. In a tsunami of grief, he quit work, dropped out, and moved back to BC to be with his parents. They were the ones who convinced him to seek grief counselling, which was where he discovered the miracle of mindfulness. After six months of practising mindfulness, he went back to school to become a psychiatrist so he could pay it forward. And on that note, would I be interested in us doing mindfulness together?

What even is mindfulness? "Uh, I've never heard of it before but, sure, why not?"

"Awesome!" He's back to an ear-to-ear smile. "We'll start with a guided meditation next session. If it's helpful, you can continue with DBT mindfulness instead of group therapy."

"Great?" Meditation—isn't that what monks do?

"The other thing I was wondering about is the treatment that traditionally works best on OCD, certain forms of cognitive behavioural therapy."

I tense. DBT, dialectical behaviour therapy, means talking about my past and learning emotional tolerance skills like whatever this mindfulness is. But other forms of CBT mean doing *wrongness*. Being forced to fuck up my rituals, like stepping on cracks at UCLA. Worst of all, stopping me from head banging, which means God will kill Mom. Panic pounds my heart against my chest, flooding me with fight-or-flight energy as I wait for what Dr. Grant says next. I use some of it up by clenching my fists and jaw 'til they ache. Don't say it, don't say it.

"Even though you've had some bad experiences with it in the past, we'd make sure everything done here was by your consent."

Shit, he's going to say it. I thought that he was different, that he respected and got me. Part of me still hopes he does.

"So how would you feel about trying some exposures?"

And pop goes my hope, bursting like a soap bubble along with my ability to be here. To share air with this shrink I can't trust.

I get up, glare at him, and leave.

CHAPTER FOUR

*R*eal world, here I come! Dr. Grant promised not to push me to do exposures and gave me clearance to go on outings, so I've kind of forgiven him. And now, I'm walking past an actual goddamn traffic light a whole block away from the Residency grounds. The sun is shining and the car exhaust from traffic on Willingdon has never smelled sweeter. My first-ever pass in the real world is a snack stroll to the Shell gas station. It's about five minutes' walking distance from Ward 2. Sweets and Jorge amble a few paces behind me while Alan and I lead the way. I'm a half step ahead of him because OCD says I have to walk fastest or I'm lazy. We chat about our families.

He's an only child like me and his family name is Lung, the same as Poh Poh's, so maybe our ancestors lived in the same village. When his OCD first showed up, his baak baak, paternal uncle, gave him lots of medicinal soups to try and ease his anxiety. I tell him about Poh Poh's mustard seed paste for super bad congestion. That gets Jorge into the convo because his tía worked at a botánica and knows all sorts of herbal remedies. Alan slows down so Jorge and Sweets can catch up to us.

For almost a whole minute I'm absorbed in Jorge's story about wormwood tea being better than Pepto-Bismol unless you drink too much of it. We all stroll at a relaxed pace. Jorge's talking so loud that I don't hear the pounding of sneakers on pavement until the fucking jogger's right next to me, panting as he passes us. A thunderclap of *wrong* strikes through me, charging my heart. I almost lose balance as I lunge into a sprint. It takes me a few seconds to overtake the jogger,

39

who balks in surprise at my glare. As soon as I'm three steps ahead of him, I swerve around and sprint back to the gang.

"What's that about?" Jorge asks, waiting a beat for me to explain myself. When I don't, he continues talking, and I ignore Sweets's concerned glance. The only reason Alan didn't run after me is because he's read about my rituals in my chart. To smooth things out between me and my fellow inmates, I buy Sweets some Skittles and Jorge a corn dog when we hit up Shell. What I really want is Diet Coke, but all they have is gross, syrupy Coke Zero. I grab a Fresca instead. On the way back there's two times when I have to run ahead of joggers. Both times I return to the group with my head hung, waiting for the ridicule. It never comes. Snacks as bribes work great.

◆

FUCK, FUCK, *FUCK*. I mean, I know God hates me and I have to punish myself or he'll kill Mom, but why this? At least Riverview, where I'd have been the exception to the adults-only rule, doesn't have *her*. Bitch Douche Bag, a.k.a. Nurse Elsie, is back from her vacation. Ward 2 is her main unit and now she's my primary, the main staff member I'm supposed to work with, since Janelle was only filling in for her. Bitch Douche Bag hands me my plastic portion cup of meds. Bitch Douche Bag gets me to open my mouth and go "ahhh" for what could be thirty seconds or an eternity. Bitch Douche Bag sits next to me every meal she's on shift to verify that I've eaten enough shitty cafeteria food. Bitch Douche Bag makes me clean up the messes on the walls from my rituals.

I gave Elsie the name Bitch Douche Bag back in Ward 1. My ex-shrink and the program over there knew fuck all about OCD and thought that enough negative reinforcement would get me to stop

A Drop in the Ocean 41

performing compulsions. Whenever staff caught me head banging, they'd knock me out as a "safety measure." For the umpteenth time, my jeans had been pulled down, one MHT's body weight pressed against my arms while another one sat on my legs. Elsie flicked the needle, and before jamming it into my ass and shooting the sedatives into my right butt cheek, she just *had* to comment on how badly I needed a shower. Because obviously being restrained and helpless, ass exposed, wasn't humiliating enough.

◆

The warm water and Vim mixture in the bucket sloshes, thudding with satisfying violence when I set it down. My red Rorschach-blot stain has started to dry after all the time it took Bitch Douche Bag to bandage my head. I press my index finger against the vertical puddle, sticky tacky. Next, I inhale its coppery musk. A different kind of helplessness washes over me as I swab the wall clean. A shadow opposite to the literally breathless, uncontrolled mess I'd been when making the stain. It is excruciating to generate enough hate, rage, and frothing conviction to fuel my head banging. The soothing catharsis of *right* only comes after I'm at full squelch. *Squelch* being the sound my reopened wound makes with each repeated smack. Full squelch happens when the scab has been pulverized and my raw skin feels every sharp, porous edge of the brick's surface. Excruciating. But at least then the squelch noise gets richer, heavier.

Now here I am with a sponge, scrubbing in circles that decimate any record of my sacrifice. Mom's not grateful, even though I'm saving her life. Like everyone else, she thinks what's *wrong* is me doing these rituals in the first place. I use paper towels to dry everything. Through my dampened, less sensitive fingertips, the sharp crevices of the bricks are barely noticeable. Only the smell lingers, raw meat under lemon fresh.

Bitch Douche Bag still isn't happy. She's come to whine about how using paper towels is wasteful, I should let the bricks air dry. The roll of paper towels now wedged under her certainly smelly armpit. She sets them down in the kitchen on our way to the girls' bathroom. Once inside, she watches with grim triumph as I dump the bucket of bloody water down the shower tub.

We join everyone else in the living room. The only free spaces on any of the furniture are couch seats next to each other. Great. A rerun of basketball is on and I just can't bring myself to care. There's fuck all to do in my room but sleep, whereas everyone here is enthralled by Kobe Bryant's fadeaway. Sweets, who finds sports equally boring, is away on a home visit. My forehead pounds. It's a dull ache about a tenth of how bad the pain gets during my worst post–head bang migraines. Closing my eyes helps. The freedom of having this ritual done is so relaxing I nod off.

When I open my eyes again, Bitch Douche Bag is hunched over a thick book. A young hero holds a glowing sword on its cover. The magical illustration is like her blowing a puff of literary nicotine into my face. My stash of books is all read, and Mom can't visit yet to bring me new ones. I'm hard-core jonesing for chapters of adventure. A summary, at least. What's happening that's got her so enthralled? Finding out requires willingly interacting with the woman who's warranted the rudest nickname I can think of. She makes everything so much worse. How can I even talk to her? Wouldn't that be like admitting she's a human being with possibly good taste in books? Hell no. I must be staring too much, because she speaks up.

"It's the fourth book in the Belgariad series by David Eddings."

A Drop in the Ocean 43

"O-kay." What do I do? Do I acknowledge her back? With words? "Uh, ummm ..."

"I'll lend you the first one, I have it at home." Her face is buried between the pages, about three-quarters through. Phew, because there's no way I'm doing eye contact.

"Thanks." I mean, what choice do I have? If I turn her down or don't say thank you, then I'm the Bitch Douche Bag.

♦

Sometimes, after the brutal catharsis of full squelch, even moments after, during the bandaging, there is a pulse. A firecracker throbbing in my frontal cortex, my brain cells exploding as they die. Whether this is from the banging or the breath holding, I'm not sure. Probably both. My evil ex-therapist from UCLA just might be right—maybe I am some sort of masochist who likes/needs pain. Not this throb though, which I dread. I'm not in control of it the way I am with other self-harm stuff. Nor is it cleansing, like the sweet sting of alcohol swabbed on with every dressing. It makes thinking or moving impossible. I'll lie down or sit with my head cradled in my hands, waiting for it to fade, hoping that when it does, I'll still remember math and what day it is, that we're in the year 2006.

The pulse wub, wub, wubs, hammering through my skull, blurring my vision. I can't tell if my rubbing the sponge around the wall is actually cleaning the last of the stain or just spreading it in circles. When I clutch it for support, my hand slips against the wet, soapy surface.

"Fucking hell," I snap, as I stumble to regain my balance.

"Oh, you're not there yet." Elsie walks toward me with rubber gloves on and an extra roll of paper towels tucked under her arm. "But you're heading that way. Literally. Your head is one virus away from rotting off your neck."

I'm hurting too much to think of some snappy comeback. Each wub is still a blow, although lessened, more a punch than a hammer strike. I just tell her "Thanks" as she helps me rinse where I've scrubbed and wipe it dry.

I start to gather the cleaning supplies when she says, "Leave that stuff for now. I need to show you something."

She leads me to the nurses' station and motions for me to come beyond the forbidden threshold, pointing at the computer. She clicks on Internet Explorer and types "flesh-eating disease" into Google. "You don't seem too concerned about brain damage or memory loss from concussions, but take a look at these." The Images page goes on forever. Endless pictures of rotting zombie skin sloughing off in places where fat, tissue, and nerves are exposed. She scrolls down until she finds one with what's left of a face, double-clicks to enlarge it. My brain pain throbs on the backburner of my awareness as acid and panic burn up my throat. Next, Elsie reads out loud the health link entry describing necrotizing fasciitis. Raising her voice for the bits about how "necrotizing fasciitis kills about one in four people infected with it." And that "death can occur within twelve to twenty-four hours."

Screw losing my memory. This thing is a skin-melting death sentence.

But it's so rare. The horrifying picture's a bajillion degrees removed from my own circumstances. Yes, it happens, of course it does. Yes, I see that it has eaten this person's face, as if a giant hand just scooped it up out of existence. No, it won't happen to me.

CHAPTER FIVE

*F*irst day of school, woot, woot! While there was some sort of schooling at the other psych wards, it was only ever teachers coming to units or a schoolroom. Here, at the Residency, there is an entire building separate from the rec building dedicated to educating us delinquents. Kids from every unit—dangerous, long-term Ward 2; docile, long-term Ward 1; and short-term Ward 3—have classes together. There's an art room with every supply under the sun, a woodworking room with constant banging noises that I will avoid, a math and science room where Sweets is, and an English and social studies room, which I'm in right now.

The teacher, Donna, is a gorgeous, smiley redhead who smells like patchouli and the sixties. Once I'm done exploring she wants me to write an essay on my goals for grade ten English. The first thing I do is check the rotating bookshelf, give it a gentle, reverent spin. My knees pop as I crouch down to take in the titles. A few of the books I've read, like the *Tao Te Ching* and *The Giver* and obviously the Harry Potters. Others I recognize, like a collection of poems by Rumi. Cool. Donna's classroom has two long tables pulled together at the corner in an L shape. A desk near the door has an ancient computer, where Chelsea plays SkiFree, and the only other desk is equipped with an even ancienter tiny TV with headphones. If Donna will let me use that computer during recess, I can type chapter five of *The Fates Unleashed* on the word processor and email myself the pages as backup.

I make my way to one of the long tables, where lined loose-leaf paper and a newish HB pencil wait for me. Goals for grade ten English, hmm. The first and last year of real school that I went to was grade

45

eight, which I didn't even finish. I first knew I wanted to be a writer at age four. My handwriting is tidier than my printing, so I start the introductory paragraph with a calligraphy capital *A*, for: "As an aspiring writer who wishes to make words her bread and butter." I don't get into the fact that it wouldn't be butter, it would be the tiniest knife scrape of margarine on rye. I don't go into my illnesses either, because why would I? Writing is one of the only things about myself that hasn't changed. One of the only things I'm ~~proud~~ not ashamed of. It's something that just is. My voice, my words—I let them pour out.

When I unhunch from my writing trance, there's someone sitting next to me. A big blond guy I've never seen before. He's reading this giant book called *The Gulag Archipelago* by Aleksandr Can't-Pronounce-His-Last-Name. He lifts his head up, and his frown reverses into a small smile, one that reaches his blue-grey eyes, the kind I'd always yearned for as a young girl infatuated with Barbie and Disney princesses. And his eyelashes—I want those even more. Damn, it isn't fair when guys have long lashes they'll never appreciate.

"Looks like an intense read," I say.

"Yup," he replies, "it's blowing my mind. This dude spent eight years in Russian labour camps where everyone worked or starved to death."

"Holy shit, guess we're lucky to be here, huh?"

"Guess so. I just got to Ward 1 a few days ago. Name's Nick. What about you?"

"I'm Mira, from Ward 2."

"The hard-core ward?" Nick's lips purse in a low whistle. "So you must be a real troublemaker, then?"

A Drop in the Ocean 47

Heat floods my cheeks, and I squirm a little in my seat. "Nawww, it's not like that. Once you get used to the whole lockdown thing, Ward 2's all right."

What I don't say is that I actually like it better there, since no one gets weirded out by my rituals the way other kids do. The way he probably would.

"Well, Mira from Ward 2, it's nice to meet you." Nick holds out his hand, squeezes mine when I offer it with a firm, friendly clasp. His hand is warm.

◆

It's no use. ARGH. Unless I'm super freaked out, I only ever bang my head inside Ward 2. I'm not ashamed (okay, maybe a little)—mostly I just want privacy. For everybody not to look at me with fear widening their eyes or disgust narrowing them, or with pity oozing through their smile. But school and rec activities mean that every unit's been meeting up every few hours, which means lots of talking. One or maybe all of my wardmates must've blabbed about how weird I look giving myself brain damage, so the whole Residency is in on what I thought was a one-time kind of joke.

"You know, Mira, you're special." Tony is a jock-bro bully from Ward 3. Him, his buddies, and Chelsea (who is cheating on Jorge with him) are already stifling giggles.

"Shut up." The force of my clenched hands bends new wrinkles in Elsie's worn paperback copy of *Queen of Sorcery*. The book is a shield, because if Tony saw my red-faced glare, he'd know he was winning.

"Special with a capital *R*." Through their laughter, I remind myself that this is shit talking lite. Wannabe gangster types like Tony think slurs give them street cred. I've heard worse, and he's using his words, not his hands, to fuck with me. Really, I shouldn't be complaining. In fact, my "retarded," gross, oozing head has probably protected me from more than the occasional grope or blow.

When I tell Sweets about it later, she says I need to own it, that no one makes up rhymes with *kike* and *dyke* at her anymore because she gives zero fucks when they do. We practise saying awful shit to one another while keeping our faces still. A Bohnes CD screams about demon friends in the background. I end up saying "avocado" three or four times, and she even uses it once on me. For the most part, though, her face stays blank. The whole time, she looks me in the eye and barely blinks. I get pretty good at freezing my expression, but she can still tell that I'm clenching my jaw.

"If you have to clench something," she says, "clench your toes, cuz your fists are a total giveaway."

◆

I hit a level of exposure therapy after the billionth time I'm called retarded. A deadening to distress chemicals firing in my brain, which is the exact technique Dr. Grant wants to use on my OCD. When the joke is sprung my way a few days later, at recess, I can even breathlessly mime laughing along. It's on its last legs, kids around the table chuckling more out of habit than amusement. One of them doesn't.

"C'mon, Tone, we all know what's really special here is your fungal toenail infection," Nick says. The kids next to Tony edge away from him, and the others snap to attention. "Promise me"—Nick clasps his big hands like he's praying—"that you'll never, ever take your socks off again. 'Kay, bro?" I chortle a little, still grimacing, because my roided out imagination can't help picturing Tony's gross toes.

A Drop in the Ocean 49

Chelsea jerks out of his lap. "What the fuck's wrong with your toenails? Why'd you never tell me about them?"

Just like that, I'm out of the burn zone. My grimace inverts as I let myself exhale.

Nick and I are out on the Ward 1 porch for his post-dinner smoke break. Everyone else, including Alan on outdoor monitor duty, has left to watch *South Park* or play COD on the PS2. It's just us, sitting on the bench with a person-sized space in between.

"Thanks for, you know, sticking it to Tony."

"Don't worry about it, that guy's such a douche. If he wasn't ragging on you, it would be me or someone else." Smoke curls out his nostrils instead of his mouth. It's what he always does when the nurses mourn his new bad habit. "I'm not smoking, I'm a dragon, see?" Now he's doing it to make me smile.

Since the sun has set, it's getting cold, and I don't have cigarettes to puff on for warmth. I rub my hands together, tuck them into my pockets to delay the freezing process. "Yeah, that's kind of his thing, I guess. Unless he wants to fuck you, he's gonna badmouth you."

"Can't say I like his taste in women."

"But Chelsea's everyone's definition of hot, mine included."

"Oh? Well, I'm not into that whole Barbie look. I like girls with dark hair better."

My heart starts thumping. I can feel my pulse throb all the way through my cold-ass fingers. They reach, without me telling them to, toward my messy dark-brown curls. Heat rushes to my head and kisses my cheeks pink. "Dark hair, eh?"

"Yup."

As I digest this, my nerves thrum. Adrenalin shoots through me as if I've been on the stepper machine for half an hour. Why didn't I put on makeup today? Why won't my legs stop jiggling? Is he looking at me? He better not be looking at me, because I can't bear looking at him. I stare down at my quivering lap while my voice goes all croaky, asking, "Is there anyone in particular that you, like, uhhh, have a thing for?" I force my gaze up in time to see Nick lick his lips.

"There's a few girls that are cute ..."

Thump, thump, thump goes my heart. Breathing is suddenly this complicated thing I have to think about doing. Speaking, even more so. "Oh, okay. Uhh, anyone I know?"

"Yeah, Kate. She's on my unit. You've met before, right?"

Womp-womp. My heart trips over itself. I look at the ground so my face won't betray me. "Kate?" Of course it's Kate. "Good ol' Kate." God, why can't I stop saying her damn name? I crush Nick's fallen cigarette butt with my shoe. "Yup, I know her. Quiet, draws in the traditional style passed down from her auntie, loves snakes."

"She's saving up to get a pet cobra. Pretty badass."

Talking about snakes, about anything at all instead of Kate? Hell yes. "My cousin has some kind of viper ..." And with that I tell him about Janis, whose pet snake is part of her burlesque act and who moved to Hollywood to become a star. He tells me about his hippie parents who built their house by hand and his shy but hilarious little sis, Emma. He lives in this tiny island town where deer eat your plants, bears shit on your lawn, and there's only one traffic light. The wackiness of our families is too absurd for me to sustain my disappointment. But it's even darker out now, meaning chilly has become freezing.

"Hey, you're shivering." Nick says. Not sure why he's surprised.

A Drop in the Ocean

"Oh, you think that's bad? Check this out." I take the now-frozen back of my left hand and place it on his cheek. This is the first time we've touched since we shook hands. The contact gives me goosebumps that have nothing to do with cold. A grin pops my dimples out when I see his eyebrows go up in shock.

"Whoa, your hand is like ice." He fake shudders, grabs my hand in both of his. "Let me warm it up."

Through the cold, I notice how rough and workworn his palms are compared to mine, probably from all those construction jobs he did with his dad. "What about my right hand?"

"I'll do that next."

CHAPTER SIX

*E*very morning of the whole eight or whatever months I was at Remuda Ranch, Mom sent over a fax. The one thing I looked forward to when I woke up was seeing the elegant loops and swirls of her handwriting. When she visited me at UCLA, I hid my head banging from her by wearing a denim hat over my swollen beluga forehead. There are no airplanes to board between us now. She's about fifteen minutes away by car. Fuck, if I ever grew the balls to go AWOL, I could walk home. Except it hasn't been home for a while. That's why she and I aren't driving there right now on our first official family pass. In Wanda the silver Honda, we cruise up Willingdon from Canada Way to north of Brentwood. Instead of listening to music, we talk. I tell her about Nick and starting school while she fills me in on neighbourhood gossip. We vroom up the slope of Capitol Hill, almost to the top. The whole afternoon stretches out before us, just like all of Burnaby sprawled below.

How can I begin to describe Mom? Words don't do her justice. Thinking of her fills me to bursting with love and shame. Sometimes she doesn't seem real, more goddess or fairy-tale queen than a living, breathing person. She slows down and backs into a spot shaded by an alder tree.

"Perfect parking, perfect parent," I say, holding my hand out for a high-five.

"Mira, don't put me on a pedestal, it's not fair." She sees my face fall and does one better than a high-five, clipping off her seat belt so she can wrap her arms around me.

A Drop in the Ocean 53

I can't help it though, the idolizing. She still loves me more than anyone else in the world. Screw mutants in capes moving shit with their minds, her love is a legit superpower. There are so many awful things I've done to her. All the rituals I've blackmailed her into participating in, all the hideous names I've screamed at her if she did them *wrong*. Yet here she is, cheek warm and satin soft against mine. Both of them wet. Sorrow and vanilla shea butter emanate from her. Beneath those, the tangy, sweet Mom smell that only she has.

We pull apart. Through sniffles we reach for our various Kleenex stashes. Her nose blow is a dainty affair, mine a snotty elephant's trumpet. "It looks nice and empty out there. I think I'm up for a walk."

She knows the drill, lets me get out of the car first before she starts walking by herself. After sprinting up the hill, I backtrack to meet her. This running ahead and coming back down is a treat. There are no doors anywhere, so I can breathe, and there are no joggers to trigger my competitiveness, so I don't push myself to run faster. A soft, pleasant ache squeezes my legs as I slow my pace to match hers. She had to do this whole trek every day from her house to school as a kid. We walk up together, her telling me stories about back then.

Houses I recognize come into view as we reach the top. We're getting closer to Poh Poh and Gung Gung's, my maternal grandparents' place, where Mom and I spent so much of our childhoods. Her until she was eighteen and me until I was three and a half, then every weekend. Poh Poh is probably there right now, making another care package for Gung Gung to give to relatives when he visits Nanaimo. Or maybe on the phone with Sister Stevens, wife to the pastor of her Apostolic Seventh-day worship church. I bet Gung Gung's napping on the black leather La-Z-Boy he got for his eightieth, or in the study upstairs playing Minesweeper on his old Power Macintosh computer.

"Do you think we should drop by?" Mom asks. "You haven't seen your grandparents for months."

My heart thumps faster as I force my feet to slow, anxiety taking over. And memories. Up on the second floor of that grey house is the room I used to sleep in, where I once felt the hand of God on my back as I prayed. The flower bed overflowing with lavender bushes leads to the backyard. Five-year-old Mira learned kindness there, perched on an apple tree as Poh Poh hand-fed a blind squirrel. That large ground-floor window belongs to the living room, where I watched Gung Gung do exercise videos, counting down the push-ups he performed on his knuckles. Where later, I counted down sit-ups, foregoing my spot on the couch and yelling out answers during *Jeopardy!*, trying for abs that elude me to this day. And the porch that leads up to the white front door, that's where Poh Poh called upon Jesus to smite Satan from me. The memory floods me until I drown in it.

I'm thirteen. I'm in pain. But most of all, I'm *wrong. Wrong. Wrong!* WRONG! I *touched* it! It doesn't matter that it was on the seventy-sixth rep, or that the back of my fingertips barely grazed the wall. I still *touched* which means it's *ruined* which means I have to do all 181 jumping jacks over again. Already raw from heaving in air, the howl I throw my whole body into grates against my throat. It brings Poh Poh running out the door to check on me. But she knows better. Should know by now to "Leave me alone!"

Except this time, she doesn't wince, shake her head, and leave. Instead, she tells me, "That's enough. You need to stop."

The thought of stopping makes me laugh until I almost lose count. I do my jumping jacks as fast and hard as I can, hyperventilating.

A Drop in the Ocean   55

Upon hearing me laugh, Poh Poh exhales sharply and makes the sign of the cross. She takes a step closer, raising her voice, which she almost never does. "Mira, this isn't you. I know you're in there. Mira, stop."

"No!"

And now she's praying, holding her hands out to God as if by raising them she can channel his annihilating, mighty white light. "Dear Lord Jesus, take the demons out. Smite the devil from your suffering daughter. Smite him and return Mira back to your heavenly fold ..." She keeps praying, quoting Scripture. Unaware that the tears and snot streaming out of me aren't from frustration anymore, but shame. Shame, because I know even then, without knowing my past life, that the only demon there is me.

We've seen each other since then. Poh Poh's resigned herself to my rituals. Waits for me to finish jumping or doing whatever it is I'm doing this month over and over without saying a word. What she says instead is that I have to love myself. That the only way to properly love others is through self-love and self-forgiveness. And this, even more than touching the wall when I shouldn't or stumbling or miscounting, is *wrong*. It's so fucked up that the thought makes bile rise in my throat, tangles my stomach with knots. Self-love is for good people, and even then it seems indulgent, selfish. For the thing that I am, it's just *wrong*.

Back in the present I purse my lips and blow through them. "I dunno, Mom, she might be having an afternoon nap." Lying is a sin; I'll add it to my thousand-paged list.

Mom must hear the funny pitch in my voice. Or maybe my rigid back and clenched fists give me away. "You're probably right, honey," she says. "Neither of us sleeps well at night, and she needs all the rest she can get. Let's go to the park instead."

I do rituals all day to save her, but she's still always saving me.

Sometimes Mom feels more like God than God does. Well, the God who got a personality makeover in the New Testament, the one full of grace and compassion and love. Mom isn't vengeful, she doesn't need me to punish myself the way he does. But if she had a Bible I'd probably have ripped it up by now. Between her wanting me to get better and him wanting me to suffer, nothing I do is good enough.

◆

I'm in the Quiet Room. Not sure how long it's been because, duh, Quiet Room. It's named for its soundproofing; yell all you want as loud as you can, and the rest of the unit might just hear a dull, muffled *mmrphff*. Gleaming, white-painted brick walls box me in and go straight down to a grey floor. The only other thing in here is a lighter-grey mattress in the same plastic material as what we kids sleep on, but thinner. The steel door, which is the darkest of all these greys, has a peephole built in. Staff use it to check on whoever's in here every fifteen minutes. Make sure we're not killing ourselves. It's the easiest thing though, to smash your head open and do some red redecorating. Like how I did a month and a half ago when I fucked up my exercises and had to punish myself. Yes, it's been that long.

I trail my fingers over the back wall at forehead height. The white paint has a glossy sheen that my fingertips slide over. It's just the tiniest bit duller where Elsie made me scrub it clean. It wasn't rituals that brought me here or Elsie who locked me in today. That honour goes to Alan.

We were playing basketball for our afternoon rec class, Ward 2 against Ward 3. I was on defence and Tony was shooting guard. Yeah, he might score a bunch, and he did, but he sucks at dribbling. I went to steal the ball from him. Wham, wham, wham, it slammed slow against the gym floor, super easy to slap from his hands. On the bounce down I shoulder checked him, which is allowed, dribbling it away on the bounce up.

"Foul, foul!" he cried, before I could take two steps.

Everyone on both teams stopped. Instead of getting ready for my pass, Jorge bent down to tie his shoes, avoided looking at me.

"That was legal, stop being such a baby," I said. He'd called me a retard for weeks—"baby" was the nicest of the names I had for him. At this point, Alan and all the kids were silent, watching both of us. A few, like Sweets, were lining up to use the water fountain.

"Take that back!" Tony strode toward me while he spoke, eyes beaming radioactive hatred.

So he could dish it, but he couldn't take it? He really was just proving my point. Everyone was waiting for the ball, and I was the one who had it. Tony reached for it. I hugged it to my chest, gripped it tighter.

Alan broke our stalemate, pointing to the clock. "Tick-tock, we have ten minutes left."

Phew, while both teams repositioned, I kept hold of the ball. I made my way to the two-point line, started settling into an aim. How many times had I practised this shot in Ward 2's caged courtyard? The corner of my mouth twitched up. We could still win this.

Tony leaned in toward me as he walked by. "That's right, keep smiling. Bet your mommy dying would wipe the stupid grin off your face."

And that's when I bashed his hawk nose with the ball.

When it fell away, his face was scrunched in pain and crimson streamed from his nostrils. Alan grabbed me before I could do any more damage, swearing as Tony's blood made contact with his skin. His face scrunched even tighter than Tony's had. Emotional pain, contamination OCD *wrongness*. Alan's arms shook as he dove straight into his pockets to squirt out copious amounts of hand sanitizer. Guilt brought me back from berserk mode to reality. I didn't have the heart to fight his pronouncement of "Quiet Room. Now!"

In an ideal world with an ideal Mira, the baby comment would've stayed trapped in my head. In a fair world, Tony would be in Ward 3's Quiet Room at this very moment, bitching about how bored he is.

I'd been using the mattress as a punching bag when the door groaned open, and Elsie thrust my journal at me.

"Here, I've found something better for you to do with your hands."

"You didn't read it, did you?"

"No, I brought it for you to use."

It took a little while for me to unclench my fists and wiggle life back into my fingers. My heart rate slowed after my breath did as Elsie examined my hands for sprains. "Thanks for getting this for me. I didn't know we were allowed stuff in here."

Once she was satisfied that nothing was broken, Elsie grabbed a green Sharpie (standard post–freak-out policy = no sharps) from her jacket pocket. "It's at staff discretion. Now how about you write down whatever it is you're feeling instead of taking it out on the mattress?"

CHAPTER SEVEN

*P*ro-D day, bitches! We're going to the mall. So maybe it's super stereotypical that I like the mall. Who gives? Metrotown is huge, with a store for everyone. It has a Chapters, where I'm gonna buy a copy of this book Dr. Grant recommended called *Mistborn*. Health food that doesn't taste like shit, like Jugo Juice and Yogen Früz. All my clothing staples. And for makeup, the holy grail, MAC!

It's not until we're in the garage, having driven around and around the same stuffed parking stalls for five minutes, that I allow my nerves to take over. My rituals are coming up. From wherever we park the van to wherever the entrance is, I'll have to hold my breath. This is everywhere, not just at the Residency. Mom and Lawrence know this ritual from years ago; they always park their cars close to whatever building we're going to. Or drop me off if they have to park farther away.

Finally, Vikas spots an empty space.

"Can you drop me off here?" I ask, when we're still within sight of the entrance.

"No can do, look at all the other cars who'll take our spot," he says.

Fuck. I consider pleading my case to him. But everybody's looking at me—whining for special treatment will just make things worse. My heart sinks further into my stomach the more rows we drive by. Our newly claimed spot's all the way at the far end of the parkade. As Vikas backs in, a bunch of kids undo their seat belts. I breathe in again and again, as deeply as I can before the back door opens. When it does, I dart out, squeezing past Nick before he gets up, already running when my foot touches the asphalt. Obviously holding my breath.

It takes everyone a few minutes to catch up to me. I spend them leaning against the door, heaving in air. My brain throbs through my skin, a pulsing that matches every twitch of my closed eyes. After, once we've made our way upstairs to the mall's ground floor, I look at the tiles to keep my dizziness at bay. The ache in my brain feels like victory.

♦

Blueberry Yogen Früz, one part tart to two parts sweet, melts on my tongue. Sweets, Nick, and I are on the second floor, each with a different snack and store in mind. Our small group with its higher privilege level needs to meet Vikas and the lower-level kids in an hour and a half. We walk slowly, savouring our borrowed freedom. Every clothing storefront has mannequins that remind me of the girls at Remuda Ranch. None of the Residency kids see feeding tubes as a status symbol. The equivalent here is the Harmlympics, with such competitions as whose scars are the worst, who's done the most drugs, and who's tried what to kill themselves. It's been so long and at least an extra twenty-five pounds since Remuda. My next lick of Yogen Früz loses its sweetness, is instead laden with calories. I need a good distraction.

"Hey." I poke Nick in the shoulder, sticking my tongue out. "Is it purple from the frozen yogurt?"

"Stick it out a little bit more."

"Ahhh."

"Not purple enough, maybe after a few more bites."

"Fine, but I'm gonna ask you again later."

We head to GUESS, where the low-rise jeans on display are 15 percent off. Even on sale they're way too much, but I can still look, dammit. *Mistborn* sways in the Chapters bag hanging from my elbow as I hold a pair of distressed skinny jeans up to my hips. How can something this ripped cost so much? While I check out last season's clearance rack, Sweets and Nick head to Millennium. That place isn't quite my scene. Besides, do I really want to watch the boy I like buy jewellery for someone else? Uh ... nope! Kate's getting discharged in a week, so it's kind of now or never for him to make a move. Sweets loves Millennium because you can never have enough pentagram chokers. The longer they take, the more MAC beckons to me from around the corner.

Makeup is kind of like armour. Put enough armour on and you're protected, put enough makeup on and I'm pretty. A bright inner eye and purple shadow bring out the amber flecks in my shit-brown irises, foundation evens out my blotchy skin, and cover-up does what its name says, covers up my flaws. This person who could be called pretty, who is obviously not me, maybe she can be confident too, look people in the eye and know they will smile back when she smiles. Maybe she's not even crazy.

"How did I know you'd be here?" Sweets asks, opening a nail polish tester and sniffing it before painting her thumbnail.

"Because you're fucking psychic." I grab the nail polish for a whiff myself. High voltage lights and mirrors surround us, along with a million billion beauty products. I smear liquid concealer on my forehead. Mom's always telling me to leave the wound alone or keep it covered by my bangs. But since it's a scab right now, the concealer doesn't sting. It just makes my forehead look almost normal.

"Did you get the ring?" I ask Nick when he pops by. He shakes his head and shrugs. Whatever that means. Nothing here interests him, and some items, like the eyelash curlers, drain the blood from his face. "That thing looks like a torture device." It turns out to be a relief when he leaves to wait by the garbage can where I tossed my empty Yogen Früz.

When we emerge, each of Sweets's nails is a different colour and I'm clutching my bag of liquid concealer and free skin care samples. I had to borrow some money from her to cover the cost.

"Stick your tongue out again," Nick says, as we join the throng of walkers going toward the main atrium. "Let's see if it's purpler now."

I cock my hips out, posing like one of the MAC models, except with an unfurled tongue instead of pouty lips.

His voice grows softer. "You're beautiful."

A fake cough disguises my snort. That same giddy rush that coursed through me when he warmed my hands comes back, heat radiating from my cheeks. "Just wait a few hours and my tongue will be boring old pink again." I stick it out and try to look at it beneath my nose. There's Sweets directly in front of us, and for once without a smartass remark. "Anyway, what, uh, time is it? The rest of the group's probably waiting for us."

"Let's go to one more store first," Sweets says.

They both giggle when we walk into Peoples, the jewellery store. God, I can't believe I'm going along with this dumbness.

I squeeze Nick's hand in warning, kick Sweets's Doc Martens. "Shh, no laughing." Everything everywhere sparkles. Precious metals polished to a shining gleam. Light dazzles and reflects from the many facets of gemstones. We make our way to the engagement ring section. Nick clears his throat to snag the attention of an elderly sales clerk.

"Excuse me, my wife and I are looking for a ring."

Her crinkly, painted lips twitch. "And which of these young ladies is your wife?" She is so not buying this. I turn back, ready to bail.

A Drop in the Ocean

Nick tugs my arm and drags us closer to the counter. I'll never get used to it, the butterfly tingles of his skin on mine. I never want to. "She is," he says, swinging our encircled hands up for the sales clerk to see. "Can't you tell?" That just makes the tingles stronger.

"Yeah, I'm their daughter," Sweets adds. And the tingles disappear.

The woman clucks her tongue at us. She points to the engagement ring cabinet. "The cheapest ring we have is a cubic zirconia composite for $750." After hearing that price we're over the whole thing and slink out the door.

I'm never showing my face there again, which is exactly what I tell Nick and Sweets while taking long strides in the opposite direction. Not like it matters. We all hear reality calling, drawing us down the escalator (a compromise—they want the elevator and I want the calorie burning of normal stairs). We go back to the ground floor to meet up with the others. Dinner at the Residency's in under an hour.

To the rest of the world, the mall is reality. Wide open space, unmedicated and unmonitored. Or if medicated, by choice, maybe through something like tea made from the dehydrated seahorses we pass. This last store we're at is the Chinese dried goods store Poh Poh really likes, from before T&T was around. We used to go here to get things like li hing mui for sore throats, candied ginger, or dried yam and lotus roots. Vikas and I coax everyone into checking it out, him for goji berries to put into a smoothie. Me, because memories.

They have a small candy section, with coin rolls of the dark-pink haw flakes that I'd never learned to like. But then … my favourite! White Rabbits. Double wrapped, first in packaging so cute it drove me nuts as a kid, then in edible rice paper. They're a hard milk taffy that sticks to your teeth as you chew and chew. Every dentist's worst nightmare. Back in the day, I could burn through a bag in an afternoon.

Three and a half dollars per package, ridiculously cheap. At twenty calories apiece I could eat six instead of two Fudgee-Os for a snack. Too bad I'm broke. I can't help holding the package, though, unwilling to put it down.

When we leave, I give the White Rabbits a goodbye kiss before placing them back on the shelf. Vikas wasn't convinced they would be just as good for him as the goji berries. I do some quick math: by the time we're all piled in the van, we'll be driving straight through rush hour traffic. Dinner will be waiting for us, cold, or ideally sent back to the caf.

I take a deep, deep breath at the central exit door, my last before sprinting toward the cement wall where our van is. Cars blur in the wake of my sneakers pounding asphalt. Where is our big blue van? Dizziness and lack of oxygen make my vision swim. Every pound on the asphalt is a personal earthquake, my heart beating so hard and so fast that it slams through my skin. My lungs go from aching for air to screaming for it. Where's the van? I need to breathe. Where's the van? I need to breathe. Where? Breathe!

And then black explodes through everything. My body makes choices for me, force-autopiloting the Mira-suit to stand still. To fucking breathe.

Returning to consciousness returns me to failure. Every neuron firing the message that I'm worse than worthless. The *wrongness* of it barrels through my throat in a banshee shriek. Things will only be *right* once I make myself pay. I rise to my knees and bat away the arms of people trying to help me. When my vision returns, I see the blue van. I've ran past it. One more breath and I'm running again, holding the air at bay until I reach the passenger's seat window, launching my forehead at it.

Bang one, a thunderbolt of pain. Bang, bang, two, three. Scab broken, bleeding freely. My hands are pressed against the window, my right arm threaded through the MAC and Chapters bags. Bang, bang, twelve, thirteen. Vikas comes toward me saying something I can't hear.

"Stay back," I warn him. "If you touch me and I lose count, I have to start over." He moves away. Someone in the distance is crying, others laughing—at least no one's trying to shove a sedative needle into my butt. Bang, bang, bang, twenty-one, twenty-two, twenty-three. My forehead slips on the glass, slick with its own blood. Big hands grab my arms and pull me, but I can't turn around. I push through their restraints. I have to get to the sacred number, the *right* number. Sixty-three this time, because six plus three equals nine. I scream at them to "*Fuck off!*" Those hands reach my head, and we battle. I'm winning, banging faster while keeping count until ... someone's palm. A hand cushions my forehead. Who would do this to me? Why do they hate me? I have to move my head to find glass again. Whoever they are, we're close enough to feel the other's breath on our skin, to smell each other's sweat.

It's Nick. Nick, inches from me. The closest we've ever been. His face all screwed up, trying not to cry, as if he were the one receiving blows to the head.

"Let me go. I have to. I'm almost done ..."

He won't.

Not until Vikas says, "Nick, leave off, you're just making it take longer for her to stop." When he does let me go, I finish in a flurry of shuddering, bleeding, and tears: fifty-eight, fifty-nine, sixty, sixty-one, sixty-two, sixty-three. And then the sixty-third bang nine more times.

On the drive home I ride shotgun so Vikas can monitor me. 50 Cent sing-raps over my sniffles as I press a dressing to my forehead. People start to talk, converse their way back into something like ease. But not me. And not Nick.

CHAPTER EIGHT

"I still don't get how eating a raisin is going to help me with OCD. It's calories I don't need." The polyester cushion squeaks as I shift my butt to a comfier position. I switch from jiggling my right leg to my left. Therapy always makes me anxious, even with Dr. Grant. At least both of us agree that Arya Stark kicks ass.

"It's a mindfulness exercise." He shakes a tiny box of Sun-Maid raisins to a salsa rhythm, as if treating it like a maraca will change my mind. "You'll use your senses of touch and taste to observe as many details as possible, then tell them to me."

I raise my bushy-ass eyebrows at him. "Is this a Jedi mind trick?"

"You don't want to do exposures, and I respect that. Those folks at UCLA should never have forced them on you in the first place. Mindfulness can help you manage the kinds of emotions that set your OCD off. Just trust me on this, please?"

"Fine." I'm not used to shrinks asking for permission or saying things like please to me. Treating me like an actual person. Plus, he's started dancing to his ridiculous raisin box music. The sheer force of his enthusiasm's wearing me down.

I grab a raisin and pop it into my mouth. Focusing on its grainy sweetness, on every dried-up wrinkle and ridge, narrows my scope of thoughts to the moment. None are left to remind me to keep my legs jiggling. Am I anxious? I'm not sure. Maybe.

Dr. Grant is too pro to straight-up ask about the incident report Vikas filled out. Instead, he gets me to spill by asking whether I had fun on our weekend outing.

"It was fun 'til I got stuck doing rituals. Pretty sure Nick is scared of me now."

Dr. Grant oohs and raises his eyebrows, even bushier than mine. "Who's Nick?"

My poker face is so non-existent. I bite the inside of my cheek to keep from grinning. "Just a boy I might like, from Ward 1. He wants to be Kate's boyfriend though." While I'm jealous of Kate, I can't help liking her. She said the legends she told me were like medicine for her, and I think stories in general might be medicine for me too.

"Well good, because you've already got a boyfriend, missy."

"Uhh, no I don't."

"Yup, his name's OCD. And from all our talks, he seems like an a-hole that you're still very devoted to."

That pisses me off, because OCD and Nick belong to entirely different worlds, different universes, even. "It's not like I like having OCD."

Dr. Grant nods. "Fair enough. But you do protect it ferociously."

I open my mouth to speak, then close it.

"Would you ever bang your head or hold your breath or jump up and down repeatedly if those things weren't your compulsions?"

"Obviously not." I glare at him. "But I'm not willing to risk my obsessions coming true just because I don't want to do a ritual. It's not worth it. I don't have a choice."

"That's the kind of thing victims of domestic violence say about leaving abusive partners. Didn't you get black eyes when you first started head banging? And your forehead was too swollen for hats?"

Sigh. I know where this is going, where every few sessions inevitably go. The OCD is not me, but right now it's the boss of me. I need to fight it, or it will take over even more of my life. Blah, blah, fight it, Mira. Blah, blah, don't be ambivalent.

A Drop in the Ocean   69

Me and OCD, we're a package deal. Take both or have none. Why the fuck can't anyone get that? Whatever anxiety the raisin eating quelled bubbles back up, transmuting into something that feels like power. Rage. Its strength sets my leg jiggling again, dulls any possibility of pain as I white-knuckle-clench my fists, nails digging deep into my palms.

"Nick doesn't ever need to know that. And I do fight the newer rituals. There's all sorts of ways I've changed on Ward 2, like how I take my shoes off to jump after lights out and don't yell anymore when people slam cupboards or dishes in the kitchen. But as for the head banging and stuff, no." My voice grows rough. "No way. I have to do them. I *have* to."

Dr. Grant's seen me full-blown freak out before. Besides, I'm not even screaming, I just turned up the volume for those last words. He doesn't cringe or yell back. He looks me in the eye, his voice as steady as his gaze. "No one's saying you can't do your rituals. But, and you already know this, anyone who cares about you gets hurt when you hurt yourself."

◆

This is it, I'm sitting down at my regular spot in English. Nick's going to walk through that door and either sit next to me like always, or—way more likely—stay as far away from me as possible. Maybe pretend I don't exist? Nerves buzz through every cell in my body. Jiggling my knee at turbo speed only burns away so much of them. All of me trembles. The more I fight it, the more it shows.

He's here, walks toward me in those ratty Adidas with the holes in the toes. Nick has the weirdest clothes. Most of the boys wear track suits and sports clothes from expensive-ass brands, mint-condition ball caps with the stickers still on them. Nick rotates between like four shirts and sweats and jeans that he cinches with a rope, not a belt. I'm in my Baby Phat denim bustier and push-uppiest push-up bra for good luck. When he reaches the chair next to mine, he puts his backpack on it. So far, so good. Without looking at me, he drags it farther away, about a foot. The metal legs grate against the floor, an awful clang that may as well be my hope dying. I deflate. *Stupid, stupid, stupid.* Oh well, at least I have my assigned reading from *Lord of the Flies* to keep me company.

I manage to get through two more chapters before I have to pee out my Diet Coke from recess. On my way out the door I give Nick a wide berth. When I get back, there's a wrinkled grocery bag next to my book about stranded schoolboys murdering each other. Beneath its larger Hon zi characters, there's the English name of the Chinese dried goods store from Metro. Every crinkle it makes as I open it seems deafening. Inside is a package of White Rabbits and an envelope with my name written on it in Nick's plain but tidy printing. My heart slams against my ribs, trying to break through them and burst out my body. I glance around. He's gone.

There's a poem in the envelope, written in much messier pencil with words scratched out. It rhymes but isn't cheesy. Okay, maybe it's a little cheesy. I'm not writing it down because it'd be way too easy for some random snooper to find. It's about how there's this whole person he sees, a girl who is caring and beautiful—I just don't get how she could be me. I want to, though. I wish I could be her. Spending time with Nick makes me feel like maybe I can. The last two lines are: "You can hide it but I know you're in pain. / Just remember that no one is sane."

A Drop in the Ocean

TIPS FOR HOT DATE WHEN NICK SAYS YES

- Dress cute but not overly sexy.
- Don't order anything messy like spaghetti or stinky like blue cheese.
- Bring mints or gum.
- Have a list of stuff to talk about.
- Watch out for red flags—is he racist? Is he checking out the servers?
- Have enough money to pay my own bill if I need to.
- MOST IMPORTANT: only get physical if I feel like it.

The mattress wobbles as Sweets stretches over and grabs her pillows. "So have you ever made out yet?"

I cringe. "Uh, avocado. Avocado!"

"That's what I thought, virgin." She snickers and throws one of the pillows at me. "This is for practice."

I bash her with it instead.

Her rebuttal is to yank the sheet I'm sitting on and sweep me down to the floor. Before I can scramble up, soft cushiony fabric smothers me.

"MMMMPF."

"What?" she says, finally lifting the pillow off.

"I'll do the stupid pillow thing." I give the pillow a quick peck, trying to keep my lips pretty as I purse them.

When it's her turn she takes a pillow and holds it in both hands. To get the best angle she tilts her head and pulls the pillow up to her face. When she kisses it, her mouth stays wide and kind of softly closes. Her tongue is out. "Remember, you have to kiss with more than just your lips."

My face must be beet red as I watch. Thank God she's concentrating too hard to notice me. "How did you get so good at that?"

"Easy, practice. Plus I pretended it was Kate when we kissed goodbye."

◆

There is a picnic table on the left side of school that's one of the places where kids chill during recess. The top is riddled with carved graffiti, the bottom with chewed gum wads. Nick and I are sitting there on either side. I keep my hands busy by folding a paper crane with a White Rabbit candy wrapper. Not as sexy as making a heart from a cherry stem with my tongue, but way better than chomping on my nails. Nick rolls a cigarette using tobacco he's gathered from butts around the property.

"Thanks for these." I wave the folded wrapper at him. "And for the poem too. Did you, uh, really mean all that stuff you said?"

"I wrote it, didn't I?"

"But like, I'm so weird. I mean, you know what I do." My right hand flies all the way to my forehead without me telling it to. I gulp, then turn the gesture into a scalp scratch.

He pockets his handmade cigarette along with his zip-lock full of tobacco. After wiping his hands on his jeans, he scoots his butt in and leans toward me. Both his elbows are on the table, his fists under his chin. "So what? The last poem I wrote was called 'Blood Mushrooms Yogurt Please.' Everyone's weird, not just the people here. We're here cuz we suck at hiding it."

"Here's better than some places. At least we get to go out, and its coed. Not like girls-only Remuda Ranch, where they shove Jesus and tubes down your throat."

"'Kay, but we can't just leave here whenever we want. Everything we do, every freedom we get, has to be approved by a board of shrinks.

A Drop in the Ocean

Ward 2 where you are is even worse, it's basically prison." Frustration sharpens his tone. Shit, he's pissed. What can I do? This isn't part of the plan.

As much as I hate my gut, I go with it. Hyperaware of my position on the bench, how by sliding up to perch on the tabletop itself, I'm close enough to see the birthmark on his neck and the individual stubble hairs around his mouth. "If I weren't right here, right now, I'd never have met you. How else in the world would I have known you existed?"

"So you get it, then? Why I had to write the poem?"

I lean in past the closest point we've been before, moving us forward from that nightmare moment and into a dreamscape. Pull us toward each other.

His lips are chapped but still soft. They're warm, much mushier than the pillow, alive while they move against mine. His breath is warm too, cigarettes and tomato sauce from the pasta at lunch.

"You kissed me," I say breathlessly. Sometimes breathlessness can be a good thing.

"No, you kissed me."

He's right.

◆

ACHIEVEMENT UNLOCKED: FIRST DATE!

I want to prove to ~~him~~ us that I can do Metrotown right. We both have an afternoon pass and more than enough change to take the bus, so no breath holding required. Yay. Since Nick told me he was dressing up, I go all out and put false lashes on, even though Mom says I don't need them. I swab a perfect Cupid's bow over my upper lip and layer the bottom one twice with the pink dazzle gloss he said he liked.

So what if we'll smush it off later when we make out? Double protection covers my forehead wound: scraggly bangs held in place by my newest Lululemon headband. I rearrange it one last time, then rap my knuckles on the Ward 1 door.

Tiny Margaret, Nick's primary, unlocks it from the inside, and there he is, his dirty-blond head almost a foot above her, his tie-dye shirt loose over his heavy frame and his baggy jeans still cinched by that same fraying rope. This is dressed up?

"You like it?" he asks, popping an invisible collar. "My mom dyed this shirt for me by hand."

God, no. "It's really bright."

An aching, giddy thrill rushes through me in the buzzing, dark movie theatre when I lay my head against his shoulder and he puts his arm around my seat. On a seventy-foot screen, we watch Amanda Bynes cross-dress her way to soccer success in a take on *Twelfth Night*.

At the sushi restaurant footsteps away from MAC, I order miso soup, a Diet Coke, and two tekka makis. I'm sipping tepid complimentary green tea when Nick tells me he's never had sushi before, ever, so what should he order? I almost do a spit take. It makes sense though, since they only have, like, three restaurants in his hometown. He gets a bento box with tempura, chicken teriyaki, some basic rolls, and a Sprite. When it comes to grabbing and holding the slippery meat with chopsticks, his efforts are almost heroic. Meanwhile, I show off being half Chinese and 100 percent Vancouverite by picking up grains of rice one by one.

"Mmm." I close my eyes in appreciation as the soft tuna of my maki melts gorgeously in my mouth. The texture is so perfect that it makes

A Drop in the Ocean 75

up for the shoddy miso soup. Raw fish isn't for Nick though, and he rushes to the washroom.

I wait.

Then wait some more before doing what I always do with my restless fingers, picking. My nails are already bitten, so I can't chew them, and I have just enough self-control to leave my forehead alone. Instead, I peel back a cut scab on my wrist. Red wells up as soon as I lift the layer of protective crust away. Nick comes back to me as I'm making a tourniquet out of napkins.

"Were they itchy?" The question under his question is why can't you let them heal? The sort of thing staff would say. It sours the chemical sweetness of my Diet Coke.

"You know, a nurse on my unit said that one day I'd call these my 'uh-oh marks.'" I sneer-snort. "As if I do them and my rituals for stupid reasons or for fun or something."

Nick's blue-grey eyes look past me, thinking. Mine stay narrowed in a glare. "I doubt anyone thinks you're doing this for shits and giggles, or that what you feel isn't valid."

Now I gnaw past the quicks of my nails. "Good, and if they do, then whatever. The only way out is through, you know?"

"Yeah, I get it. You think one day there'll … be a different way through?"

What comes out of me isn't a real word. I stab a tekka maki with both chopsticks, crush and smush the rice and the pink jewel of tuna at its centre into flat, sticky smears. "What about you, why are you even here?"

Nick's jaw clenches. He takes a few long, loud slurps of his Sprite. When he does speak, he hunches over, voice gravelly. "I get mad, okay, and sad. And I do dumb things because of that."

"Oh."

Both of us stay silent, Nick not quite glaring, automatically popping California rolls into his mouth the way he did popcorn at the theatre. Meanwhile I'm so done with eating. My insides keep sinking, like they're falling into this pit that never ends. Petty bitches don't deserve nice things like dates or Japanese food. Nick's chair scrapes loudly against the floor.

"Gonna grab a smoke."

The server asks me if I want a refill twice before Nick comes back. When he finally does, we talk about other things until the bill comes. I don't fight too hard against him paying for me, because it's nice to know he wants to. That he saved up our Residency allowance (ten bucks a week) for a few weeks, specifically for our dinner. A few steps out of the restaurant brings us to store after store of distractions. By the bus ride back, we're both chill again. Me resting my head on his shoulder as we sit turns into us making out before returning to the Residency and our units.

CHAPTER NINE

*H*e's making me breathe today in therapy. Right now. Fuck my life. I hate breathing. Sure, the only times I don't breathe are when I'm running from door to door, or car to door, or banging my head, but in this moment, as Dr. Grant tells me to keep filling my diaphragm with breath, the breathing is *wrong*! I get all trembly after my fourth inhale and try to stop the trembling by clenching. In Poh Poh and Gung Gung's first language, Cantonese, the word for four sounds like the word for death, and that is just too much. That same brain- and heart-exploding, certain-doom *wrongness* surges through me. It doesn't go away until dizziness replaces it and my lips quiver, begging for me to release my exhale.

"Okay, okay." Dr. Grant puts up his hands in a whoa-girl gesture. "We're done with this exercise. I need you to tell me what's going on. What are you feeling, what do you notice in your body?"

Talking means breathing, and then I'm sniffling, doing both. "My heart, it's stampeding. I can feel my pulse throbbing at my wrists, at my neck. All this energy and heat just storming around inside me because of how *wrong* it was to breathe a second ago, when all you wanted me to do was breathe. But now I can. Now breathing's okay again. And, um, on that note, my breath … It's narsty-ass coffee breath."

A small huff of laughter. "It's not that bad, trust me, nothing like my wife's morning breath. Can you back up a bit, though? Can you tell me if that limbic fear feeling crops up a lot when you're not engaged in rituals?"

"That *wrongness*? Lots. I'll be doing something like walking and notice a landmark, and then I have to run until I reach it. Whenever

I drop something or miss a pass, like in badminton or tennis, I have to stretch to punish myself. Or I'll make a typo and have to type the whole sentence over again as fast as I can without mistakes, three tries max." Punish myself, the magic number three. I don't need Dr. Grant to point out OCD's footprints trampling over new parts of my life.

"So you always go with the urges, then?" he asks, voice neutral, no judgment. "Whenever you get them?"

"It's my go-to reaction, like a reflex. Not going through with them would take all this effort, and I'm tired." I hate how my voice quakes as I say that last word.

"You know how we talked about sticky thoughts? How trying to ignore or fight them only makes them worse because you're giving them more power?"

I nod slowly.

"Well, these are like the ritual equivalents. Baby compulsions that you go along with even though they come from nowhere. If you never stand up to them, they're just going to make your world smaller and smaller. It will suck *so* much in the moment, but you can choose to break the anxiety-action-anxiety cycle before it even begins."

"With the sticky thoughts, I get not taking them seriously. It makes sense that I have to acknowledge them but not react to them or I'll feel worse, but this? I know exactly what to do to make things *right*. It's such an easy fix."

"Not a fix, a trap. Try powering through the anxiety when it's at its weakest. Notice it just like you'd notice a sticky thought, then move on with what you were doing before instead of following the urge. Remember, you always have a choice."

"So choose to be anxious? Choose to feel shitty and to fail on purpose? Choose *wrong*?"

A Drop in the Ocean 79

"It gets easier. Choose to fight OCD and the *wrongness* weakens every time. The choice will never get easier than in those moments when the compulsions haven't taken root. Think of it this way ..."

Dr. Grant goes into this analogy about how obeying OCD is like a trail in a forest. One I've walked for so long that I've worn it into a path. It's smooth from constant use, part of my muscle memory. Fighting OCD is another path, one that I'll have to make from scratch: hacking away the branches, tripping over roots or fallen logs, and maybe even getting stuck or lost. But every time I do choose that fighting path, it gets clearer and easier to walk. It can become ingrained in me as much as the obeying path. Can be my new automatic route, my new normal, as long as I keep walking it. Over and over, the way I did with the old one. Giving in to the rituals will be the exception. Doing the hard, mindful work of fighting OCD means I could live at home. I could go to regular school, then university, learn to drive, get a job. My life on that path would be a whole world with endless possible directions, not a one-road prison.

"Wait up, you said OCD was like an abusive partner. How can it be both someone who beats me up and a path in a forest? Those are way different metaphors."

"That's why you're the writer and I'm the dude figuring out your meds. How's your dry mouth from the clomipramine, by the way?"

♦

It's amazing how much meds can fuck or unfuck you up. Or often, both. Besides clomipramine (an antidepressant) and clonazepam (a benzo), Dr. Grant has me taking this thing called divalproex (an anticonvulsant) mainly prescribed to treat bipolar. Sweets was on it too, until Dr. Park switched her up to lithium. Not enough, though—she hasn't left her room at all this week except for school and food. Standard depressive cycle behaviour. I knuckle out the rhythm of "The Beautiful People" on her door. "Come watch *Cube 2: Hypercube* with us on Ward 3. We can bet on who dies first."

Silence.

"Sweets?"

More silence. Which means only Jorge and I end up migrating across the parking lot and down the hill to Ward 3. It's the smallest unit, but it's got the biggest TV. Ward 1 is doing their own thing, so no Nick. On the bright side, Tony got discharged last weekend, yay! Noor, who's taken his place, is the reason Jorge's been gunning so badly for us to do an inter-unit thing. She's super pretty, which has me worried that Nick might like her, because I would if he and I weren't a thing. She and Jorge snuggle up on the couch. Chelsea's not any kind of problem since she's been gone for about a month. If Chelsea were here, she'd probably make fun of Noor for her eye twitching. Not anything psych related, just plain blepharospasm. A name that cracks us all up.

I try to get her and Jorge to bet their allowance on who they think will live the longest. They turn it into a bet for sex favours.

"Oh, c'mon, Mira." I can hear the eye roll in Jorge's tone. "Like you and Nick won't be fucking in a few weeks."

The terror of that sends my fingers scrambling to my forehead, where I get lost in the rough bumps and divots of my wound. The dried blood and skin layers are as much a trap as the hypercube is. One I'm at home in. I sigh in relief when I hear that tearing sound I love, scab scraping off skin.

Back on Ward 2, I don't bother with shock rock tunes, just rap on Sweets's door, thonk thonk, and barge straight in.

"What's wrong with everyone here?" I flop down on her bed.

A Drop in the Ocean

"What's wrong with you?" She rubs her swollen racoon eyes, smudging liner and mascara from days ago deeper into her face.

"Everyone's so horny all the time that it makes me sick. If I have to choose between being obsessed with screwing or being obsessive compulsive, then I'd rather bang my head forever."

"Tell me you didn't wake me up just to say your life plan is Riverview?"

"Obviously not. It would be nice to have fewer rituals so I could live at home. As long as I could keep most of them, like the ones that protect Mom."

"What does Dr. Grant say? He's the expert, right?"

"Apparently obeying OCD is this path in the forest I've been walking my whole life and fighting OCD is a new path that will get easier the more I walk it."

"Why a fucking forest? What is it with therapists and their nature analogies? Why couldn't it be a grocery store?"

"I like the forest better. Nature is pristine, not perverted. If I lived in the forest I wouldn't run into people buying condoms or lube in the pharmacy aisle."

She snorts. Okay, so mood wise, still a little cunty. "The forest is a sexfest, Mira. Every flower you smell is your nose buried in a plant's reproductive organs. Animals hump in every inch of it."

Ugh, I can't help thinking about the sachet of dried lavender from Poh Poh's garden in my underwear drawer. How I squeeze it and inhale deeply whenever I put on new clothes.

"Ha, check out your face. You look like someone just strangled your dreams."

A dull, throbbing ache in my lower stomach woke me up this morning. I scratched the sleep goop from my eyes and headed to the girls' bathroom. Nothing's better than a good morning dump. Maybe this one will knock my weight back to something less disgusting. Ha ha, NOPE!

No poop babies plopped off at the pool. Instead, red drops. I wipe between my legs and there's more red. A rusty red and a copper smell I know too well from my forehead that shouldn't be coming out of me from anywhere else. I got it when I was twelve, lost it when I was thirteen—it's been over three years since my rag.

"Fuck!" My first yell isn't even that loud, but it's amplified by the echo of the bathroom, which is gratifying. My forehead screams at me to slam it against the white-painted walls. The porous brick underneath would sponge up my blood and head meat while making a great full squelch sound. But Dr. Grant's stupid speech about how the best time to fight an urge is when it's new keeps me frozen. Hands braced on the wall, back and neck bent so close that my bangs brush against its glossy whiteness, a noise like the death rattle from *The Grudge* comes out of me.

If I do bang my head now, I'll be adding another session of banging again tomorrow and for the rest of however long I wake up to red doom this week. And then a month from now. And, unless I get a hold of my weight, every other month afterward. Weak. Fat. WORTHLESS. WRONG. If I'm a cup, *wrongness* fills me to overflowing. Demands some sort of atoning action. I compromise, smashing my left fist into the wall instead.

"FUCK!" Turning pain to rage is how I power through more of it. Angry voices join mine, the voices of Dinah and staff that I can hear through the door and walls.

A Drop in the Ocean   83

Dinah's knuckles stampede on the door. "Tweak in your own damn room, I've needed to pee since I woke up."

"Not tweaking." I take one of those deep breaths Dr. Grant is such a fan of, turn the volume knob on my voice down to normal. "Almost done. Use the boys' bathroom if you have to go so bad." Inhaling back into my body, I notice a throbbing in the knuckles of my left hand. When I try to bend my fingers into a fist, the throbbing turns into fire. I can't close my hand. Shit.

By my next breath, Dinah's back to yelling through the door. "Nuh-uh, don't wanna get sperm on my pussy. I'm staying 'til you let me in."

Laughter echoes through both the girls' and boys' hallways. Dinah's being cute-ridiculous as opposed to scary delusional-ridiculous. I brush past her and her furious glare, angling my left arm behind me.

By keeping quiet, my broken knuckles stay a secret through most of breakfast. I feed myself a piece of toast with my right hand, keeping my swollen left one resting on my lap beneath the table. That same strategy gets me through math and science. There are a few questions I don't get and leave blank. Better to fill them in tomorrow than to call the teacher, Doug, over and risk interrogation. Art therapy is where things go to shit. You can't make clay sculptures with one hand. Ten minutes into the hour-and-a-half block, I get sent to Ward 2's nurses' station.

"My, my, Miss Mira, what are we gonna do with you?" Elsie places the ice pack over my left hand, which I hold still on the counter. Its cool weight soothes the throbbing of my knuckles immediately. She bandages it up with tightly woven gauze. "Stay here keeping your hand iced for twenty minutes."

Okay, so I know what Elsie told me, but she's in the bathroom or something and Nick and Sweets are waving at me through the window. It's been at least ten minutes of me sitting here like a lump. My hand's probably fine.

"Holy shit, really?"

"Why not? Today feels right." Nothing else has worked.

Nick beams as he fist pumps. "Fuck yeah! Let's pop that weed cherry."

Sweets, who knows me better, who's seen me hack myself hoarse and complain about contact highs, raises a single eyebrow, the left one, with the piercing. "You're sure about this? I won't wake up tomorrow morning to you screaming and then taking forever in the bathroom? What was that all about, anyways?"

"Nothing." I frown at her, kick a bit too viciously at some rocks. They tumble down the grassy knoll beyond the Residency's property. Nick looks at us, his smile gone. In a low murmur he can't hear, I say to Sweets, "Please shut up. Promise I won't bitch at you when I'm sober."

She shrugs, takes a long drag from Nick's joint before passing it back to him. "All righty then."

I start off shotgunning. Nick exhales the smoke from his hoot into my open mouth. Beneath the bud lies the salty-sour pheromone mix of pure him. Another high I've yet to get the hang of.

"Okay, okay. This isn't a rom-com," Sweets says, when a couple more shotguns turn into Nick and me making out. Sweets holds the smoking two-thirds of a joint out toward me. "So you're gonna inhale, then hold it in for as long as you can."

A Drop in the Ocean

I go for it. Skunky, berryliciousness bursts through my taste buds. Smoke gathers down my throat, trapped there by my clamped lips, building, billowing. How long do I do this for? Are they trying to kill me? My whole throat dries up, heat clawing my poor windpipe until ...

Blood rushes to my head and smoke explodes out of me. I hack and wheeze for minutes. God, I suck at this. Every time I exhale, needles stab their way up my throat. It hurts way worse than holding it in.

"Coughing's good, coughing's fine." Sweets squeezes my shoulder in an *I got you* kind of way.

Nick tries to de-awkwardize the moment. "Y'know, they call it blueberry kush cuz it's a pot plant crossed with a blueberry bush."

"Yeah, sure." Sweets catches my eye and rolls her hazel ones. "Anyways, let's get outta here. There's this cool skate shop we could bus to."

"No bus," I say. "What if I'm obvious? They'll kick me off and then we're screwed."

"Relax, your eyes are barely bloodshot. I have some sour apple breath spray to mask the smell." She unzips her lips-shaped purse and brandishes a candy bottle at me.

"How 'bout we walk to McDick's?" Nick asks. "Tonight is spaghetti, and the last two times it was like eating tomato sauce with worms."

"Eww."

With that, we're on our way.

We walk a few blocks beyond the tech school, skirting a crowd of students. No vice squad police step out of the throng to arrest us, even though my pulse is still throbbing, three beats to every one step I take. Nick and Sweets walk behind me, owning the sidewalk. Both nonchalant yet impassioned while debating the merits of growing versus shaving your pubes.

"Guys, guys, I don't feel anything. Why don't I feel anything?" I shout over my shoulder.

"You're so cute when you're flustered," Nick says when they catch up to me. Sweets taking a while I understand; I can rest my chin on the top of her head. Nick has no excuse. He's a giant who walks slower than anyone I've ever met. At least they've stopped talking about treasure trails.

"Mira, don't freak out." Why is Sweets talking to me like I'm a toddler? "But you're kinda freaking out about not freaking out. And that means you're high."

"Yesssss!" It takes us a few times because hello, we're high, but we manage to coordinate a three-way celebration high-five right as the bus pulls up. Two stops and half a block later, we're at Brentwood with its McDick's on the ground floor.

We wait in different lineups, racing to see who'll reach a server first. An old couple ahead of me finally finishes arguing with the manager and moves aside. Oops, guess my cheer was too loud. Countless heads turn my way. Guess I was being … obvious?

I burst out laughing. Take as long with my giggle fit as I did with my coughing one. And these are foghorn-sounding, body-heaving laughs. Ones that cause both Nick and Sweets to lose it. I stagger over to Nick's line, where a bored-looking server waits for us to finish. Nick supersizes everything. Meanwhile Sweets is so picky that I totally get why server dude keeps sighing. She wants extra this, half sauce that, substitute blah for blah.

"Oh, and uh, an Oreo McFlurry," I add.

"What size would you like, ma'am?" server dude asks, with dial-tone flatness. Did he just ma'am me?

A Drop in the Ocean 87

"Small, duh." Do I look like some stuffy old matron to him? With the thought of matrons comes the thought of grown-ass womanhood, and with the thought of womanhood comes the thought that drove me to weed in the first place. Why the fuck did I order a McFlurry? They must have a billion calories. No wonder *it's* back.

"Hey, got a stomach cramp," I tell Sweets and Nick once our order's done. "Why don't you split my ice cream? I might be a while on the toilet." Before they can reply, I'm off to the bathroom.

After slamming the stall shut and lining the seat with toilet paper, I allow my shaky legs to collapse on my fat ass. Yup, *it's* still there, a coppery ooze. My body's biggest fuck you yet. Since this morning's pad is soaked, I wrap toilet paper round and round my underwear for protection. Waves of nausea slosh in my stomach. All the while, I'm floating above myself. Like how I sometimes do when I hold my breath too long or bang my head too hard. That disgusting, person-shaped sausage casing can't possibly be what I'm made of, what constitutes *me*. God, it's exhausting, hating myself this much. Still, though, I'm more relaxed than I've felt in years. Body so slack when I return to it that it's not tense enough, clenched enough, to hold all that loathing. I lean on the wall, ready to snooze, to lose consciousness so that old me and high me can both shut off.

A mother and daughter murmur in the stall beside me, a middle-aged woman inspects her makeup at the counter—I see her through the crack in the door. Time stretches, thin as an elastic band about to snap, while I wait for everyone to leave. Does the daughter know how lucky she is to be spending time with her mom? Can't the woman with the makeup tell that her foundation's too light? Once everyone does leave, I do my jumping rituals, then speedwalk from door to door without washing up since the sinks are right below the mirror and I just *can't* right now with my reflection. Instead, I keep my eyes magnetized to the raggedy laces of my Skechers. Good thing Sweets and Nick aren't waiting on the ground floor. It means I can sneak in a makeshift handwash with water from the soda fountain and antiseptic from the wall dispenser without feeling too embarrassed. Next, I clomp upstairs to find them.

It's easy enough to spot the only person with neon-pink hair and a scarlet lips purse. "What took you so long?" Sweets asks when I reach them.

"Why didn't you guys have the McFlurry?" Next to empty wrappers, it stands full and ashamed, melting into vanilla cookie soup. Fuck, it looks good. I've gone as many years without McDonald's as I have without a period. Uh-oh, the grease and meat smells circulating everywhere are equally delicious. Must escape. I pile the McFlurry and empty wrappers onto a tray, ready to head to the nearest garbage bin.

"Mira, wait a sec. I know I'm not the best about being 'open'"— Nick makes air quotes around the word—"or whatever, but even I can tell something's up. If I eat some of this gross Oreo stuff, will you? Watch." He grabs the McFlurry cup and brings it to his lips, the spoon hitting his nose as he takes a big gulp. "Mmm, not bad."

And just like when he's warming my frozen hands, that giddy, aching rush comes back.

He cares about me. My *boyfriend* cares about me. My best friend does too. I blink a little, eyes weed dry, trying to process everything. Here. All of us here, sitting together. Out in the actual world. And damn, it feels good to be sitting back down. Another wave of giggles sweeps me up, the ice cream smushed all around Nick's mouth and dribbling down his chin suddenly hilarious.

A Drop in the Ocean

"Give it." I zoom the spoon to myself, making airplane noises. "Fuck, that's good. Fuck, that's delicious." This creamy Oreo-chunk mush is the best thing I've ever eaten. It tastes like summer birthday parties, like wholesome-ass satisfaction.

"Bet you haven't had one of those for a long time, eh?" Sweets nods toward what's left of my McFlurry.

"Yeah. It's my second second-first."

"Huh?"

These people are my people. They know me and despite it all love me. "I got high with you for the first time ever, to forget about my first second-first."

"Still not sure what you're saying." Sweets nibbles on her last few fries.

"You heard me screaming this morning because I found out I've got my period. Again. For the first time since my whole eating disorder thing."

Nick hunches closer to me, grasping for my hand. "But isn't that kinda good? Now you can have babies again if you want." His sticky fingers ick up mine.

"Hell no." Sweets saves me from having to reply. "I never want to be a living dead mombie. Rather be a cool aunt."

That sparks a whole new convo about various cool relatives and cousins. I exclaim at the appropriate moments, add a sentence sometimes. Really though, I'm focused on scraping the last spoonful of ice cream into my mouth. Surprised and kinda thrilled that I don't feel that guilty.

CHAPTER TEN

Mom's taken me on a special-request pass to see Gung Gung. He's dying.

Gung Gung is eighty-three, and this is his second heart failure. I could try and puzzle out the meaning behind that number, why even though it's odd (the way all of my ritual reps are) it's probably the worst and last year of his life. But I'm too tired to procrastinate with what Dr. Grant calls magic numbers. OCD doesn't get to take centre stage. Besides, I'm so numb I can't be anxious. Jumping in the hospital bathroom a few minutes ago, the magic of numbers felt realer than the thought of Gung Gung getting discharged from existence.

Then I see him. He's propped up by pillows and swaddled in blankets on his hospital bed, less than ten white hairs hanging over his scalp. Tubes are everywhere, around and inside him like he's hooked into the Matrix. It's these tubes that do me in, have me in tears as soon as I walk through the door. I know first-hand how much IVs and feeding tubes suck. But those things don't turn your every breath into Darth Vader's. Only ventilators do that. His isn't a full mask that suctions and obscures his face. Instead, I can almost see his lips through the mouthpiece and the medical tape strapped across his jaw. That makes it worse, because I see enough of his expression to tell that just existing, the effort it takes, brings him so much pain.

"Hi, Dad, Mira and I are here to visit with you," Mom says in the soft, cheery tone she uses specifically for old or sick people. It's what I heard whenever I phoned her from UCLA, an octave and a half lower than her tone for talking to cute animals or little kids.

A Drop in the Ocean   91

Gung Gung's cloudy eyes open wider, creasing as he smiles as much as he can through the mouthpiece. Antiseptic stings our nostrils while harsh lights illuminate but don't warm us. A symphony of beeps and IV drips with that hideous ventilator shunting as the bass carries on all as we smile back. I smile so hard that the tears still forming in my eyes squeeze out and fall down my face. With a shaking hand, I brush away snot dribbling from my nose and mixing with those tears.

Then Gung Gung raises his hand. He spreads it out toward us and pulls it in before letting it collapse back onto the bed. *Come closer.*

We do. Mom goes to his left and I go to his right. I crouch down low, close enough to smell his putrid sweat. I clench my jaw as my lips quiver in their upward curve. Bend lower so our eyes are level and I can see the story on every line of his face. My stinging eyes close as I press a kiss onto his cheek. Wet, salty. He's crying too. He cranes toward me, fighting against the tube that breathes for him to kiss me back.

The Gung Gung in my heart is a quiet but vibrant man who holds his broad shoulders proudly square. He has most of his thick salt-and-pepper hair and walks with purpose. A lot of my childhood's happiest moments are with, for, and because of him. I can't write them all down, but here are my top nine: Breakfast oatmeal races—who could cram the most steaming Cream of Wheat into their mouth first? Him picking me up from school in his white camper van. Parking at McDonald's and handing me a toonie for our half-vanilla, half-chocolate twist cones because me going in was faster than the drive-through. Our trip to Harrison Hot Springs, where I slept in that big van's built-in bed. Eating a tomato slice for the first time when we went out for burgers with war vet Uncle Fred. Both he and Gung Gung had eaten banana peels as kids when there was nothing else, so I didn't want to let them down. Visiting a bunch of other uncles and aunties around Lunar New Year and how they pressed lei si into my hands—my favourite envelope ornamented with two graceful rainbow-feathered fung wong, tails curling into a cloud. The way he beamed when I beamed as soon as he opened the front door, back from a trip to Nanaimo. Returning from one trip, he'd held a white poodle stuffie with red bows on her ears in the crook of his elbow. "Guess what I got for you, Mira?" Sounding out the words of his tiny printing before I could read well on my own. He'd used a multicoloured pen to spell out each colour with its match in ink: red, black, blue, and green. The back-and-forth game of parroting his sounds—yat, yi, saam, sei, ng, luk, chat, baat, gau, sap—and copying those tidy pen strokes with crayon until Gung Gung had taught me how to count from one to ten in Cantonese. And number nine, or gau: how thrilled Poh Poh was on those rarest of times when he would say mealtime grace.

◆

On the kid and teen psych ward at UCLA, we played a fuck ton of Texas Hold 'Em. I always lost because my poker face is epically non-existent. Back on Ward 2 I go straight to the bathroom to improve the hand I've been dealt. I scrub off the blood from the car head banging and what's left of my makeup after crying all my mascara and liner into oil-spill streaks down my face. At least I don't look like a horror movie villain anymore. Nothing can hide how red and blotchy I am or the bloodshot puffiness of my eyes. I bet Jorge will take one look at them and demand to know when I toked up and why I didn't share. He isn't who I need.

I don't know what I'll spill to Sweets or Nick, only that they'll make it better. I yell at Sweets through her door above the stereo

A Drop in the Ocean

blasting death metal to meet me outside. Nick I find chain-smoking on Ward 1's porch. One look at me in all my post-weeping glory and he says, "We're climbing the Buddha."

Is that slang for some sort of sex thing? "Excuse me? Sweets is on her way."

"Even better."

What the fuck? "What does climbing the Buddha even mean? My gung gung—" And then the waterworks switch back on. My eyes become leaking faucets, my lips press against each other, holding in a moan.

"Just walk with me, it's not what you think." Nick grabs my hand with both of his and squeezes it. The goosebumps I always get when we're close to each other, that heady rush, slip through my cry circuit and reroute my reflexes. I'm still sad, but now I'm walking with him as he leads me toward the school building. I'm waving at Sweets as she heads down the Ward 2 steps to catch up with us. She has her damn stereo with her and holds it balanced on her shoulder like an eighties homie instead of a hard-core goth. I tell them the whole Gung Gung story as we walk through the courtyard in between the math and English classrooms to the garden area, where a Buddha statue sits at the foot of a Japanese maple tree. Unlike its shrub-sized cousin a few feet away, this one is full grown. Its leaves fire-glow red and orange instead of light green, thick branches reaching past the eaves of the school's flat roof.

"See, Buddha. We don't really climb him, pretty sure that would be sacrilegious. We climb the tree behind him, then jump up for a bird's-eye view of Crazy Camp. Everything feels smaller, in a good way, from up high. At home I head into the woods, here I head to the roof. Whatever's bugging me loses its bite when I see the forest and the mountains past the high-rises. Maybe it'll be like that for you too."

"And music. Everything's better with the right kind of music." Sweets brandishes her stereo. I can see how heavy it is by the way her arm muscles bulge holding it up. "How 'bout a rooftop dance party? Your gung gung won dance competitions and stuff, right? Let's tear it up for him." She hands the stereo to Nick and scrambles up the tree.

Wait up, why does he get to have the portable arm workout? As soon as the urge materializes, the words spill out my mouth. "I wanna hold the stereo."

Sweets frowns, her unwounded forehead furling. "No way, you'll break it. Nick's a big dude, he's got this."

"I'm strong enough to carry it," I shout up at her back, as she jumps from the branch to the roof.

"And if either of you break it, you buy me a new one," she says from her new perch up top.

Five dollars plus change sit in my wallet, in my purse, in my drawer. Definitely not enough to replace Sweets's baby if I drop it or a button falls off or something. It's either turn this into a fight or ignore the *wrongness* to check out a place I've only seen in my head. The Buddha by my feet has the softest smile. His right hand slices the air with a graceful bend, more like a blade of grass than a sword. Donna taught me that this gesture is the abhayamudra, for fearlessness and fierce compassion. All right, Mr. Zen, ~~maybe I can~~ I will let go just this once. The Japanese maple's bark is smoother than the oak tree by Ward 2 that I climb so much. Even easier to get a good grip on.

"You need a boost up?" Nick asks, setting the stereo I'm beginning to hate on the ground.

A Drop in the Ocean   95

Too late. I'm already crouching, then standing on the branch closest to the roof. It's the easiest thing to fly for one step. I'm surprised by the springiness of the asphalt roof shingles when I land next to Sweets. Nick's up a moment later, and we set off to explore. The school building is connected to the rec building by a skinny corridor of offices. Only staff are allowed to access the corridor, but we stroll above it, taking in the dusk. The orange and red of sunset lines wispy clouds I can almost touch, fights against its fading to a blue darker than Nick's eyes. I know it's cheesy, but they're the colour of a storm at sea. Sneaking glances at them instead of watching my footing makes me stumble. We're on the gym roof now, though, so even if I fell it wouldn't be off the ledge to my fucking death. Nick puts the stereo down in the centre of the roof, and Sweets fiddles with the FM dial, switching from the Fox 99.3's mosh pit music to the Beat 94.5, which plays the hip hop you hear at clubs.

"You're welcome, kiddos," she says, wiggling her eyebrows. "Let's see you drop it like it's hot."

Nick laughs and I groan. We kind of just shuffle side to side and bob our heads at the beginning. I'm trying to find the beat and remember the moves Chelsea taught me, mostly different ways of emphasizing your boobs or your butt. Then "Promiscuous" comes on. That's my song! I'm feeling it, channelling the playful sexiness of the music and the words. I bend my ass close to Nick's hands, something I've never done before. Lean into him so his warm breath pricks up the hairs on the back of my neck and my arms. His nearness makes me shiver as we hold each other and move together in this new, good way. Is this what grinding is? Are we grinding?

A few songs later and Sweets caves—she's dancing too. All her moves are goofy shit like big fish, little fish, cardboard box; the shopping cart; and the funky chicken. I do my dorkiest disco arms, and Nick pulls out the YMCA. My abs are getting a workout from how much I'm laughing. Kids from Ward 3 come out way below us for a smoke break, and we yell at them 'til they dance a little too. The chill in the darkening air refreshes my lungs and skin. We get a double dose of Nelly when "All Good Things (Come to an End)" plays. The sad, slow guitar strumming gives us the chance to take a breather.

"I wish I were Nelly Furtado," I say between pants. "She's freaking gorgeous and talented."

Nick steps closer to me and hunches a little so we're face to face. "Forget her. I'm all about that sexy backup dancer on the roof."

I'll never get used to his outrageous compliments. I never want to. I put my arms around his neck, where they slide a little against his sweat. He puts his arms around my waist and grazes his fingertips just a little lower than my hip. Because I only went to half a year of high school, I didn't make it to any dances. I'm glad of that now instead of sad. The sky, so close above me, and an audience of one beats a crappy crowded gym any day. I rest my cheek against Nick's chest, my cheekbone on his collarbone, his heartbeat a steady pounding in my ear that I match my breathing to. Please, please be wrong, Nelly. Please don't let this end.

On the way back down, we talk about theme songs for our lives.

"I wanted 'Take Me Away' by Fefe Dobson to play. Cuz that would be mine," Sweets says, scuffing her Docs on the asphalt.

"Really? Not 'Liii-thhheee-ummm'?" I hold the notes for as long as I can.

"Naw. A love song to sorrow? Uh-uh. I get it, just like everyone on Ward 2 gets 'Locked Up' and every kid at the Residency gets Gnarls Barkley's 'Crazy.' But it's not my personal pick. What about you?"

Young Mira would have said "Reflection" from the *Mulan* sound-track before Sweets even finished asking. This Mira says, "'Worthless,' from *The Brave Little Toaster*."

"What the hell's the Brave Little Toaster?" Nick asks. At the same time, Sweets makes a wrong answer buzzer noise. "Nope. Try again."

I ignore her. "It's this cartoon about some household appliances who adventure in search of their human owner. The toaster is the main character."

"Since we're talking about toast," Nick says, "I was on this med at home that turned my brain to mush. I couldn't remember the word *toaster*, I called it the thing that makes toast."

"What med was it?" Sweets asks.

"Thorazine?" I guess. That one fucked with my bladder, which I'm never telling anyone.

"Risperidone."

"Oh my God, I hated risperidone. It made me so angry and dizzy all the time." I think back to how slow I was. How anytime I moved it felt like I was forcing myself through mud.

"When I was on it, it made me puke," Sweets says, grinning as wide as I am. It's weird, because all three of us are stoked about how much we hate this pill. My people know what risperidone's like. It sucked for them too!

"Okay, Nick, your turn. What's your theme song?"

"Uh, it depends. When I'm upset its Korn's 'Coming Undone.' For life in general, maybe this song my dad likes called 'Wheel in the Sky.' He played it for me on our road trip to Prince Rupert. It's kind of about how life keeps going on, no matter what happens."

"Deep," Sweets says.

I nod. Mm-hmming like I know what song they're talking about.

"On the way back, he gave me driving lessons and we jammed out to 50 Cent's 'Get in My Car.'"

Now that song I do know. "Really? He was okay with that?"

Nick laughs a little. "His hearing's bad so he didn't understand the lyrics."

Some sort of spell breaks after we climb back down and walk out of the school courtyard to the parking lot. Everything is regular sized. My grief returns, looming beyond any mindfulness bullshit or any other thoughts in my brain. We were fucking around on the roof while Gung Gung's dying. Sweets and Nick tell me not to feel guilty about having fun. I still do, but the group hug helps.

◆

So we got in trouble for dancing on the roof. The Ward 3 kids must've ratted us out. Staff have been upset at me a lot before, but it was always because of my OCD or ED. Forbidden from screaming at people if they slam the doors, banned from hiding my food in my pockets. Shit like that. This time it was for doing something fun and normal.

"But it wasn't a safety hazard, we were fine."

"What if you hadn't been?" Elsie yelled. She was glaring, but with eyes so wide I could see the whites all around her pupils. "And it could've taken hours for us to get to you. Who would've heard you screaming for help?"

"We were having fun. Why would we scream?"

"Because a few years ago, a patient fell from up there. They denied it, but I'm pretty sure they were in a scrap and got pushed."

"Oh." The awfulness of that statement leaves me lost for words. When I find them again, I say, "Even if we hated each other, Nick and Sweets would never do that."

A Drop in the Ocean

I get why Elsie was so upset now, though. Her anger, like mine, has dissipated. It was fear at what could have been that made her grip so tightly to my shoulder after patting it. "I'm not saying I think they would, but if something like that had happened, we would've been helpless to stop it. Horrible things happen all the time. It's not fair, but it's reality. You can never be too careful."

I can't believe I used to think Elsie was cruel, or that Bitch Douche Bag was some sort of scathing insult. And it wasn't just Elsie. A while ago, I was staffist. Positive that all staff were out to get me. Really, though, they're just people. Not some amorphous blob of malevolent authority figures. Guess I should listen to them more.

CHAPTER ELEVEN

I don't want to do fucking CBT." It comes out louder and gruffer than I intended. So much so that Dr. Grant backs up from leaning toward me. "But," I continue, "I'll look at a few of those stupid handouts in your booklet."

A wide grin replaces the shock on his face. "Well, you certainly took me by surprise. Way to go, superstar, what changed your mind?"

"Just be happy that I'm even doing this, okay? Don't ask why."

"I trust that you'll tell me your motivations when you're ready." Trust, when you're ready … he's doing the therapist version of Mom saying she's disappointed in me instead of saying she's pissed.

The way I play up my eye roll makes me dizzy with zero payback, as it does fuck all to his placid expression or what he has to say.

"In the meantime, read the introduction and do the first two homework sheets for our session tomorrow."

◆

Shaking, shaking. Why am I doing this? Why am I even here? I grab life by the balls and turn the shaking into turbo-speed knee jiggling.

"I love me a good earthquake," Elsie says. She's here to make sure I'm accountable to my treatment. Which means she made me dig out the CBT booklet I buried under clothes in my dresser drawer yesterday. The "homework" I've been avoiding like the plague that it is. She gathers the introduction handouts that I've already read, strewn over the dining room table, into a tidy pile.

None of it is that new to me. It goes over what CBT, craptastic brain torture, a.k.a. cognitive behavioural therapy, is and how the main part of it used for OCD is exposure and ritual prevention. Even at thirteen, all I had to do was see the word *exposure* to know it was bad. People die from exposure. Most of the time it's exposure to the elements. OCD, though, is supposed to die if I'm exposed to all the things that trigger my rituals while I purposefully don't engage in them. The part that makes it exposure is that it's not just once. It's over and over and over until I get bored of the trigger and we move on to the next one. How the hell could I ever be bored of things that feel so *wrong* it's like me and the entire universe are exploding until I fix them with rituals? It's not that I like banging my head or jumping or holding my breath. It's that I have to.

I flip through the rest of the booklet, skimming across paragraphs. Most of it I'm expected to fill out. Sure, Elsie looking over my shoulder at this stupid blank grid must be thinking, *Oh, that's not so bad, all Mira has to do is list stuff that makes her anxious and write down her compulsions.* Wrong. Filling out this sheet means saying yes to the *wrongness*, means murdering ritual after ritual until eventually we get to the ones that will lead to Mom's death if I don't do them. Which may as well mean murdering her.

I don't want to waste journal pages on craptastic brain torture. It's where I store my soul. I can read older entries and see proof that I can be happy, that there are things worth getting up in the morning for. And of all those things, writing is my raison d'être. Or raisin duh etra, as Nick calls it to make me laugh.

He's another reason for living, reason maybe my existence isn't so *wrong*. Mom, Poh Poh, Gung Gung, Sweets, Lawrence, Dr. Grant, even Elsie humming off-key beside me—they're my raisons d'être too. Having Gung Gung struggle against the machine keeping him alive just to kiss me is my raison de this bullshit. He loves me enough to fight and win over that kind of pain. I know it would hurt him even more to see how much I hurt myself. So many people who love me keep begging me to power through CBT. I don't deserve to be normal, to not suffer. Except right now I'm making the people I love most suffer because of my OCD. I order them around to appease my rituals, I scream and lash out at them if the rituals go *wrong*. Learning parts of CBT might be worth it if they take away parts of the pain I keep causing.

So here goes: not every single ritual or puzzle piece of my OCD, but enough collected in one spot to start seeing the whole of it. How the obsessions and compulsions all interlock and fit together along with my SUDS (subjective units of distress) level for each trigger.

A Drop in the Ocean

Compulsion or Situation	Subjective Units of Distress Level 0–100
Someone standing while I sit	70
Someone exercising better or more than me	90
Banging noises (slamming doors, clanging pots and pans, construction)	70–200 (depends on duration, loudness)
Screwing up (taking break, slowing down, falling) while rec exercising	200
Exercise rituals—abs or jumping jacks (morning, night)	60–80
Screwing up while ritual exercising	70–100
Heavy thing I need to lift	60
Jumping after using bathroom	60
Stepping on crack or touching object/area when I shouldn't	60–80
Banging head 111 times (morning, noon, night)	70–100
Holding breath while running (cars, doors)	80
Banging head during Mom visit	70–200
Banging head because I screwed up	1,000
Screwing up urge (baby compulsion)	80
Touching and/or miscounting	90–130
Breathing when I shouldn't	100–150
Stretching because I dropped something	60–80
Turning off and on all light switches 15 times when needed	40–50
Opening and closing all doors I enter/exit: once for staff-unlocked doors, 3 times for non-locked doors	80–90

Thoughts, Images, or Impulses That Cause Me Distress	Subjective Units of Distress Level 0–100
I am stupid (not good enough at school)	50
I am fat (can't count ribs in mirror, weight too high)	50–60
I am lazy or weak	50–60
I am weird / a freak	50–60
I am worthless	70
I am evil or selfish	70–90
Feeling like I screwed up a ritual	60–80
Knowing I for sure screwed up a ritual	80–200
Not exercising as hard as I can	70–80
Wondering if I hurt someone's feelings	70–80
God is against me	70–80
I have to punish myself, make myself pay, or God will kill Mom	1,000
I don't deserve to live and everyone would be better off (and secretly relieved) if I died	90–100
Images of who I was and what I did in past life	90–100

A Drop in the Ocean

Perpetuation of Compulsions	Subjective Units of Distress Level 0–100
If I am too slow I have to do more, faster	50–60
If I breathe while running or head banging I have to redo	50–60
If I screw up an important ritual I have to head bang	70–80
If I think I'm selfish I have to do more	70–80
If I touch something I have to redo	70–80
If I stumble I have to redo	70–80
If I drop something I have to redo	80
If I miscount I have to redo	80–90

◆

As a hard-core Christian, and then as an anorexic, I'd never been super stoked for Halloween. Taking Satan and calories out of it really sucks away the joy. This year is gonna be different. No trick-or-treating, because while other kids do that with staff, us higher levels are getting dropped off at Playland. Pickup by curfew.

My thin embroidered costume flats slap the pavement as I run to the van. Our ward's late because Elsie discovered that Franco's SweeTARTS are in fact E. Since I wimped out and refused the half tab he offered me, I'm the sole Ward 2-er allowed on pass. Nick whistles in that weird way he does, blowing air through his curled tongue, when I give him a winded twirl. I'm Mulan with the white face paint, heavy eyeliner, and crimson lips from when she met the matchmaker. Except I also have a sword, because her kicking ass was the best part.

"Nuh-uh," I poke Nick with the plastic blade as he pulls in for a kiss. "I spent way too long on this for you to kiss it off in thirty seconds."

"What if it was longer than thirty?" Shit, that's a good point. I have all the stuff to reapply.

Distraction time. "And you're s'posed to be a ...?"

"A vampire," he says, fishing out super fake plastic fangs. He crams them over his real teeth and mumbles something indecipherable.

"What'd you say?"

He takes the fangs out. "Duh."

"Duh what?"

"Duh nothing. That's all I said."

"Those fangs have gotta go." I convince him to toss them and be a zombie instead. We spend the rest of the car ride in makeover mode. Corpse-pale skin with bruises, blood, and open wounds—it's not that different from me after a bad head bang. My fingers fly to my bangs. I fluff them out while checking my forehead in my mirror, making sure they cover my scab. Nick catches my frown in the reflection and winks.

"You look great, babe."

After we get dropped off, the smokers have time for two smoke breaks while I keep our place in the ticket line. Having *Assassin's Apprentice* to read keeps me from dying of boredom. Stamps on our hands and the tickets and other stuff in my purse, Nick and I say bye to the rest of the group. First ride: Music Express. Some of the songs from our rooftop dance party play as we're spun, jostled faster and faster, along a diagonal slope. Whenever we hit that tilt, gravity becomes the perfect excuse for me to fall onto him. In the tunnel part, the way-too-familiar chorus of "Locked Up" blasts out at us. We lose our shit, me laughing 'til I gasp because right now, we're not. We're

A Drop in the Ocean 107

actually free for the next three and a half hours. Psych ward Cinderellas at a Fright Night ball.

We don't have enough money to play any of the games, so Nick never gets the chance to win me a stuffie. But we do hit up the Corkscrew, which I never knew was a "fuckin' icon," as Nick says.

"Haven't you seen *Final Destination*? The third one came out a few months ago. This was the ride they all should've died on."

On the ride, the wind lashes my skin. It roars deliciously in my ears from how high and fast we're going. Nick has his hands up and adds his own roar of joy. I close my eyes as we spiral upside down and rocket downhill. He asks me if I'm scared. No, I'm at peace.

It's times like these that I wish for death. After a really good day, when my rituals have gone well and my relationships even better, perishing in some kind of disaster I have no control over feels like the perfect way to go. Everything ending on a high note, me having ruined nothing, hurt nobody, exiting existence. It's not like my anorexia antics, trying to trick God into thinking it's not suicide by slowly starving myself to death. Or even the too-cowardly-to-kill-myself-but-not-wanting-to-be-alive angst I'm used to. Pretty sure it's too positive a thought to call suicidal, especially if it was something like this roller coaster derailing. But what about Nick? Then he would die too, along with all these other people. Fuck, maybe I should stick to wishing for a heart attack or dying tonight really peacefully in my sleep. That would work.

My strategy for the haunted houses is to keep my hands on Nick's large shoulders and stare straight at the ground when things get too scary. In the ones with strobe lights, I switch to studying the embroidery on my flats to keep from getting dizzy. Yeah, some of the special effects are pretty fake, but I have a big imagination, and *The Ring* gave me nightmares for months. I own that. The third house has this gory scene with fake bodies that look way too real. It doesn't help that a little boy races from room to room, wailing and screaming for his "Mumma, Daddy, Mumma!" The first time Nick hears the kid shout, his shoulders tense. A few rooms later we catch a glimpse of the kid, who's crying too hard to see where he's going, bumping into people and furniture. Instead of asking for his parents, he whimpers, "Ow, ow, ow, ow."

Nick crouches so he's at the kid's eye level. But before he's even said a word the only thing left of the kid is the sound of his footsteps pounding away. Nick, still crouching, rocks once, back and forth. His shoulders are quaking. As he gets up, I grip onto them. His pulse jack-hammers against my fingertips.

"The kid'll be fine," I murmur, kneading my knuckles into his back.

He shrugs my hands off. "Yeah, sure."

Outside of that room, Nick stays fight-or-flight rigid, ready to right-hook someone at any moment. He's not making fun of the haunted houses' cheesy backstories or complaining about how we haven't been jump scared by an actor anymore. Instead, when we run into Fright Night staff we ask if they've seen a little boy crying. No, they say, they haven't. When we finally get outside after double-checking every room again for the kid, it's drizzling. My flats get soaked, but I'm happy to be moving on from our fruitless search. We're near an alleyway that's been turned into a parking lot. Only one more haunted house to go.

"You want that massage now?" I ask, reaching for Nick's shoulders.

"Don't!" He shoves me away. A stumbling backstep saves me from falling on my ass. I keep the *what the hell* to myself. Nick strides ahead

A Drop in the Ocean

of me as we cross the parking lot to the last Fright Night attraction. What can I do?

We're halfway through the parking lot, and it's gone from sprinkling to spitting. The Playland logo searchlight lands on the triangular blob we're walking toward, illuminating a striped circus tent. A freak show theme? Please be a freak show theme and not—Pennywise and the Joker step out of the Staff Only trailer at the parking lot's edge. Clowns. Fuck.

"Let's skip this one."

"What?" Nick snaps. Like I've just told him to go fuck his mother.

"I said"—and now there's a bite in my voice too—"let's skip this one."

"Why?" He slows down so we're walking at the same pace.

Pennywise and the Joker are both within earshot as I say, "Because I hate clowns."

The two actors stop. They whisper to each other before sauntering our way.

"So you hate clowns, do you?" Pennywise asks.

The Joker laughs. Kind of a "har, har, har, hyuck." I'm not sure if it's supposed to be demented or murderous—maybe both?

"Hey." Nick's hands are balled into fists. After a few brisk steps he's all up in their faces. They're older than him and there's two of them, but he's around their size and something so much worse than pissed.

"What the fuck, man!" Pennywise raises his hands. He's painted half his face into an open-fanged mouth, which makes looking at his actual mouth within the makeup mouth really fucking trippy. "We're just doing our job."

The Joker is no longer laughing. He shakes his index finger at us, tsk-tsk-tsking.

What kind of prick scares someone not even in the park and then tries to act all superior about it when people get upset? "Nick, don't," is all I say, though. Because he's bent down and found a rock the size of his fist. "Just ... wh-why do you need that?" I grab him by the shoulders and try to get him to look me in the eyes. He snarls and shakes me off. Both clowns are hustling back to their carnival tent now. I gave them the few seconds they needed to get away.

"Look what happened. You thought I couldn't take them, didn't you?"

"I just, I—"

"*Shut up!* Shut. The. Fuck. Up." Spit flies out of his mouth an inch away from my face. Maybe my heart is pounding fast, I can't tell, because it's falling into this hole in my gut that I didn't know was endless. All of me falling as I cringe and wince in my costume lie. I'm not Mulan. I'm not even brave. Nick shakes his head and mutters something I can't hear. He stalks back the way we came. Five feet behind, I follow. At the Staff Only trailer, he stops. He lifts his hand with the rock in it, sharp edge out.

SMASH. The loudness makes me cry out. There goes the front window, glass shattering. In the moon and the roaming signal lights, I see a spiderweb of cracks ripple out from its broken centre. Should I be glad or sad that there isn't an alarm bringing crowds our way? Maybe glad. Because security would pin him down. If he struggled, they'd club him or tase him. I do what little I can to protect my ears, dulling the sound violence by keeping my palms pressed hard against them. Nick keeps going. SMASH. The hood of the trailer has a giant dent. SMASH. It has another. He can't see me, but I cringe with every hit. Moan like the little boy from earlier while backing farther away. A banging noise is a banging noise is a banging noise, no matter who makes it. And the fact that it's Nick being out of control sparks two kinds of *wrongness* through my brain. SMASH. There goes the left side-view mirror, beheaded in one stroke. My legs tremble, only steadying when I crouch and make myself as small as possible, hands still clamped on my ears. His blows, their force, over and over, reminds me of Metrotown when he saw me head banging.

"Let's go!" I force myself to yell from the ground. "We're going to get caught."

He's panting, the smashes less frequent, not as forceful. He drops his hands to his knees for a sec and heaves in a few deep breaths. When he gets back up, he glances my way. It's progress.

"Security will come, or police."

"What are you doing? Why are you so far away?"

"You're banging and it's scary."

"Jesus Christ." Another hard smash of the front window. Shattered glass sprinkles the concrete. "I thought it was just when people slammed doors."

"Banging noises. Any banging noises."

He smashes a little softer. Red from his bleeding knuckles smears against the off-white of the dirty trailer.

"Your hands!" I grit my teeth and do the opposite of what my survival instincts want by walking toward him. "Nick, you're hurt. We need to leave."

He continues with the half-hearted smashes, only hitting things that make a softer shattering noise. There goes the right side-view mirror. There goes the right headlight.

"Either we leave now, or I'm screaming 'til someone comes." To prep for screaming as loud as I can, I swallow spit for a few seconds. My throat's still hoarse from yelling at Fright Night shit. These will be actual words I want people to hear instead of shrieks I'm ashamed of two seconds later. I step farther away from Nick, making sure I don't turn my back on him. On my fourth step, pain slices through the sole of my right foot. Glass.

"Ow-wuh!" As I yelp, I hop around on one leg trying to see the damage in the damn dark. My flat's thin rubber sole is punctured in a few places where the glass stabbed my foot. Balancing properly now, I trace the damage with my fingertips, past the cracked rubber to my sock, soggy with blood.

Nick's sneer contorts to confusion, then to open-mouthed alarm when he realizes what's happened. He tosses the rock and doesn't look back, jogging over a few steps until we're almost touching. "Your foot's bleeding." His voice has softened back to sounding like Nick. "You need to sit down."

If I don't put too much weight on my right foot or step on its side or heel, I can still walk. I do that, hobbling away from the trailer, knowing in my gut that he'll follow. "So? What about your knuckles?"

"Okay, okay, sit down on the curb. We'll both bandage up."

With what? I'm about to ask, but he's already tearing his shirt into strips. My knees give way so fast when we park our asses down. Both of us grunt, our muscles relieved to be resting. My energy drains along with my adrenalin as we sit that way for a while. I keep a two-person-sized space between us, just in case. He tries to close the distance and I flinch. Resigned, he doesn't try again. After what feels like ages, Nick, actual Nick, starts talking. His voice is soft and husky.

"I never wanted you to see that."

I stay quiet but nod so he knows I'm listening.

"It's like I become this whole other person and just explode. That's even what they call it."

"Like, why you're here?"

"Yeah, partly at least. Intermittent explosive disorder, depression, being one of the youngest kids in town to have his stomach pumped for booze."

He'd told me the truth about his diagnosis, then: *I get mad and sad and do dumb things.*

"That boy in the haunted house, the one who was crying ..."

He stops bandaging his hand, lifts his hunched neck to look at me. Does nothing else but look, with full attention. And his eyes are so sad and so raw that my heart breaks.

Fuck it. Fuck learning the tragic backstory about why he looks the way he looks right now. All I want is for him not to. Not to hurt. Not to talk about it unless it's his choice. "You know what? As long as you promise never to scare me like that again, you don't have to force yourself to tell me about your past. I get it. And I get it because I know I'll never get it, because I never went through what you did. No one but you has. Does that make sense?"

His eyebrows furrow, a question forming on his lips. Before he asks it, I continue.

"No one but you's lived your life. No one can live it for you. But I'm here to do what I can to help."

Without speaking, he grabs both my hands in his. Although I still flinch, I don't pull away. We look down and study them together. His are cartoon puffy, knuckles swollen. Where they're cut up, the blood's started to dry and coagulate. Mine are, like always, cold. Not for long, though, as he rubs them and warms them with his breath. The activity gets his blood flowing, which makes one of his cuts reopen. It spills scarlet down the back of my hand.

"There, now we've both bled on each other," he says as I wind a shirt strip around his right palm.

"So we're even?"

"Not even—ha ha—close."

I groan at his pun. "How do you mean?"

"Well, I'd spend the rest of my life cleaning up your blood."

"Promise?"

"Pinky-swear promise," he says, so we do.

We leave after we've both bandaged each other up and his shirt no longer covers his wide navel. We're half an hour late to the pickup spot. Some of our ordeal must show through, because Margaret doesn't penalize us when my only explanation is that we "got lost." Instead, she marches us to the van, where the others are waiting. We sit in the very back, sandwiched between some Ward 3-ers. They chatter about the rides while we lean against each other and just breathe.

CHAPTER TWELVE

*N*o one's found out. Nick said he googled it at school and there were like two online articles about vandalism at Playland. A trailer is among a bunch of damaged property listed. I guess Nick's broken his knuckles before, so one of the nurses bandaged it up properly without prying too much. When I asked how often shit like this has happened, he admitted Playland was the worst he's ever gotten. Promised he'd never get that worked up again. He better keep his word, or else ... Well, let's not even go there. Meanwhile, I swore that I would take what happened to the grave, not even hint about it to Dr. Grant, who's under a confidentiality oath. Every hour, the secret swells up in me. It's been less than a day, how the hell do I keep it in for the rest of my life? I need to tell someone or I'll burst. And by someone, I mean Sweets. After what Nick calls the billionth time of me begging him, he caves. We can tell Sweets together. We've done enough rule-breaking shit as a team to know that she can keep a secret. Besides, she owes me for buying her disposable razors. (She's only allowed to shave with the shitty electric razor under staff supervision because duh.)

Something's off with her, has been for a while. Who knew the main side effect of lithium was bitchiness? When we talk, Sweets answers in clipped sentences or doesn't answer at all. I keep asking her what I did to make her so pissed. "Nothing, okay? I'm just not in the mood for you." And stuff like that is what she says when I apologize. It's like she's a few steps farther away from me than she really is, even when we're sitting next to each other. What's weird is that it's not a depressive cycle. She's actually being nicer to the staff and pretty much the same to all the other kids.

Nick and I are strategic. We wait 'til she's alone for her traditional post-lunch vanilla Prime Time. The rest of the unit's smoking at the back exit so they can shoot hoops if they want. Not her thing. Nick has a fat doobie rolled to help the news go down easier. She turns our way, exhaling a wisp as we walk to Ward 2's front entrance. I wave so hard my arm gets sore. She rolls her eyes and turns toward the wall. We keep walking her way.

If booze is liquid courage, what's weed? Skunky courage? "Can I have a hit now?" You probably can't get the munchies from a few puffs.

"No." Nick tucks the joint back in his jacket pocket. "The point is that we light it and blaze together."

On the fourth step I stumble a little, because my legs are shaky. Sweets watches us while smushing her Prime Time under her black spike–studded platform shoe.

"Hey, we need to tell you something."

The left side of her mouth quirks up in a sour half grin. She sighs and snatches the joint from Nick's outstretched palm. "Me first."

"It's a really big deal, can we go somewhere private?"

Fruity Pebbles, which smells a bit like the cereal but mainly like weed, overpowers the burnt vanilla in the air. She holds the toke in for almost a minute. The cloud she exhales makes me cough. "I know you ooze drama so this may come as a shock, but what you're going through isn't always the biggest deal at any given moment." There's a flatness in her voice I'm not used to, beneath all the snark.

"Fine then, go first. What's up with you, Taryn?" I hit the *T* sound hard. Nick's staying out of it, all his attention fixed on the joint handed back to him.

A Drop in the Ocean 117

"No, you killed the moment. Just spill or leave."

I raise my eyebrows at Nick. *Should we?*

"It's about Halloween," he says, passing me the joint. Smoke scrapes my trachea as I toke up. "When we were at Playland, I kind of lashed out."

Sweets stomps forward, lurching into Nick's face the way he did with the clowns. The top of her head, elevated by her platforms, barely reaches Nick's chin, but damn, she's scary. "If you hit her, I swear to God ..."

"No, no, no." I put my arms between the two of them because that's all that fits. Really, I want to squish them around her in a giant hug because she does still like me. Or at least cares about my well-being or whatever. Enough to take on Nick, which means she'd still be pissed if she knew just how frightening he'd been. Which means she doesn't need to know every last detail. "It's not like that. He trashed a trailer, not me."

"Huh?" The murder is gone from her glare.

"Not *trashed*. And I wouldn't've done it if those clowns had left Mira alone."

He brought up the clowns. I follow his lead and tell Sweets about how they were being total pricks. The joint's down to a cherry when it reaches me again. She and Nick have moved on to cigarettes, and we've told her a Disneyfied version of the full story. She waves her Prime Time at us.

"Anyways, what I was gonna say before is that I'm getting discharged in five days."

"We'll miss you, but congrats," Nick says.

Whereas I yell, "What the actual fuck?" My heartbeat launches into overdrive. When I inhale to slow it down, I glare betrayed rage at her, shaking my head until it gets woozy. Right, I need to exhale. I do, then keep taking loud, deep breaths before finally saying, "Why'd you wait so long to tell me?"

Sweets meets my glare, staring me down until she hisses in frustration and glances away. "Because I knew you'd turn it into a ginormous deal the way you are right now."

"Isn't it?"

"It's supposed to be a good thing, right, Nick?"

Nick clears his throat and looks pleadingly at both of us. "C'mon guys, this doesn't need to be a fight. Going home is the end goal of being here. It's what we all want."

I turn to him, hating how he's stuck in the middle, how he's taking her side. "I'm not saying I want Sweets to stay here forever. Just that *friends* aren't supposed to keep news this big from each other. We came clean after one day of having a secret. How long do you think she's known about her discharge?"

"A week, okay, a week," Sweets snaps. "And I'm outta here. I don't need to be interrogated by my *friends*."

After she leaves Nick tries to make me feel better by warming my hands. He wants to cuddle and make out, but I keep remembering how these softly speaking lips screamed at me, how these arms wrapping around me and these gentle hands smashed a trailer. That, plus him backing up Sweets means for once, I'm not in the mood.

◆

Since I can't rely on my friends it's good that I have family. Things with Sweets are mutually strained now. Which is fucked, because we might never see each other again. Obviously we're not doing anything as preppy or cheesy as getting BFF jewellery from Ardene or Claire's.

A Drop in the Ocean   *119*

There'd have to be some kind of Sweera (Sweets + Mira) equivalent. I want her to write me a goodbye message at the very least. Not yet, though, because Mom and her "surprise" should be showing up at any moment.

Seriously? Where is she? It's 3:38 p.m. I can understand being up to five minutes late, but eight—that's three whole extra minutes. And this is Mom we're talking about; she's never late. I rub my hands against my arms, trying to warm away the goosebumps from the drafty-ass air conditioning. It's my first time in the family meeting lounge, one of the rooms in the corridor between the school and the gym. Next door's conference room is basically this giant round table full of fancy office seats.

Here in the lounge it's supposed to feel comfier, "intimate," maybe. The furniture is nicer than anything anywhere else at the Residency: a flat-screen TV complete with DVD player across from a jumbo leather couch, a medium-ish square table with neatly stacked board games and art supplies, and chairs almost as nice as the ones in the conference room. There are even decorative freaking cushions. Should I use them as a kind of extra layer for my freezing, bare arms? Nah.

There's a faint rap at the door and a familiar high, musical voice. "Knock, knock."

Then a lower, croakier one. "Can we come in?"

"Poh Poh!" I rush out of my seat and fling open the door.

Poh Poh totters in on bird-thin legs, clutching Mom's right arm for support. This is the first time in nine months that I've seen her. The last time was when I'd just flown back from UCLA neuropsych. Since then, she's gotten tinier. While I fixated on the flatness of my stomach as a tween, she literally didn't have one. Not since 2000, when doctors found cancer there and removed it. Her deep, tawny skin curves gauntly inward on her neck, and her collarbones stick out like pencils. Unlike Gung Gung, she still has most of her hair. She dyes it but doesn't bother with perms anymore. Below are sparse, pencilled-in brows and very few eyelashes, the rest burnt away during a child-hood kitchen fire. Her eyes, though, they're the same. Clear within the creases of crow's feet and laugh lines, not yet clouded with cataracts. The best thing is the way they shine, especially when she smiles.

We hold each other, squeezing tight. Her grip's so strong, as if no time's gone by since she taught me to make pie dough. Me holding the rolling pin and her hands holding mine, the dough flattening smooth under the countertop powdered with flour. Neither of us wants to be the first to break the embrace. We don't have to, as Mom comes in for a group hug.

"This is the best surprise ever," I tell them.

After a second round of hugs, they let me scooch chairs from the table closer to mine. I get caught up in lifting them above my head. Moving things = exercise, so I have to do it. It's one of those baby rituals Dr. Grant wants me to fight. But my family is used to me doing things like this; they have to love me no matter what, so I don't hide it as much. I don't even think about refusing or delaying the urge until my ass is back down in my chair. At least Dr. Grant would be proud that my fingernails are intact, my hands occupied by twirling the pen I brought with me.

"What's new with you?" I ask Poh Poh. "Have you done anything cool or exciting these past few months?"

"Auntie Ruby"—who's really my great-aunt—"came over from Vic-toria, and us sisters all got together for a lunch date at Oakridge. The

A Drop in the Ocean

arthritis in her hands is acting up, so I added her joint pain to our daily prayer circle. We pray for you too."

Great, God stuff. The pen becomes a blur as I tap tap tap tap tap it against my leg. Poh Poh doesn't get that God made me this way as punishment. She's the one who's always saying he doesn't make mistakes.

"Oh. Tell everyone thanks."

Silence brews until Mom clears her throat, hefting up a large tote bag.

"Here's the second part of your surprise." She takes out our family photo album and two russet-red leatherbound ones I've never seen before that are even bigger, setting them in the centre of the table. "You've been asking all sorts of questions about what Dad was like when he was younger. This pair of albums from the attic can help you peek into his past."

"I'll be your tour guide," Poh Poh says.

The first russet album's pictures are all black and white. There's a chubby, smiling baby in the arms of a woman with the same full face and fuller lips. A studio photo where the woman is seated, adorned by a long strand of pearls and a flower broach, with a baby girl in her lap. A toddler girl stands next to them while the boy from before looks old enough for preschool. Above them all stands a man with round glasses, a suit, a bow tie, and a pocket watch. None of them smile.

"That's your gung gung after his one-month. Held by his mother, your taai mah. The one beside it is a family portrait."

After that comes a *Vancouver Sun* article, "12 Troupers Call Her Mother," along with photos of even more children, seven, and Taai Mah posed in a row. All of them wear intricate costumes, sequined and flashy even in black and white. Gung Gung, the first-born, is the tallest, a wiry youth smiling so wide his jaw must hurt. In the photo below it, he's the base of a three-person pyramid, his posture perfect while lifting two younger siblings. They hold up their arms like Olympic gymnasts do after a routine.

"Holy shit."

Mom nudges me under the table. "Swearing," she whispers.

"Sorry, Poh Poh. I've heard the stories growing up, but seeing these pictures adds a whole new level."

Poh Poh smiles. "A portion of his act was to light a match on the ground while riding his unicycle. Another was tap dancing with his sisters."

Parts of Gung Gung I recognize, like the slicked-back, side-parted hair, the thousand-watt smile so different from his solemn studio portrait. He's got to be thirteen or fourteen here, still a beanpole. Where are the muscles? Where's Poh Poh, for that matter?

"How old were you both when you started dating?" I ask her, as we flip past pages of vintage race cars. He was a race-car driver too.

"We were in our twenties," she answers.

"What? That's old enough to be in university. I couldn't wait that long to date Nick."

"Her boyfriend from Ward 1," Mom explains.

I know my smile reveals the dimples I've inherited from Poh Poh. "He's awesome, we've been going out for about a month."

"A month," Poh Poh sniffs. "You're too young."

Mom distracts her before she can disapprove any more. "Wow, look at that photo of you and Dad at Stanley Park."

In the next few pages Poh Poh and Gung Gung smile beside each other in photo after photo of Chinese restaurant tables. Sometimes they sit at round tables with Lazy Susans at dim sum, other times

A Drop in the Ocean

they're in banquet halls surrounded by twenty-plus family members and friends. Poh Poh fills us in on what occasion each feast was for, who's who, and how we're related to them. I stare longest at the precious few of her and Gung Gung on their own. Him, grown into the broad shoulders I recognize, holding her in front of the Lions Gate Bridge. Him on a cushioned armchair, with her balanced on its right arm. My favourite is the album's last photo. The way they're posed and dressed makes them look like a fifties movie star couple. Gung Gung's svelte in a tailored black suit and tie, while Poh Poh has a Lucille Ball perm, dark lipstick, and a pinstriped dress. It's a studio portrait, so their smiles are stiff but genuine, creasing the corners of their eyes. I can tell that they make each other happy.

We haven't come to it yet, but the photo I like best of us three is significantly goofier. An only slightly balding Gung Gung sits on toddler Mira's left, and a healthy, exuberant Poh Poh on her right. All of us have our mouths open, the two of them probably saying "cheese" while I nibble on my finger with my perfectly straight baby teeth. As for their teeth, you can see dark-silver fillings. Both of them are too swept up in the moment to care. Something about their expressions reminds me of the fifties movie star shot, except more. Truer. Freer, maybe. The corners of their eyes are creased with wrinkles but mostly from joy.

The next album begins with more fifties, white picket fence stuff. The two of them holding baby versions of my oldest aunt and uncle, their house in the background. Another has Poh Poh resplendent in an off-the-shoulder dress, hair in soft waves and classic smoky eye makeup.

"You were so beautiful—you still are," I say. I reach over to squeeze her hand, but my fingers close on empty air. She's wiping her eyes, sniffling.

"That was his favourite dress on me." There's a gurgle to her words, from the snot she's too ladylike to brush off with the back of her hand like I would. Mom's already offering a Kleenex from her stash.

"We don't have to do this anymore. You've told me lots." The tears mean she's triggered, but she's doing what she always does, sacrificing herself to make others happy.

She breathes deep, lets out a quavering exhale. "It's fine."

"No, it's not. Not if I'm making you remember all these things and you're sad because of how much they've changed." How selfish am I? This man I've known for sixteen years has been the love of her life for over sixty. Whatever I'm going through is small fucking potatoes compared to her pain.

"Life is change." Poh Poh blows her nose, using every centimetre of Kleenex so she doesn't need a second. "God blessed us with a long time together. Besides, something can be worthwhile even if it's painful. Sharing Gung Gung's life with you is how we celebrate it. He loves you so much." She squeezes my hand the way I'd wanted to hers. "He'd want you to know."

"Then tell me everything."

Poh Poh's lips quiver as she forces a trace of a smile back on her face. "First I need to use the ladies' room. I'll be back in a moment."

Mom shoots up from her chair and holds her arm out for Poh Poh to take.

"It's okay, Sarah, I know where it is."

I keep quizzing Mom about what kind of dad Gung Gung was while we wait. It blows my mind that the mostly silent senior I've known him as thrived in high-adrenalin situations. What cool father-daughter memories does she have? Did he teach her circus tricks? Apparently, the whole breakfast oatmeal race tradition was

A Drop in the Ocean   125

her idea, except Gung Gung never noticed her trying to keep pace with him.

"Okay, then, did he read to you at bedtime or teach you how to drive in one of his fancy cars?"

Mom sighs. "Dad's role in parenting was to be the provider. He worked overtime as a denturist to keep all of us fed and clothed."

"What about the weekends? Or when he got home, did you play games together? You know, mah-jong, cards?"

"Uh-uh." Another sigh as she shakes her head. "First off, Mum's church didn't approve of games, it was too much like gambling. Second, after being the provider, Dad was the disciplinarian. When he did get home, Mum would tell him if me or any of your aunts and uncles had misbehaved. If we'd been really bad, he'd rap his knuckles on our foreheads."

I push past my bangs, feeling how my forehead scab aches to be picked. "So you never got to spend time with him?" My dad lives all the way in France, a legit reason for not really being in my life. Gung Gung had six kids, six chances to be there.

"Not that much. Gung Gung might have had an exciting past, but it was really Poh Poh who raised us. He put food on the table. She kept track of that food, shopped for it, cooked it, then cleaned it up afterward. Gung Gung was the head of the household, and Poh Poh was its heart."

"Oh." I hate chores—cooking, gardening, cleaning, laundry. When I was little I didn't know they were chores, only fun games Poh Poh and I played together.

Mom's eyes dart to the door to check if we're still alone. "Don't tell anybody, but when I was sorting out junk in their basement, I found a university scholarship letter with Poh Poh's maiden name on it. She couldn't go because she had to make money to help her parents and younger siblings. All my life, she never once mentioned applying for post-secondary. I only found out by accident."

There are whole other sides to who Gung Gung and Poh Poh are. Not grandparents or even parents, but people barely older than me with dreams like mine, totally separate from having kids. Gung Gung got to live out some of his dreams, having audiences look up to him, racing and buying sports cars. Whereas Poh Poh was overlooked. Sacrificing her dreams to support her birth family, then starting and raising a family of her own. If you're a woman, that's what's expected of you. Too bad no one thinks child care and cleaning are glamorous.

"That's awful, she got in and couldn't go."

"It is, in ways that aren't her fault. Now shh. You know how she hates anyone fussing over her."

"My lips are sealed." I mime double-zipping my mouth shut.

When Poh Poh's back, we look through the rest of the albums. The decades are easy to tell, worn head to toe by my family. Gung Gung in corduroys and a toque absorbed in a game of Whac-A-Mole, my aunties in bell-bottoms and flower headbands. Mom on her first day of kindergarten in a blue dress. Gung Gung in a fuchsia shirt when my cousins first start to show up as babies. Poh Poh's lipstick of the very same shade in the nineties when me and the last of the cousins are born.

"Look at how cute your waves are." Poh Poh coos over the photos where Mom's shiny black hair curves and wisps at the nape of her neck.

"What do you mean, cute?" Mom says, her voice rising. "You know I *hated* that haircut because it made me look like a boy."

There's a gasp from Poh Poh. "No one thought that."

A Drop in the Ocean 127

Oops. "You mean that kid in the striped shirt and white shorts next to Auntie Lynn is Mom, not Uncle Gordon?"

"Of course it's me," Mom says in a high voice, cheeks red as if she's just had a glass or two of booze.

In that same high pitch, Poh Poh exclaims, "Mira, that's obviously your mother."

I nod, smart enough to know when to back down. "Now I totally see that it's Mom."

Poh Poh pats my hand. *Good girl.*

The last picture in the album is one I haven't seen before. It's at Poh Poh's tiny church all the way in Langley. She'd drive us there and back every Saturday for worship service. There's the pulpit and choir stand, and I can name every member of the congregation singing praise. Even though it's been five years since I went there, it's as if time has frozen. Pastor Stevens at the pulpit still wears his cross-print pocket square immaculately folded into his suit. Sister Stevens, his wife, still stands in the spot of honour, first row centre of the choir. Next to her is Poh Poh, and next to Poh Poh, where I used to stand, is a pretty brunette in a matching lavender sweater and skirt. Her cheek rests on Poh Poh's shoulder, the family resemblance undeniable, both with the same beatific grin.

"Is that Rachel?" I splutter. "In my spot at choir?"

"That girl is such a blessing, she's been my church companion for over a year now. Next service, she's giving a testimonial." Poh Poh's eyes shine as she caresses the edge of the photo. Perfect freaking Rachel, the youngest, churchiest, and favouritest of the Lung cousins. I remember when Poh Poh used to look at me that way, and when she stopped. It was when I turned crazy. Suddenly, a headache pounds dizziness at my temples. I think about how much worse the ache would be if it were electricity instead. How that was what the head of the psych department at Children's Hospital wanted to do to me.

"So you said ECT helped Auntie Edith?"

"What's ECT?"

Mom's voice goes quiet and grim. "Shock therapy, electroconvulsive shock treatment."

"Ai ya!" Poh Poh heaves a sigh and wilts into herself, head bending like a flower past its prime. "Let's not talk about such things." After a pointed stare from Mom and me, she goes on. "Yes, that's what they did in Essondale for her depression. Then she was able to go on with the rest of her life. But you don't need that, do you, Mira? You're getting better here, aren't you?"

CHAPTER THIRTEEN

Fuck! Double fuck actually. Usually jumping's not a problem, just exhausting. Not this time, this time I TOUCHED THE WALL. Fuck walls! As punishment, I've extended my wound up high into my hairline by blunt force slicing it. I switched up my flat wall surface for one of the sharp-ass corners where walls from two different directions join. My scalp's split at the seams in a perfect line. Now that it's scabbed over, I pull back my hair and there's this thin red treasure trail that widens into the blob of my wound.

If I go to the nurses' station, they might want to give me stitches. Fuck that even more than walls. I'm not bleeding anymore, and I've smeared a bunch of Polysporin over the whole shit show. All I need is something for the pain. Something to kill the pounding and the heat that comes with each shooting ache. Ice. A fuck ton of it in a zip-lock bag, that'll do the trick.

In the kitchen I open the freezer door to blessed cold. God, I wish I could just live in there. I crack out the ice cubes left in both trays into my zip-lock. Pop one in my mouth and crunch. I'm so lost in the relief that I don't notice Sweets coming into the kitchen until she's ahemming at me with her arms crossed over her chest.

"Whaddyou want?" I say, slurping up the cube in an effort not to waste the water I've melted with my mouth.

"Goddamn, did you take a razor to your scalp?"

"Shut up." I jerk my head toward Janelle, who's monitoring this wing of the unit. Yes, my bangs are in place, a little bit sticky from dried blood but covering everything. "How can you see that—isn't my hair in the way? Anyway, I always bang my head."

129

Sweets's indigo lips twitch into a smirk. She leans in, opening the fridge so the noisy fan blocks staff from hearing our convo. "You forget how short I am. When I look up, I see under your bangs. Also, that scalp thing is new, it's on a different part of your head." She keeps looking at it, as if she's concerned. Great, so now she wants to be friends again and I'll have to recount every humiliating detail.

"It was from jumping *wrong*. Let's not talk about it."

She rolls her eyes. "Fine by me. Just grab me the ice tray, I'll take what you didn't use."

"Oh sorry. I had to refill both of them."

"Shit."

From my zip-lock, I grab four of the bigger cubes. "Take these."

"I'll need more than that. Why not come with me and use the pack on our walk?"

Do I want to be walking or doing anything other than lying next to the fridge? No. But do I wish things between us BFF crazies could go back to our version of normal? Yes. And am I curious? Hell yes.

"All right, you lead."

Sweets gets the okay from Janelle and we're off. As long as we're back half an hour before lights out, we can bum around wherever we want on Residency grounds. We walk side by side, me with the ice pack on my head, her with both hands buried in her baggy cargo pants pockets.

"Should we get Nick?" I ask. We've passed the parking lot and are coming up to Ward 1. Thank God he doesn't live on our ward, where my weirdness on an hourly basis would scare him as much as his Playland outburst frightened me.

"He's already waiting." Sweets leads us left, then down the knoll. Away from the school, toward the back of the Residency, where the

A Drop in the Ocean

cafeteria and a soccer field are. On the other side of the soccer field is actual juvie. The girls and guys there live on separate wards and only socialize a few hours a day. I guess that's another thing to be thankful for, not living there. Rule of threes, what's my third thankful thing? The ice. It's staying nice and solid. Meanwhile what has melted hasn't leaked all over me. Sweets double bagging it was a good call. I tell her so and she grunts in agreement. Every few minutes I lift the bag away when the cold starts to ache instead of soothe.

Our search leads us past the soccer field to an overgrown grove that's shared Residency/juvie territory. Nick calls out to us from beneath the branches of its largest shrub, completely hidden. We squeeze through the foliage into a leafy den. He's spread two of the thermal blankets you can get from the laundry room over the ground and is sitting on one, cross-legged. On the other rests a lighter and bottle of Everclear, the colourful corncob of its label bright against a black background. Corn? I guess you really can make booze out of anything.

"Hey babe, what's that for?" I ask, popping a squat next to him. Sweets fishes stuff out of her pockets before joining us.

"Jinking, obviously," Nick says. When I still look confused, he explains, "Smoking joints and drinking."

Sweets punches him in the arm. "Nuh-uh. It's for sterilization. Why didn't you just get rubbing alcohol?" She places an ink bottle, a travel bag of cotton batting, and a round sewing needle container alongside the Everclear. Ink is for art, a needle can be a pen nib, fire can cleanse that nib, alcohol can cleanse an unconventional canvas, and my ice can numb that canvas's pain.

"You're going to tattoo yourselves, aren't you?"

"Yup, and we'll party with what's left of the Everclear. That's why I didn't get isopropyl, that shit will kill you if you drink it."

I give both of them my best laser glare, but my frown melts from anger to pain.

"Don't worry, give us the ice and you can bounce. We won't let you get in trouble," Sweets says. "And don't talk shit about my subscription to *Inked* anymore. It had this great DIY stick-and-poke article that I read enough times to make me a pro at this."

"No, you idiots. Tattoo teardrops on your face for all I care." They better not. "It's just, don't do stuff like this without me. We're supposed to tell each other everything."

Nick and Sweets exchange a look. "Staff are bound to notice our new ink jobs, we're like, guaranteed gonna get in trouble." Sweets speaks slowly, as if I'm too naive to figure that out myself. "You sure you're okay with this?"

I think about how tattoos are like jewellery you can never take off. How Sweets not-so-secretly thinks I'm a prude. How when my whole unit got in trouble for taking E, they lost off-unit privileges for seven days tops. How Sweets will be leaving forever. "Only if I get one too."

"Congrats, babe, you're a secret badass," Nick says, reaching over and scooping me into his lap for a kiss. When he has enough cash to get inked by an actual pro, he wants "you have one lives left ... ♡" in pixelated Nintendo font down his forearm. Existentialism via video games, it's super him. He's this amazing mix of smart, goofy, and caring. During moments like this, who he was at Playland and who I am when I'm banging my head feel like versions of us from an alternate universe.

Sweets takes out a few needles and examines them before settling on one that's medium sized. She burns it for five seconds in the lighter's

A Drop in the Ocean

flame. Next, she hikes down her left sock and cleanses a spot on her ankle with Everclear. She pours just the tiniest bit of ink into the lid and dips the needle in. "Since you are my 'besties'"—she makes air quotes with the needle in her hand and ink flies, splatting black on the blanket—"I'll do me first as the trial run. I practised on some orange peels that turned out pretty good."

I watch her stab herself over and over with the tiny, sharp point. Each stab makes a dot, and when she gets the hang of how it feels, she makes smaller dots to connect them all together in a line.

"Doesn't this mean that you can't be buried in your family's cemetery?" I ask.

Sweets shrugs. "I'm pretty sure Hashem would be fucking stoked that I'm making cool art with a needle and not slashing into myself with a blade. Besides, my family only practises on and off." She balances on her right leg and raises her left to give us a better view of the finished product. Five rays of a pentagram, only one of them wobbly, spread out right above her ankle bone. The whole star is barely bigger than my thumb. After a last look, she ices it and nods. "Yup, I made the right call. Thought about cutting, pretty pissed I have to leave, but then I was like, there must be something better. Something I can do instead that doesn't make me feel like shit the instant it's done." Her being such a giant bitch lately makes way more sense.

Nick swabs a spot on his right shoulder where he wants two crossed arrows. "Is your home life really fucked up?" He asks what I didn't have the nerve to, what she's never talked about for the three months I've known her.

"It's not like my parents beat me or anything. Or that I'm worried about getting raped by some goof neighbour." Sweets jams the needle into Nick's skin fast and hard, until red wells up where the black should be. "Home isn't home, that's all."

"I feel like that sometimes," I murmur.

"Same," says Nick.

"Your parents don't treat you like a burden, though, do they?" She looks up from her handiwork and quirks an eyebrow at me. "Your hot mom comes to see you every week, and she'd come more if she was allowed, I bet." Wait up, she just called Mom hot? Which is an objective fact because she used to model but ... gross. I make the BFF choice to bite my tongue as Sweets continues. "They don't get me, I don't get them, and that's that."

We're silent for a while as Sweets dips the needle back into the ink before beginning on the second arrow. Then I ask what's been haunting me these last four days. "What about us? We get you, we love you. How are we gonna stay in touch when you're all the way in West Van?"

"Well, we're not allowed to visit anyways," Sweets says, "not for three months. Residency rules."

A staff member must've told me that during intake, but that was back when I was on Ward 1. Way back when I didn't trust anyone or even have friends to miss. "That's such bullshit! Why does that rule even exist? Why make people cut ties with the only other people who've been through what they've been through for three whole months? Especially people who don't want to go home in the first place."

Before I can rant more, Nick squeezes my wrist, increasing the pressure until I look at him. He mouths, *Not now.*

A quick glance at Sweets and I totally get Nick's point. Her hands are shaking too much for her to continue.

A Drop in the Ocean   135

"Three months isn't that long," Nick says. "That's not even a full season of *Survivor*." The fact that he watches and likes that show gets us talking about reality TV, which gets Sweets to calm down and admit to liking *American Idol*. By the time we're debating whether *Canadian Idol* is better or worse, she's chilled enough to start inking again. One of the feathers still comes out super thick compared to the other. She thickens up the former one to make them even but goes too far. It's the same trap I fall into when I try to do winged liner. She settles for almost identical. Phew. Nick gets the mostly melted ice. Now it's my turn.

Fucked up thing about me number one quadrillion: the itty-bitty needle jabs from the stick and poke freak me out worse than a regular head bang. They're such different kinds of pain. A regular head bang, like this morning's before the jumping catastrophe, is boring. My whole forehead wound is pretty desensitized. This spot above my right wrist, though, it's virgin freaking skin. All unscathed, capable of feeling the slightest twinge. Acid in my stomach sloshes up my throat as I watch the rapid in-out of each poke that sticks the ink under my skin. With my eyes averted I can dissociate a little, lose the squeamishness that comes from studying my body too hard.

"Do you want it bigger?" Sweets points to the tiny black cross that you'd mistake for a birthmark from far away.

"Sure, a little bigger." This tattoo's meant to stick out a bit. A souvenir from the dopest people I've met in my life during one of its shittiest years. "Can you make it into a star or an ankh?"

"Just lemme refill the ink." Sweets handles the bottle with deliberate care, tipping out another small splash. She hums a little as she widens the top part of my cross, stops humming a second later when I stop breathing and Nick hisses under his breath. We all heard it. A rustle. Feet kick up loose rocks, then we see the feet: leopard-print Nikes. Shit, it's Janelle.

We scramble to clean up as silently as possible. Sweets pockets her supplies while Nick hides the Everclear in one of his jacket sleeves. Janelle calls our names, her voice growing fainter as she walks off. Still we wait, whisper-counting to one hundred before fleeing the shrub. Every piece of evidence from our tattoo sesh gets chucked in a nearby trash can. With a sigh, Nick tosses the Everclear in too. It lands against the metal bin with a thunderous clonk after all our quiet. I look over my tattoo as we cross the soccer field. It's no longer a cross since the top part is pointed and kind of oval. But it's not really a star because the other points haven't been made into rays, and it's a little too uneven to be an ankh. Whatever it is, I'm proud of my Residency prison tat.

◆

The Band-Aid over my star/ankh peels off with a lovely, sticky tug against my skin. It reminds me of being in grade two and pouring Elmer's liquid glue on my hand or doing a peel-off skin care mask. Those long minutes it takes for the damn things to dry, so worth it for the seconds of catharsis from ripping them off. Everything else about today sucks. Sweets and I huddle together on the living room couch where *Edward Scissorhands* is playing, from the DVD box set of Tim Burton films Nick and I bought her. (He's not here because he's stuck on his unit doing therapy stuff.) Instead of a thank-you hug I got glared at, Sweets holding the gift bag as if it were full of preppy princess accessories. "What'd you get this for?" Now, she pokes around at her second piece of black forest cake, smearing the whipped cream with her fork. My heart feels like the maraschino cherry she's smushing, a piece of bright-red mush. This discharge party blows.

A Drop in the Ocean

I've lost count of how many times I unhinge my jaw, about to launch into a weepy goodbye: *Will you miss me as much as I'm gonna miss you, you mouthy goth goddess?* It always snaps back shut, my teeth clanking against each other, because what if she says no? I get the whole *I'm gonna be distant so I don't miss you* logic, but come the fuck on. These are our last few hours together. Of our lives maybe, because what if she goes back to the real world and wants zero reminders of Crazy Camp? Add the no visits between former and current patients for three months rule, and even if she intends to stay in touch, shiny normal life could distract her from ever following through. That's why the rule's around, to make sure former Residency kids put the past behind them. Fuck, tomorrow I'm part of Sweets's past. The real world on its own is tempting enough; teeming with distractions and potential friends she could make who don't freak out. Bile lurches in my throat as I examine my quarter-eaten cake slice.

I get up with a groan and shuffle over to the kitchen to toss it in the trash. When I come back, I witness Franco's farewell. An energetic wave and two entire words: "Bye, Taryn."

Jorge comes over next. "Never thought I'd say this, but some of your heavy metal shit ain't that bad." He stands back a little, then belts out a dead on "Oh-ah-ah-ah-ah" like in Disturbed's "Down with the Sickness."

Sweets sings a few bars of the chorus, smiling a real smile for the first time today. Should I join in? I open my mouth, clank it back down on air. Let them have their moment. She and Jorge bump fists. He closes in for a hug, tells her, "Keep doing you, muthafucka."

Maybe it's good that I waited. Jorge getting all sappy can be a gateway goodbye, prepping the way for mine to get full-blown sentimental. I'll give her some breathing room before breaking the ice with the perfect sarcastic comment about the movie. Us laughing can launch into me saying how much I'll miss her sense of humour and how she's like my big sis even though she's younger and smaller than me. Is it weird I'm so into control that I'm micromanaging my conversations? Oh well. Onscreen, robo goth Johnny Depp delights the neighbourhood with his barber skills. What can I say about dogs getting haircuts to make Sweets laugh? Too late, Dinah's here now, snipping the moment like one of those oversized scissorhands.

She stares, very hard, at Sweets's scars. Her face winces into that same expression of yikes and ouch that she wears whenever Sweets has her arms bare or I pick my scab. It doesn't take as long as it usually does for her to tear her eyes away and meet our gazes.

"You look like him, but your hair's nicer, and he's good at hair. Are you good at hair too? Which one of you is better at hair?"

"Me," Sweets says, before I can speak.

"Great, then can you braid mine?" Dinah plops on the floor in front of Sweets. She gathers her spiralling coils in a gleaming cloud that falls past her shoulders. Sweets finger combs them, deftly easing knots apart, grimacing when she has to tug hard. She separates Dinah's hair into increasingly smaller sections. The finished product is a fishtail of woven strands that V into each other, starting wide from the top of Dinah's head and narrowing down to the small of her back. She looks like a freaking mermaid queen. I clear my throat when Dinah's done examining her fancy braid in a hand mirror and squealing over how pretty it is, about to ask if Sweets wants an ol' fashioned three-strand braid. (The only kind I can make.) That's a good entry point into a heartfelt goodbye, right? Some bonding over haircare?

Missed my chance. They're already exchanging seats. Sweets grunting as Dinah combs her bob and we all hear her brittle dyed

A Drop in the Ocean 139

hair crunch. The finished product is a loose mess of erratically woven strands. Sweets oohs and aahs over it, gives Dinah a hug. I shake my head. The frontal cortex part I bang tells me I shouldn't be jealous; the reptilian amygdala part that triggers my OCD tells me fuck her, fuck them both, and fuck this movie with its overblown campiness.

A small eternity passes. Dinah's disappeared down the girls' wing and Franco's shifted to lying down on the other couch.

"You want me to fix your hair back to how it was?" I ask. This could be it, the Hallmark goodbye moment.

"No way," Sweets snaps. "Dinah worked hard on this for me."

Again with the attitude. I smooth away my snarl. Just because she's pissed at me for whatever reason doesn't mean I need to be pissed back. "Okay, it's just that it looks a little messy and I could make it better."

"It's not always about you, Mira."

Great. She's basically telling me I'm selfish, which is what my OCD screams at me all day, every day. "What's that supposed to mean? Whatever I do or say, you keep shutting me down."

"Then why am I watching this movie with you?" The way she says it, it's like sitting here is torture. Not a chance to watch one of her fave childhood films.

"A movie from a box set Nick and I bought you as a goodbye present and you're acting like you hate it." I have to grit my teeth to keep my voice at normal speaking volume. Even then, it comes out gruff.

Her lip curls as she moves to the end of the couch, "No, I'm not."

"Well, you're acting like you hate me."

And now she sighs, shaking her head. "God, you're dramatic. That's exactly what I don't want. Not today."

Today. Her last day here. Now, hours before she leaves. My anger ashes out, and ashes are what I taste as I say, "What do you want, then?"

"To watch this fucking movie. Can we?"

"Sure."

More small eternities pass before Sweets slides back into her spot from before our tiff. She sees me watching her shift closer, gives me a small grin. I grin back. It's the closest right now that we'll get to saying sorry. When I refocus on the screen, Johnny Depp is in an artistic frenzy, cutting a gorgeous ice sculpture. What if I just bit the bullet, apologized, and then we had our heartfelt goodbye? Naw. The moment's not *right*. Maybe more time will soften us up.

Now Johnny Depp's running away, freaking out. Definitely not the *right* moment. But what if it never feels *right*? Because when is it ever right in the first place to say goodbye to your best friend? For the sake of the show, which Sweets is finally getting into, I decide to wait until the end. That way Sweets can't say my drama distracted her from enjoying it. Besides, when the movie goes back to Granny finishing her story, that will leave us on a high note. The film equivalent of peeling Elmer's glue off your hand. By then I'll take the plunge, no matter what degree of *rightness* the moment holds. Ex-boyfriend dies, and I start thinking of jokes about Hollywood kiss scenes. Cheesy music plays. Below it, there's the vibrating thonk of steel bolts shutting. Sweets goes rigid.

Shit.

"Taryn, your parents are here," Alan yells from the front door.

Sweets shuts her eyes, scrunches her face like she's in pain.

Shit, shit, shit.

"'Kay, I gotta go." She throws her arms around me in a stiff, quick hug.

This is it? This is it! My sluggish pulse quickens to a trot. "Hold up, don't they want to come in? Can't they give you a minute?" I

A Drop in the Ocean

lean as far as I can away from the sofa to see what's happening at the front door. Her dad pulls up the sleeve of his power suit to check his wristwatch. Her mom, who wears her beige shawl over a flower-print dress like sable fur covering a ballgown, has her arms crossed over her ample chest.

"Where are you, honeybear?" she calls out in a strained falsetto.

"Honeybear?" I repeat in horror.

"No, they won't come in cuz they're afraid of us ... I mean you, y'know, criminal youth."

I grunt in protest before memory kicks in. Right, Ward 2 kids are all juvenile delinquents to the rest of the world.

Sweets goes on. "Keep in touch, all right? I wrote my digits and my email in your journal. The Residency can't stop us messaging." She's speaking into my shoulder because I've sprung my arms around her and won't let go. She hugs me back, her chest rising for a deep, shuddering breath. As she exhales, she turns, propels herself out of my grasp and off the couch into the first steps of a speedwalk to the door.

I want to yell, "I'll miss you." Or "You've changed my life." Or some sort of anything. But then I see how, after she smudges her liner wiping her eyes, she checks to make sure there were no witnesses. My teeth clack against each other as I clamp my mouth shut.

◆

Sweets's Note

MIIIIRRRAAAAAA!

What the fuck do I even say? You're my psych ward sister! We've put up with each other's weirdnessess, me ignoring your forehead, u still chillin w/ me thru mania and melancholy (I'll always remember u saying think of dogs and fruit, lol!) But never ever defined each other by what shrinks call us. Someday I hope u can do that 4 yourself.

When u do have those thoughts of being a bad person, tell your OCD avocado, b/c it's not u at all. There's this 80s hit u might like that could be your life theme song, "Running Up That Hill." Recovery feels like that sometimes, running up a hill or mountain where u have to trust that there is a top, even when u can't see it. Listen to it when you're sad since I won't be here to nag u about self-care shit like brushing your teeth.

Anywayz, you're the total package, a babe w/ brains and a badass. And what makes u the baddest of asses is how much u care. Being nice, giving a shit when life sucks, takes serious lady balls, aka ovaries. Don't ever lose that.

Luv u 4eva, Sweets

P.S. Sorry I've been such a cunt lately.

P.P.S. U better message me, bitch!

CHAPTER FOURTEEN

A grunt.

A GRUNT.

That was the last thing I ever said to Sweets, and it wasn't even a word. Why couldn't she say all the nice stuff she wrote down to my freaking face?! Thank Jesus, who I don't hate at the moment, that I have therapy today. I march into Dr. Grant's office already talking as I'm opening his door.

"You know how we were talking about stuff being meta? How meta is this: I feel bad about feeling bad."

"Can you give me some specifics?"

Dr. Grant is wearing a new aftershave, and its factory floral musk overpowers the room. Is it Axe? He's a psychiatrist, he should be smart enough to know never to buy Axe. "Can we open a window?"

"Sure."

While he undoes the window lock, I study the ragged edges of my fingernails and find them lacking. Perfect to nibble on as I explain, "You were right about Sweets, she was acting distant to cover up how sad she was to leave. She wrote a bunch of heartfelt things in her goodbye message to me. Guess I should be grateful, right?"

Dr. Grant glances up from the carnage of nail ends I've put on his desk to look me in the eyes. "But you're not?"

"I am." I exhale a long, snarling sigh. "Not as much as I should be, which is what I feel bad about. I'm disappointed with how Sweets let things end. They could've gone so much better."

"We all have our defence mechanisms. It sounds to me like along with her sarcasm, Taryn's aloofness before discharge was how she tried to protect herself." He puts out his hands in that whoa-girl gesture when he sees how vigorously I nod. "Don't quote me on that, though, I'm not her therapist, I'm yours. And I've got a cool bit of DBT to tie into our CBT today."

What? "For fuck's sake, I'm telling you about how my best friend left, and you want to cognitive behavioural therapize me right now? You're joking, right?"

"No, Mira, you know I'm a psychiatrist, not a human being. We shrinks are incapable of humour or caring."

"Can we skip craptastic brain torture today, like, considering the circumstances?"

From the way Dr. Grant folds his hands on his desk and how very neutral he keeps his expression, I know what he's thinking: *There goes Mira with her number one defence mechanism, anger.* "It's not actual CBT, just a list. No exposures for now, not until you say they're okay. I promise."

Another list. How can I get something out of this besides feeling like shit afterward? "What's this list about? If we finish it before the hour's up, can I leave early?"

"Really, am I such bad company that you want to run out of here the second we're done?"

"Okay, not leave early, but talk about what animals we'd want our familiars to be if we were medieval European witches?"

"Maybe."

"Fine, I'll take a maybe."

"Cool. The list is a simple table. Pros and cons for engaging in self-harm compulsions. What's good about them, what's bad about them, along with pros and cons for fighting against those kinds of compulsions."

"Whoa, whoa, whoa. No."

"Why not?"

"You know I *have* to bang my head. That's the deal I made with God: punish myself to keep Mom alive."

"Okay." Dr. Grant nods, lips pressed tightly together. "I thought you might say that. Then I remembered what happened a few days ago when you touched the wall while jumping."

"The gash smash?" (The name we came up with to describe my knife-slice forehead scab from using wall corners.)

"Yes, the gash smash. And the time before that, when you didn't hold your breath as long as you'd planned to. It fits a pattern of yours to head bang immediately after feeling like you've performed a compulsion inadequately."

Failure. That's what those are examples of. Times when I fucked up and needed to pay for it. Nails bitten to the quick, I've switched over to the hangnails growing like weeds from my cuticles. One strand of skin keeps peeling as I rip, revealing raw pink underlayers. "That's enough examples, I get the point."

"I'm not saying you have to stop the head banging this instant as much as bringing up the fact that these occasions have nothing to do with God hurting your mother. A thing that in and of itself, you can't prove."

My nails dig into the meat of my palms from how hard I clench. "If you could feel what I'd feel you'd know it's true."

"Okay." Dr. Grant stays silent for a few moments, and we both breathe. His breaths are deep and even. As time passes, my short, shallow ones follow suit.

After some more full breaths, he continues. "How about we make the lists? That's all. What would be good or bad about using DBT skills instead of head banging when you're dissatisfied with how you've done your rituals?"

Self-Harm Rituals— Pros	Self-Harm Rituals— Cons
- 99.99 percent sure God will kill Mom if I don't	- I can't prove for a fact that God will kill Mom if I don't, so I may be doing it for nothing
- Way to punish myself	- Can damage property (dents in drywall), which leads to interpersonal and law problems
- Bad person if I don't	
- Calms me down fast (immediate release from distress)	
- Feel exhausted after, so harder to get upset about other things b/c I'm drained	- Causes brain damage and concussions
- Hurting self instead of others, unless I am restrained and forced to stop against my will	- Visible physical injury, ugly scar, possibility of flesh-eating disease
- Able to be quieter when I do it in public	- Causes physical pain, headaches, blacking out
- Automatic response to many triggers (ingrained compulsive pattern)	- People see this as histrionic and miss my message
- Clearly communicates I am upset	- Doesn't actually help me process distress, just reinforces OCD cycle
- Shows people I am serious about triggers	- Causes loved ones emotional pain
- Feels less helpless than being sad or in pain	- Causes negative perceptions of me as dramatic, "retarded," manipulative
- Makes emotional pain physical and concrete / easier to process	- So drained afterward I shut down
	- Hurts my self-respect
	- Feel guilt, shame, and humiliation after

A Drop in the Ocean

Resisting Self-Harm Rituals—Pros	Resisting Self-Harm Rituals—Cons
- Takes my power back	- Using skills is harder / less immediate than self-harm
- Gain more self-respect	- People might underestimate my level of distress—how will they see how much pain I'm in?
- Less physical pain	
- No wound on forehead, nothing to pick at	
- Less chance of brain damage	- Requires more focus, more work to overcome OCD urges
- People may view me as a mature person	- Feel guilty, lazy, worthless for not punishing myself
- Less damage to property leads to less interpersonal or law problems	
- Short term: less shame and guilt	- Have to deal and sit with unwanted emotions like sadness throughout rest of the day
- Long term: feel proud of myself	
- Not drained the same way after feeling distress, can move on with my day	- Skills might not work as well as self-harm at calming me down
- Family can be proud of me	
- More in line with my goals and values	

There's a decent amount of reasons why I shouldn't head bang if it's not to save lives. More than I thought. And I did manage to punch the wall instead when I got my rag. Maybe, for very minor ritual screw-ups, I can do progressive muscle relaxation. That's when you clench different body parts as hard as you can and then release them to relax. Another pro: all that tensing of different muscles must burn calories.

CHAPTER FIFTEEN

WHAT TO TELL GUNG GUNG:
- I love him
- Thank you
- Favourite things about him
- Favourite memories
- What he taught me
- More thank yous
- More love
- How he lived a good life
- Okay if he goes

Did I just hear my skin sizzle? Hot coffee sloshes out of my cup, scalding my trembling left hand and arm. Fuck. The jitters from what some call too much coffee are almost always worth it. Except when they're not. Every atom in my body vibrates with nervous caffeine energy, overflowing past that sweet spot so that functioning is harder, not easier. The last thing I need for what might be the last time I ever see Gung Gung.

"I told you not to get coffee." Mom holds her hot chocolate with immaculate stillness. Poh Poh hobbles a few paces behind us. Her tremors—from old age, not caffeine—aren't as bad as mine, which means her Lipton green tea stays in its Styrofoam cup. The staples at her house are oolong and jasmine, stuff Timmy Ho's doesn't have. Just like with so many other things in her life, she makes do.

After you've been to enough hospitals, they all look the same. I could swear that the modern art prints in this hallway are identical to

148

A Drop in the Ocean 149

the ones they had in UCLA. The same sluggish dread and powerlessness I felt there return, leaving me hollow. Falling with each step I take. I try to ground myself in sound. Poh Poh's quiet shuffle, Mom's confident click clack, my squeaky sneakers, and sporadic footsteps from passersby become a background percussion to the pounding of my heart. Gung Gung's been moved from cardiology to the ICU. Somehow, the flu he caught while recovering from his heart failure turned into pneumonia, and he's worse off now than when he first got here.

I open the door to the room he shares with two other people. Curtains provide a semblance of privacy. His bed's at the back, where open shutters let in weak sunlight. A banner hangs on the wall with "Get Well, Gung Gung" written in fancy calligraphy. I roll my eyes, recognizing perfect Rachel's cartoon roses sprouting from every letter. Can't there be one thing she isn't good at?

My spark of annoyance fizzles out the moment I see Gung Gung. Despite having been warned, I wilt when I see his closed eyes, the hollows under them dark as bruises. He's still unconscious. He's also lost weight and grown sickly pale, a stick figure of the man who gave me piggyback rides until I was seven. Two years after Mom refused to pick me up anymore because I was a Big Girl. Am I a Big Girl now? Fuck no. The waterworks have been activated. I snuffle at the foot of Gung Gung's bed, holding the sorrow in as much as I can so that Mom has quiet as she speaks to him.

Poh Poh rests on the chair near the window. She looks at me looking at her and leans toward me, stretching her gaunt arm out to pat my leg. I grab her hand—it's cold. So cold and wrinkled and small that I wonder how she's not shivering. I take it in both of mine, hold the fragile treasure the way I would my favourite glass Christmas ornament, then step closer. Near enough now, I lift her hand up and blow warm air on the parts of it I'm not kneading. I know what to do from all the times Nick's warmed my hands.

"Mmmm." Poh Poh smiles and squeezes my thumb in gratitude. "That feels lovely, thank you for spoiling me." She calls this being spoiled? It feels so dinky and stupid, the smallest of gestures. Warming her hand takes me less than five minutes, while each arthritic finger I rub she's worked to the bone taking care of this family. Gung Gung's the same way. He rarely talked about growing up with only banana peels to eat. Or quitting car racing to work extra hours making false teeth. Not even about the times—yes, plural—he left his office on Pender to find his car tires slashed or "go back to China" keyed into the hood. Mom was the one who told me those stories.

Right now, she's crouched near Gung Gung's ear, speaking too softly for me to hear. She plants a last kiss on his cheek before coming over to where I am at the foot of the bed.

"Your turn," she whispers.

I go up, try to memorize every plane and angle of his face as I look past the ventilator, beyond the tubes. As if looking hard enough can freeze him in time, so even if he's asleep like this forever, unaware of the world, at least he's still alive. I do my best to see every detail so that they can live on in my memory. The way Gung Gung's skin is rough like old leather, Mom's pink lip gloss still glistening on his right cheek. The biggish mole he has on his opposite cheek, closer to his chin with the "good luck" hair growing out of it. How every sunspot, every wrinkle, tells a story. How no one knows them all but him. If he lives, I'll make him talk. Make him tell me the narrative arc of each birthmark and about every one of those pictures in the albums I flipped through. I'd fill as many journals as it took to get the stories down. But all I can do is give him what I have. My story of us.

A Drop in the Ocean

"Hey, Gung Gung, it's me, Mira. I love you so much, I don't even have the words for it. And words are my thing." I rasp a short, dry chuckle. My hands don't know what to do. They hover around his pillow as I consider fluffing it, but that might hurt him. Can I squeeze his shoulder, or would that screw with one of the machines? Caffeine keeps my fingers trembling as they clench and unclench. "I'm old enough to realize how lucky I was to have you as a grandpa. You were so busy working when Mom and the others were young that you never actually got to raise them. Maybe that's why you always spoiled me, gave me twice as much love. Whatever the reason, I'm grateful." Except it gets lost in translation, the "ful" after "grate" garbled by me choking back a sob. Mom hands me a tissue box so I can continue. Trumpeting out snot every few sentences.

I tell him what I said I would a few paragraphs ago. Love, thank you, favourites, lessons, more thanks, more love. Mention how I am proud, proud as fuck (except I don't swear) to be his granddaughter. That unlike Lawrence, who thinks Gung Gung in his twenties looked like Marlon Brando, I think Marlon Brando looked like him. But that my favourite thing about him has always been his quiet.

There are less than a handful of people I can stay silent around. I get nervous when I have to sit still, especially when someone's there to talk to. If they're there, I talk. Fill what feels like emptiness with words. With Gung Gung, it was never like that. We could sit together silently for hours, me writing or drawing, him reading the newspaper. Those times filled me with actual rightness, nothing to do with OCD. Calmer and deeper in joy than fun times with friends. We were each other's home. I wait in that quiet with him for a moment. Both together, home, still. I hear his ventilator and the gurgle of phlegm in my own exhales. My heart breaks with love. Then I tell him if he needs to, he can go.

Everything feels wobbly and underwater. On Jell-O legs, I quiver my way back to Mom and Poh Poh. The two of them talk from some far away distance until Mom nudges me forward, toward the door. Poh Poh stays behind. She barely has to hunch to be eye level with Gung Gung as she speaks softly to him in Cantonese.

Once we're out of the ICU, the grilling begins. Mom wants to know about my meds—are they helping me sleep better at night? Are there any bad side effects? Hell yes. The far-awayness fades as I launch into a tirade about weight gain. We're nearing the modern art hallway again, full of people on pilgrimages to the cafeteria. I speed up the way I always do walking through crowds.

"At least none of these make you swell up like a tomato the way penicillamine does," Mom says, lengthening her stride to keep pace with me. Out of the crowd, a twenty-first-century Disney princess runs toward us. Cousin Rachel.

"Auntie Sarah, I can't believe I ran into you!"

She makes a shrill "eeeee" noise as she thrusts her arms around Mom, who coos back, "Hey, sweetie." Their embrace goes on for longer than the quick squeeze I gave Mom after my car door rituals. The two of them even look more like mother and daughter than Mom and me. Their hair frizz free and shining, like they've just shot an Herbal Essences commercial. I scrounge up a smile and wait my turn. After some shoulder pats and I love yous, the two pull apart. Rachel fixes her clothes as she breaks out of the hug, relaxing into a debutante posture. Then she sees me. Her eyes widen.

"Oh, Mira. You're here." Her voice trembles a little with ... fear?

A Drop in the Ocean

My arms are out as I step toward her, ready to get the obligatory hug over with. She flinches, backing away.

Screw the fake smile. As I widen the distance between us, I do a quick pit sniff before remembering that I have coffee breath. "Do I smell bad or something?" I try to make it sound like a joke.

"No, it's not that." Rachel's hair swishes with the vigour of her head shake. "You smell fine. Great, even. It's just, you look different."

She's right, I'm probably twenty-five to thirty pounds heavier than I was when we last saw each other.

I mutter a gruff "Thanks" to shut down anything else she might say about me being fat. If my hug effort was half-hearted before, this time it's quarter-hearted.

But still, she cringes away from me.

"Okay, fine." I keep my distance from her.

Mom looks back and forth at us, her eyes narrowed. "What's going on, you two?"

"Not a thing," Rachel says, "except I just realized how late I am!" She emphasizes the last three words, as if her lateness is a scandalous crime. "Bye, you guys, it was sooo nice to see you." And now she's not quite running away.

Mom and I give each other a look. I scowl as I scoff, "Weird. Why didn't she want to touch me? I have mental illness, not cooties." The scoff is a front. Mom's smart enough to know that, but also smart enough to not engage with it.

Her expression is infinitely sadder as she replies, "I'm not saying the way Rachel acted was right, but you scare people, Mira. And when people are frightened, they put up walls."

As much as I resent perfect princess Rachel, it still kicks my heart in the ass to think that she's scared of me.

"How about I give you a hug, hmm?" Mom wraps her arms around me and squeezes. She smacks a big kiss on my cheek. "The next time you see your cousins, tell them about what you're going through. Sometimes people just need to hear the whole story. It's like Oprah says, 'When you know better, you do better.'"

"Speaking of Oprah," I say, "you know what would be a great interview? Her and Gung Gung."

She goes, "Aww," and pats me on the back. The same sad smile blooms on both of our faces.

◆

In fantasy novels they're always talking about the power of names. Naming someone or something can shape their nature, and discovering someone's true name gives you power over them. Common first quests often involve finding or earning your true name, which is usually three or more syllables long with some sort of epic meaning if you're the main protagonist. Take my protagonist, Evvy. Her full title is Evasanline, it means "midnight star beloved" in the Old Tongue, the language of creation. But since spell-check hates me, it always wants to change her name to Vaseline. Google says Mira means different things in different languages. Story of my life, things being complicated, no one right answer. In Romance languages Mira is related to "wonder." In Eastern European languages it means "peace." In Hebrew, "bitter." In Albanian, "kindness." In Sanskrit, "ocean." The story Mom always told me was that it was a compromise. Dad wanted Jezebel, she wanted Christiana. Somehow the intersection between such hella different tastes was Mira. No one right answer, so settle for what you can live with. Also the story of my life.

A Drop in the Ocean   155

During English, when Donna isn't looking, I switch out my required reading, *Brave New World*, for *The Naming*. The paperback spine tears a little in protest when I bend Alison Croggon's masterpiece flat on the table so only the pages are visible. I wince, unwilling to risk looking at the damage. *Brave New World* is the most FUBAR dystopia I've ever encountered. Where being a mother is the worst thing you can be, and where people are genetically engineered into racist fucking castes. The main magic in *The Naming*, where Maerad escapes enslavement and grows into her bardic destiny, is, well ... it's in the title, lol. Nick sees everything because he's in his usual spot beside me. We meet each other's eyes. God, his are gorgeous. I raise a finger to my lips, *shhh*, then nibble it to be sexy. He winks.

When Nick and I meet after lunch, *The Naming* comes with me. He might have to go to the washroom or something, which means I can read while I wait for him. By now, I'm balls deep in the novel's lost school of Pellinor lore. I plop into his lap as he finishes his smoke. For a little while, the only sound is him puffing and the rasp of paper on paper as I turn pages. He puts it out by stamping on it, and I feel his body tense as he gets ready to stand up. I refuse to move. He gets the message, sighing and settling back into his seat.

"Naming, eh? Is it a the-more-names-the-better kind of thing?"

I force my eyes up from the page, dog-ear it to mark my place. "Not exactly, it's more accuracy based. Magic has its own language, and you activate it by speaking it, by Naming."

He mock sighs. "That's too bad, cuz I got all the names."

"How many?"

"Five."

"Five names, pretty cool." I snuggle into his chest, tilting my chin on his left shoulder. "Know anyone with eight?"

"No way, six is getting excessive. But eight, pffft, that's ridiculous."

"Mira Meilin Anne Coralie Lung Kong Durand van Kraft."

"Jesus, that's a mouthful. Was there a bulk sale the day you were born?"

"Hey!" I punch him with no force. "I'm your girlfriend, you should know my full name. That, like, makes it official."

"More official than this." He grabs my head and pulls my mouth to his. When he starts to break away, I don't let him go. We get our breath back and he says, "Well, for it to be *official* official, you should know mine. Nick Travis Stephen Walsh Haighley."

"Nick Travis Stephen Walsh Haighley," I echo back to him. "I think I can remember that. You remember mine?"

"Mira Meilin Anne Coralie Lung Kong Der—uhhh, shit."

"Durand van Kraft. Van Kraft is my stepdad's last name, so it's not on my birth certificate."

"Are all those names on your ID and stuff?"

"No, Gung Gung gave me the name Meilin when he saw me for the first time, but that wasn't until Mom and I moved back to BC." Gung Gung. It's the first time I've thought of him today. The butterflies lingering in my chest from our makeout sesh poof out of existence. My stomach plunges, my eyes burn. I blink back the tears. There'll be time to cry later, after lights out and my last head bang. In one fluid motion I cross my arms, hiding how I squeeze the skin of my wrist from Nick. The burn between both nails brings me back to the present. "How about you?" I say, to distract us both. "Who chose Nick, your mom or your dad?"

"My ma always liked the name Nick. It says Nicholas on my birth certificate, but that just makes everyone think Santa Claus or Nicolas Cage." Both of us laugh, more out of nerves than humour. He can

A Drop in the Ocean

sense something's off, because he's not an idiot. He clears his throat. "Your granddad, he sounds like a cool dude. He seems—"

"Yes, he is." I kinda yell it, get the words out before he can finish his sentence. "A cool dude. You both are." Voice back to normal, I say, "But you're not getting out of learning my names that easy." Names = safe convo territory.

There's relief in Nick's voice too. "All right, give me some extra incentive."

"How 'bout a bet?"

The wager goes like this: we memorize each other's names by Friday. If he forgets or mispronounces one of my names, we go for a hike as our next date. If I mess up his, then we stay on Residency grounds. Boo. Considering what's at stake, memorizing Nick's name is my top priority, screw grade ten English or kinetic molecular theory.

◆

Subject: Rawr
Date: Thu 16 Nov 2006

Sup Babe?
You've been gone 10 days and it feels like 4EVER!!! Everybody misses you esp. me. Saw my gramps @ the hospital, he's in a coma. Life's been the shits except 4 Nick. U better be having as much fun as possible in the real world for me. When I get discharged we HAVE 2 meet up, maybe go clubbing?! I'll do a mosh pit if u get us IDS.

Love u lots,
Mira

◆

Checked my emails, checked Facebook, now what? Franco is on my left chuckling at Salad Fingers on YouTube. Jorge is on my right, headphones plugged into his computer's audio jack, his body blocking what's probably porn on the screen. Something he's okay watching now that Elsie's no longer on the prowl, monitoring our internet use. Nope, she's making use of Net Plaza herself two rows ahead of us, consulting Google for desserts.

I sneak looks at other customers' screens as I walk over to her. Anime, the *Vancouver Sun*, business emails, Craigslist. Nope, nothing interesting. But maybe that's a good thing, because what the fuck would I do if I did see someone buying AK-47s or bricks of coke online? Tell the one bored teen at the front desk with the Goku hair? Unlike Goku, he'd die in a fight even quicker than me.

"Hey Ce'Nedra." (She calls me that because apparently I'm stubborn, like the dryad princess in the Belgariad series she lent me.) She's clicking on a link to "The best ever authentic English trifle recipe." The page loads an image of a terrifying dessert Tower of Babel. There's fruit, whipped cream, custard, sponge fingers, Jell-O, more whipped cream, and more Jell-O. Who came up with this?

"Hi Polgara." I butter her up by calling her the name of the Belgariad character we both like best, a badass sorceress. Then give her a big hug, close enough now to notice that the Jell-O layer has fruit petrified in it like bugs fossilized in amber. I swallow a gag. How much must Elsie hate the people she's baking for? "Wow, that looks so … fancy. What's the special occasion?"

"It's my nephew's twentieth birthday. His mother, my sister-in-law, is dead set on making him diplomat cake, so I'm doing one better."

"I'm sure he'll appreciate all this effort you're going to for him. You must be his favourite aunt, just like you're my fave nurse."

A Drop in the Ocean

Elsie rolls her eyes, exaggerated, but with a smile so that I don't take it the wrong way. "I'm old but not dumb. What do you want?"

"That's why I like you, you never bullshit around."

Her loud harrumph earns us a glare from her nearest computer neighbour. "Yeah, yeah, what is it?" she asks.

"Well ..." I've had enough of looking Elsie in the eye, but I'm not about to subject myself to more images of that pudding layer thing. I examine and scrape my nail beds instead. "Since you're asking, I need an overnight pass."

"Sorry, but no."

"You don't even know why. Let me explain the situation to you first."

"Does it have something to do with your granddad passing on?" Damn. How can she say that and stay deadpan? As if she'd just asked me what time it was, not whether someone I love has died.

"My gung gung"—I accentuate the double *G*'s, the subtext: *not granddad*—"hasn't passed on. But he might. At any moment, he might. I want to say goodbye to him before he does."

Elsie frowns and cocks her head to the side. "Wasn't that what you just did?"

"He was unconscious."

She winces.

I jump in before she spouts some vague platitude about better places or living a full life. "Which is why I need a pass for as long as possible. The whole weekend would be even better, overnight at least. I'll spend every hour I'm not asleep at the hospital so when he wakes up, I'm right there and we can have closure." Mental health professionals love the c-word. (Closure, not cunt.)

"Where exactly would you be sleeping?" The wince has been replaced by raised brows, greying just like the hair on her head. "I highly doubt they'd let you sleep on the floor of the ICU next to him."

"They might. If not, I could stay at my parents'." I'm on round four of nail patrol, eradicating any last traces of overgrown skin at the bottoms of my cuticles.

"You mean the place you haven't set foot in for three years, where all of your obsessions and compulsions started?"

"Two and a half years, not three."

"Sure." Elsie's eye roll this time is less friendly, more infuriating. "You want to stay overnight, possibly two nights in a row, in arguably one of the most triggering spots on the planet for you, even though you haven't yet visited home on a day pass. Have you talked to Sarah or Lawrence about this, at least?"

I get it, I really do, all the good points she's raising. Why can't she get mine? Gung Gung is dying. Doesn't she see how desperate things are? "Let's phone them together."

"We're on an outing, you'll have to wait until we get back on unit to call them."

"As in you'll call them with me?"

"I can see about getting you excused from class and sending you out on a few day passes."

"That's it?"

"Maybe two or three this coming week, depending on what the rest of the team agrees with."

There's this rushing I feel, my blood surging and hurtling and screaming through my veins. My core tightens, then my chest, my limbs, until I'm shaking. What if that was it? "No. That's not what

A Drop in the Ocean 161

I—no!" What if that really was goodbye and Gung Gung didn't even look at me? Didn't even know I was there?

Goku hair leans over the counter toward us. "You okay?" he asks.

Elsie smiles and sweeps her hand in a *no big deal* wave. "We're great," she tells him. To me, she says, "You're not getting an overnight until you visit for a smaller period of time first. And it'll stay small until you can reliably have visits where everything goes swimmingly. Then you'll have to make a safety plan with me and Dr. Grant that outlines how you'll manage the hardest parts of your day, like the head banging."

God, this again? "I'm still doing the head banging, that never changed."

"And that's why my answer can't change either. I respect how terrible this is for you, having to let go of your gung gung. Of course you want to be with him as much as possible. But have you thought about how all of this is affecting your mom? Every time she visits her daughter, she also has to witness her hurting herself. Now her father is dying. I know you downplay the length and intensity of your head banging on unit to her. I know part of that minimizing is done out of love. Do you really want to put your mother through two full days of your head banging at its worst, morning, noon, and night?"

A low moan slips out of my throat.

"Then there's your stepdad. You two aren't so close. What is it you were telling me? That he cares about the house more than he cares about you? I doubt he'll take very kindly to you slamming your head into the drywall with the same kind of force as a boxer throwing a punch. The more you progress in treatment, the more your privileges, like overnight passes, will progress in the Residency program. At the moment, kiddo, you're just not there."

After hearing Elsie speak, it's amazing how quickly my rushing blood thickens, turns to pudding, then solid, like the Jell-O in that nightmare dessert. I want to yell about how I wish it were *her* mom's dad dying. I want to storm out of the dinky internet café, slam its door so loud that every computer monitor rattles. I want to hear the hundred crystalline shatters of me hurtling the nearest monitor, SMASH, onto the floor. Arms straining against its weight and then nothingness.

But I don't. Because those things would just prove Elsie right.

♦

A lime-green Post-it note on Dr. Grant's door says, "Mira, please go to the soccer field for therapy." WTF is Dr. Grant up to? Only one way to find out. Outside, I shiver a little in the morning breeze as I walk past the parking lot. If Nick were among the cluster of kids smoking on Ward 1's porch, he'd run over and insist on warming me up. He's got science right now, which means I have to make do with rubbing my hands against my arms and squeezing them into my sweater sleeves. When I reach the field, they're almost back to life. Cold bites the tip of my nose and the tops of my ears instead. There's a whizz in the air, a whistle that loudens and spins from a blur to a football flying straight for my face. I put my arms up to catch it, but my fingers are still too stiff. I fumble and miss.

"Motherfucker!"

Autopilot takes over. My legs stiffen as I bend straight at the waist, stretching my arms until my palms brush the damp grass. The twinge of pain in the backs of my knees tells me, yes, I've done the ritual *right*. I stay that way for a count of one, two, three. One, two, three. One, two, three. By the time I'm up, football clutched in my right hand, Dr. Grant is yelling-distance away from me, getting closer.

A Drop in the Ocean 163

"Do you touch your toes like that whenever you miss the birdie in badminton?"

Ah, someone must've complained about my constant stopping to stretch during the doubles tournament whenever I made a fault.

"Not my toes, the floor. It's a deeper stretch."

"I see, and why does your OCD tell you to do that?"

"Punishment for dropping things."

Dr. Grant's eyes widen, and for half a second his lips sag into a grimace. I blink and it's gone.

"It's not that bad." I shrug my shoulders, shift the football from hand to hand. "If I drop something or miss a catch, I do a forward bend for three reps of counting to three. Not the end of the world."

I know what my old Remuda Ranch therapist would say: *Denial is not just a river in Egypt*. Ha freaking ha. Yes, I am aware that OCD gets me to bend over forward and be its defence attorney.

Dr. Grant says, "What if you dropped something on purpose and didn't stretch? Is that a good middle path between exposure response prevention and flat-out giving in to the OCD?"

My heart starts to trot. "How do you mean?"

"Play catch with me, and after a few throws, intentionally miss one of my passes. Think of it this way: you're getting to be outdoors, doing physical activity instead of sitting inside talking about your childhood. What do you think burns more calories?"

"Obviously being out here. But I'll only do it once, and first we warm up by throwing it properly."

There's athletic artistry to throwing a football. You have to have enough power and aim behind it so that it goes where you want it to, while also curving your hands and your fingers just so to make the thing spin all the way in the air. Before the Residency, I was a football virgin. Since then, I've played flag football a few times without utterly humiliating myself. As a noob, my aim is still a little off, meaning that every few throws I send his way, Dr. Grant speedwalks to catch the ball. For a self-proclaimed nerd, he throws with a surprising amount of accuracy—oof, the ball thuds into my chest—and power. I curve my spine into a *C* and crunch to absorb the force. Movement has burned away my chill, gotten adrenalin pumping pleasantly through my veins. My body wants to settle into a rhythm, except my brain knows what's coming. Dr. Grant's losing patience, crossing his arms over his chest as soon as he's done tossing the ball my way.

"Last one?" he keeps asking.

To which I say, "Not yet."

We pass back and forth four more times. Him getting more impatient, holding on to the ball for longer and longer before throwing it back. The nervous energy builds until my pulse throbs through my skin. If I'm going to have to fuck up on purpose in a few short moments, may as well aim for perfection while I can. I throw a beauty that plops right into his arms.

He walks toward me, football tucked between his right hand and hip. "I'm not throwing the ball anymore unless you miss."

I flinch, caught in the knee-jerk belief that missing means fucking up. Failure. Then there's the alternative meaning from the deal we made. "I guess it's not like I'm making a mistake if my whole goal in the first place is to not catch the ball?"

He sighs. "One day, you and I will have a talk about reassurance. But for now, let's just think of this as value clarification. No, it's not a mistake. You want to miss. You need to miss to win against the perfectionism at the root of this compulsion." He bends his knees, settling into a throwing stance with the ball in his palm. "Before I throw this, tell me what your subjective units of distress level is out of a hundred."

Great, another decision I have to make that involves precision and possibly fucking up. A jolt of irritation creases my forehead. My scab crinkles. "Uh, my SUDs are at an eighty-five." I focus on the football, remember I'm not supposed to catch it, and turn my gaze into a murder glare at Dr. Grant. Dizziness pounds in the back of my brain.

"Remember to breathe." The ball is up, arcing toward me. Don't catch it, don't catch it. The point is to not catch it. I take some shuddering, deep breaths, notice how they're way longer than my sprinting pulse. When the ball is the closest it will get to me, I thrust both my arms down and to the side. MISS. The goal is to MISS.

And the football's on the ground.

"Great job." There's this crackly note of pride in his voice that pisses me the fuck off. How can he pile on the praise for this oh so casually, knowing how hard it was for me? Does he think I'm stupid, that I don't realize how ridiculous it is to be so distressed over not catching a fucking football? The ground wobbles. No. It's my legs. I'm shaking. God, why am I shaking? I need to leave. I walk toward Dr. Grant because it is away from the football and the terrible temptation of stretching.

"What are your SUDs at?" The congratulatory crackle is gone. Dr. Grant reads my mind, or more likely my face, because he jogs and retrieves the ball before I go all forward bendy and self-punishy.

I pick up my pace, fall in step beside him. "112. If I got any more anxious, I'd puke or have a seizure or explode."

"But you didn't."

For a psychiatrist who went to Stanford, he sure is dumb. "You're making this worse." The more distance I put between me and this field of shame, the better. Too bad I can't ditch him so easily. He's right, I didn't puke or have a seizure or explode. In fact, my heart's sprint is winding down, I'm no longer wobbling, and my SUDs have lowered to a ninety. It helps that Dr. Grant isn't shoving congratulations down my throat. He isn't even beside me anymore. I turn around, and his eyes latch onto mine.

He pants a little between words as he says, "Mira, stop walking so fast."

I keep the same pace. "I always walk faster when I'm anxious, you know that."

"Fair enough." His occasional panting is the only noise as we make our way back to the parking lot. By the time we're walking through it, he's breathing evenly. Meanwhile, my heart rate's winding down from canter to trot, and my SUDs are at a seventy-five. Because I know he's going to ask about them and I just want it over with, I tell him they've gone down.

"How does that make you feel?"

I shrug. "I dunno. You told me they'd lower, but I didn't think it would be that fast."

"Sometimes it won't be, and that's okay too," he says. "No matter how high your SUDs get, anxiety can't kill you. Remember that."

◆

Nick gets a B on couples homework. He pronounced Coralie *Carolie*.

"One syllable off out of eight names, not too bad," he says.

"Nick Travis Stephen Walsh Haighley." His five names are my rebuttal, stuck in my head forever, where they belong. Where we belong is in North Van, scrambling up a mountain through lush forest trails. Doing something active off the property for our date, making

A Drop in the Ocean 167

it memorable. Where we are is the Ward 1 bench, sitting on our asses. Stale cigarette smoke engulfs me as Nick puffs on his nasty hand-rolled butt joint. I cough loudly.

"I'm not a fan of you smoking at all, but dude, just take my twenty bucks and buy a pack of real smokes. That thing is beyond gross."

Nick's pecs, which are my pillow, stiffen. His voice is clipped. "Like I said already, I'm fine."

"No, you're not." I grab at the cigarette, growl in frustration when he moves it above my reach. "And I'm not either, I'm bored as fuck. You said you needed to rest today, that you had a migraine. How does smoking make your headache better?"

He hunches away from me to have another puff, shielding his precious butt smoke with his right hand. "Better than having a nicotine fit on top of a migraine."

I retort through action, squirming between his arms, clawing at the cigarette in his left hand. He pushes my hands away, but I won't let go. My grip slides, rolling his sleeve up midarm until he hisses in pain as my fingertips sink into a patch of oozing skin. I look down just in time to see at least five blobs too big to be mosquito bites. While most of them are sullen red, two fester with white-yellow pus. What are they are the size of? Cigarette ends.

"Uh, what are those?"

Nick takes the smouldering butt smoke, now only a butt itself, and slowly brings it centimetres away from the fresh skin on his opposite arm's wrist. Raw hurt lances through my heart. He scoffs, tosses it on the ground, and grinds it to pulp. "Now you know what it feels like."

I scoot up off his lap as if it were the smouldering butt. "What's that supposed to mean? Since when have I ever put out a cigarette on my arm? Never. I don't even smoke."

"You know what it means. Except I stopped and you don't. Because I can't stand you looking at me the way you're looking at me now."

And I do know what he means. The first time he ever held me: my bleeding head between his palms, both of us battling on the van in Metrotown's parking lot. Me screaming, breaking through his grasp to *keep banging it*. Treating something he cares about worse than shit. I squeeze my eyes shut, squeeze my whole face tight against bitterness, like I just bit into fu gwa. If I thought I wasn't fine before, I am whole echelons of not fine now.

"I don't hurt myself to hurt you. You know that. You said it yourself at sushi, this isn't for shits and giggles." My voice shakes as I continue. "It's not some sick game I play to get reactions out of people. When I'm banging my head, does it look like I'm having fun? I *have* to."

Nick's voice shakes too. "No, you don't."

Yes I do! That's what I want to say. Scream. Scream in his face, to be exact. Along with my standard rant about punishment and past lives and saving Mom. But this isn't about me. It takes every ounce of that mindfulness DBT shit Dr. Grant has such a hard-on for to say this instead: "You didn't have to hurt yourself either, so why did you? Was it because you were angry and needed a distraction?"

We're both surprised that I didn't defend my rituals. The shock leaves Nick quiet. He shrugs, no comeback except honesty. "More like I could tell I was on my way to getting pissed off real bad. Felt it building and my nerves winding up … Usually I toke to take the edge off, but I'd run out of weed."

As he talks, I study his burn holes. They remind me of craters on the moon, all round and indented.

He sees me staring and shoves down his sleeve. "Anyways, the doc and my folks keep bugging me about being sober, so I wanted to try

A Drop in the Ocean

some other way to get rid of the feeling. Something that wasn't getting high or drunk or destroying property. I figured, why not make it physical, make it, y'know, outside myself so I don't have to keep it all pent up inside? Does that make sense?"

"Yeah, lots of sense." To show him how much sense he makes, I sit back down next to him. Right now doesn't feel like a hop on his lap moment. Instead I settle for putting my face so close to his our noses almost touch. If I wanted to, I could count every teeny micro pore from in between his eyebrows to where his nostrils flare. God, he's gorgeous. Especially when he's trusting me with these parts of himself like this.

"That's it." His eyes half close as a soft, sexy grin spreads across his face.

"What?" My pulse does the hundred-metre dash. I feel it through my throat, my wrists, my thighs.

"That's the way I want you to look at me all day, every day." As we close in for a kiss, I swerve to my right. My puckered lips pass his face and left shoulder, and I grope at that left sleeve again, this time on purpose. Once they're exposed, there's no way to miss them. One by one, I kiss his burns.

"Fine, then I get to kiss yours." And I let him. He kisses every uh-oh mark on my arms, even the barely-there scars where my neck meets my shoulders. His lips on this new part of my skin raise goosebumps, tickle with a good, tender kind of ache. I press in closer, and he kisses up my neck. With both hands he brushes my bangs to either side of my head. It's really happening. He's willing to kiss my forensic-scene forehead.

I duck down, murmur, "You don't have to," to the holes in his sneakers.

He cups my chin in his hand and tilts my face up. His blue-grey eyes smile directly into mine. A sad smile. One that gives my heart the same kind of tender ache my body feels. "I want to," he says. Then gently sweeps my bangs to the side and lowers his lips.

Most of the skin on my forehead is desensitized, so maybe I'm just imagining it. Two soft bumps that press and smush against my scab. I don't let him linger there long before grabbing his face, attacking his mouth with mine. Beneath the cigarette breath is the salty-sour taste of pure Nick. Mmmm. My kiss goes from soft to hard and greedy. I press all of me against him and he presses back so we're as close to each other as possible. Body heat and the equal force of how we push into each other melt me. Time melts too.

CHAPTER SIXTEEN

With Jorge as my grade ten bio buddy, science is never boring. It's never really productive either. This class, we're all about that binomial nomenclature, and Jorge is whupping my memory's ass.

My curls swish against my shoulders as I shake my head. "Nuh-uh, there's no way you already know it that fast. Again."

"Kingdom, phylum, class, order"—Jorge whispers something to himself, then counts the rest out with his fingers—"family, genus, species."

I turn to Doug, who stands over us. "Are those right?"

"Yup, those are correct."

"It's something to do with what he was whispering, isn't it?"

Doug smiles and adjusts his clear-frame glasses more snugly on his nose. "I bet our boy has himself an acronym. A mnemonic device helping him remember the exact order of the classification system."

Jorge burps, diffusing shepherd's pie and Sprite throughout the air. He tilts back in his chair so that it balances on two legs. "Yeah, I got a system, but it's all English. None of that old-timey medical language shit."

Doug's smile flips; his excited tone sours. "Well, enlighten us then. And how many times do I have to tell you, don't lean like that."

I bite my lip to hide a smirk. English is my jam. Duh, I know what acronyms are. I know what literary foils are too. This pair have enough antics and banter to start their own sitcom. One I get to watch live. All they're missing is a fun pun name and theme song.

"Fine." The chair lands upright on all four legs with a thud. Jorge says, "King Phillip Came Over For Good Sex."

Doug clears his throat, then chokes on his own ahem. "Good snacks, people, good snacks. King Phillip Came Over For Good Snacks."

Jorge snickers, leaning back again, except this time he tilts the chair too far and topples over. There's a much bigger thud and swearing before their inevitable argument begins.

"What did I tell you two seconds ago?"

"Don't talk down to me, bro, I'm not stupid."

I'm plugging my ears, trying to read my textbook when I hear a brusque tap, tap on the door. Elsie walks in. Suddenly, both guys are using their indoor voices. Her and her half-second knocks—there's barely space to breathe before she's barging in on you. I guess that's how she catches everybody doing shit they're not supposed to. My ears pop as I uncover them.

"Mira, you have a phone call."

Weird, she called me Mira, not Ce'Nedra. "Who is it from?"

"Your mother."

Even weirder. I tilt my head to the side. "Isn't she at work?"

"No, she's at the hospital. Come with me, please, you need to speak to her." *Hospital.* Just that one word and the way she says it. How beseeching she is with the rest of the sentence, how sadly she looks at me, makes me guess what it is. *Please be wrong, brain, please be wrong.*

On the walk back to Ward 2, then through the unit to the phone in the day room, Elsie lets me grip her hand. When I let go of it, I see angry red nail indents from where I've clawed into her. She returns the squeeze in hug form before giving me privacy.

My legs collapse onto the armchair next to the coffee table, where a box of Kleenex has been strategically placed by the phone. There's always a box of Kleenex by the phone, in every psych place I've been to. This time, the box is three-quarters full, waiting for me to use it

A Drop in the Ocean   173

up. If this call is what I think it is, one box won't be enough. *Be wrong, brain, be wrong.* I know I told him he could go, but I'm not ready. I'm never, ever going to be.

"Hi Mom, what's going on?"

Her voice is gentle, soft. "I'm so sorry, babe." But the pain it holds leaves it broken. "Gung Gung's passed away."

♦

Fuck Dr. Grant! I trusted him. I thought that he had my back, that he wanted to help me. Instead, he's made things shittier than I could ever have imagined. I'm beyond anxious, past trembling, guts in free fall like I'm plummeting through a vortex in space. I may as well be. Because despite the service being a half hour's drive away, I don't have the balls to go AWOL and crash it the way a ~~good~~ better granddaughter would.

He's not letting me go to Gung Gung's funeral. It's in three days, but Dr. Grant never works weekends, and Monday is when it's happening, so that's too late. Now is the only chance I get to change his and Elsie's minds.

What makes this whole thing even more surreal is that she's on my side. Her eyebrows tilt up in sympathy as she says, "We were reviewing your progress these last few weeks. Despite everything you're going through, there's a lot of it. You're working hard, my dear, and it shows."

Dr. Grant jumps in, back to his overly optimistic self. "We want to keep your momentum going. How do we do that on Residency grounds?"

"You can't!" I look from one to the other. "I'll be Miss Recovery 2006 if you let me mourn my gung gung. I don't need an overnight pass, just a day pass. Hell, I don't even need to go to the memorial feast afterward if you're worried about eating disorder bullshit. The service will only be like two hours, three max."

Dr. Grant's gone grim again, which means he's about to tell me no.

"Come on!" I splutter. "There must be something I can do, some way you can make sure I'm in control and let me go. What if—what if staff came with me?"

I can see the light bulb moment as it sparks in Elsie's brain and shines across her face. "That's something I'm willing to take on, Simon." Elsie uses Dr. Grant's first name, equal to equal. He doesn't reply, but a new line in his forehead appears as his frown deepens. Elsie clears her throat and turns to me. "Mira, would you and your family be okay with that?"

Would Mom and Lawrence be okay with that? Second cousins whispering about how crazy Mira needs a handler? "Yes, of course they would." Everything hinges on Dr. Grant, and my voice quavers as I ask him, "Let's do that, then, okay? I go to the funeral, just the funeral, and Elsie comes with me?"

Dr. Grant is pale. His bright eyes are as sad as Elsie's when she told me about the phone call. He shakes his head, excruciatingly slowly, back and forth.

There goes my stomach again, plunging past rock bottom. "C'mon, you both said it yourself, I'm doing all the right things, including the CBT brain torture. The funeral itself will be like an intense therapy session, something that you feel awful going through but that's necessary in the end." I put my whole soul into my pleading eyes. Feel all of me clench with the effort of how badly I need this. "I bet there'll be all sorts of mini exposures during the service that I'll be stoked to do, because that's how I get to say goodbye to my gung gung. I didn't get to say goodbye to him when he was alive." Elsie looks down when

I stare at her before lasering the full power of my hurt at Dr. Grant. "You *owe* me."

"You're right," Dr. Grant almost snaps, "we do have a responsibility toward you. You're certified in our care. As for exposures … mini?" He laughs darkly. "Are you kidding me? The funeral will be teeming with family members who trigger the hell out of you, and you've yet to have a visit home with your immediate family."

I bite my lip, clinging to the physical pain. Using it to keep worse pain at bay.

Elsie reaches for my hand. It takes every ounce of strength and trust in me to suppress my flinch and let her squeeze my knuckles. It takes more strength than I knew I had to accept a Kleenex from Dr. Grant. He takes one for himself too. Once he's done sniffling into it, he speaks in a softer tone.

"It's not that I want to deny you the chance to say goodbye to your gung gung. It's that OCD wise, you're nowhere near ready. Nor is Elsie, who hasn't been trained to conduct CBT. I can't in good conscience throw either of you out in the middle of the ocean when you can barely tread water in the kiddie pool with me. I did that once, let a patient go on a triggering pass against my better judgment. You know how it ended? With the kid in an ambulance and trauma for everyone involved."

"But I'm not that person. I'm me. I thought that you got me, that you understood." The last word comes out vehement and guttural as my voice erupts. I strangle it back to something closer to speaking than yelling. "Don't you know how important this is?"

"Doesn't matter." Dr. Grant's tone is firm, final. "It's not worth risking your safety."

"Fuck you." I shove my chair back, get up, and leave.

I know, I know, I know that Dr. Grant's doing what he thinks is best for me. Something bad happened to someone else once upon a time, and he doesn't want that for me. Doesn't want me to flip shit at a funeral in front of a hundred of my relatives and Gung Gung's octogenarian friends. He's worried about me hurting myself along with my reputation among my tribe. The people I'm going to spend the rest of my life with post-Residency. If I bang my head and people see, or even if people see the aftermath, then it's over for me. Fuck, forget self-harm—jumping is noisy enough to get people talking. Or getting in an argument with Mom and Lawrence. Or confiding in an overly gossipy auntie. If I get caught doing any of those things or a whole bunch more, I'm screwed. He doesn't get what I've known for over four years: it's too late to keep my head above the water. One day when I was twelve, I obeyed an urge. I don't even remember what it was. Only that something was *wrong*, so I performed a compulsion to fix it. I've been drowning ever since.

♦

Subject: ♡ hrt brokn 4 u
Date: Sun 26 Nov 2006

Holy shit Mira, I'm so, so sorry.
Ima jump thru the screen and into the Matrix to give u the HUGEST hug. xoxoxo. I know your gramps was a cool dude cuz u told me about him. He would want u 2 be safe before anything else, so he's all good about the funeral. Besides, u can still have 1, like all by yourself, becuz love never dies, and what's so special about a body anyways when nobody's home? U can talk 2 him from anywhere.

Life in the real world is OK. If I get good grades my parents r gonna buy me a car!!! Dad says I gotta take driving lessons and get legit good at it 1st. Then when u get out I can drive us places!! U got a discharge date yet? Til then, guess I'll keep missing the shit outta u.

HUGZ!
Sweets

♦

The music here is so anti-Ward 2, crooning sixties soft rock that makes the Beatles sound edgy. Mom and I are at Paint Your Art Out. I'm bitching about the music but really, it's the prices—forty bucks for us to paint one tile each and get them fired. Major rip-off. Special glazes for an extra five? Fuck no. I tsk, sucking the last bit of caramelly goodness from my Werther's Original. Mom took an extra lei si envelope for me. The candy, Gung Gung's favourite sweet, was its sugary content. At celebrations like Lunar New Year, lei si is red for good luck, full of money. At funerals, it's white, the colour of death, with candy to take away death's bitter taste.

"Stop counting calories and just eat it," Mom had said, sighing as I fiddled with the wrapper. "You're not supposed to take the candy home with you, it's bad luck."

Home with me, as if the Residency were home. Mine, not hers. I'd tossed the wrapper on her side of the table and chomped, cleaving the candy in two. Which is why I have so little of it left. Another trace of Gung Gung slipping away from me. I dip my paintbrush into the rinse water and swirl as sky blue bleeds from its hairs, then dissipates into the murk.

Over guitar strums, Mom recounts the service. "Of course Carine wanted fifteen minutes for her eulogy, and the whole time she talked about herself."

About a hundred people came. Everyone from family to Gung Gung's Chinatown buddies to his dental clients to Poh Poh's church pals to the neighbours on Capitol Hill. Pastor Stevens's sermon was short but moving and made no mention of how Gung Gung himself wasn't a member of the flock, nor even a Christian, for that matter. Poh Poh kept her cool through all of it up until the send-off hymn, "Amazing Grace." Her tears were silent. No one noticed them but Mom, who sat beside her and kept dry eyed. "I was too stressed to cry," she told me. Afterward, a slide show that Mom, Lawrence, and Uncle Ken put together played highlights from Gung Gung's life.

One of the slide show photos, which were sourced from those albums Mom and Poh Poh showed me, was of Gung Gung driving his favourite race car. A teal-blue Austin A40 convertible that he'd rebuilt for high speed. So aerodynamic that it didn't even have doors or windows to cause drag. As sleek as it was, I can't help picturing the image as Gung Gung driving a giant blue-green sausage. A sausage with a face. Two round headlights at either side of the giant grille look like eyes, the grille a fencing mask snout, and the racing plate a mouth. The front wheels, farther back and sticking out, could be its ears.

A glossy reprint of the photo rests on my side of the table, propped up against a paint jug for reference. There's no way I'm fucking up my tribute tile by trying to paint the car from memory. I sketch the proportions out first while Mom freehands her tile, a landscape scene with a cherry blossom tree. She uses the teeniest-ever paintbrush to make the tree branches. The ends curve up into lines as thin as eyelashes.

"Were people upset that I wasn't there?" I ask. "Did you tell them how hard I fought to come?"

"In my eulogy I let everyone know, like I promised."

My right knee goes from bored jiggle to turbo speed, exercise-exorcising my nerves. "Okay, well, what *exactly* did you say?"

Mom's voice rises along with her eyebrows. "What we agreed on. How much you loved Gung Gung, but that you're away in treatment for an ongoing medical condition."

Phew. I dial down the jiggle and my chair stops vibrating.

"Anyway," she adds, "hardly anybody asked for follow-up information and no one was angry with you. They were all too busy being scandalized by Janis's plunging neckline." Janis with the viper burlesque act I told Nick about—duh, her dress had cleavage.

"What about Rachel, was she there?"

"Obviously."

"Let me guess, her outfit was timelessly gorgeous and her eulogy got a standing ovation."

Mom ignores the jealousy dripping from my voice. "None of your cousins got to speak. We only had the funeral parlour booked for two hours. She might've said more at the feast, but I wasn't at her table." The feast. At least I didn't have to sit through that. No making up excuses about why I've been MIA from family gatherings or inventing symptoms for some nonpsychiatric medical condition. One small blessing.

I pencil in the race plate's number, fifty-two. It's a lot rounder than the way I normally write—the sharp corner of the five is curved almost as much as its bottom—but it looks good. The graphite gleams as I trace the number over again, darker.

"Did they have beef tomato chow mein?"

"No, first we had sugar water soup, tong seoi. And a bunch of Dad's favourite dishes."

"So there must've been spare ribs?"

"Uh-huh, and Uncle Hugh has the sauce on his slacks to prove it. You know how messy he is."

My stomach gurgles as I picture tender honey-glazed pork falling off the bone, slathered in hoisin sauce. I clench it and think about the calories instead, how many hours on the stepper Dr. Grant saved me from. I only half listen as Mom fills me in on the gossip from everyone at her table, on which stories of Gung Gung they told and whether they remembered them the same way she did.

As I move from sketching to painting the first layer, my eyes keep shifting to the racing plate. Number fifty-two. Was that Gung Gung's lucky number, or was that the rank he placed at? Because fifty-two isn't that lucky, and even out of one hundred it's not a great score. No, Mom tells me, she doesn't know why his race car had that number. Nor does she ever remember him racing. "He put all that aside before I was born." Gung Gung had more than one race car; he even built some by hand. Did they have other numbers, or was he always fifty-two?

Fifty-two. Five-zero and two. It's not a number I like that much. A far cry from my faves, nine and three. The number itself is even, not odd, meh. At least five and two add up to seven, an odd number. Still, nothing special. But as I mix blue and green to get the A40's shade, I count my swirls: one, two, three, four, five. One, two. Five times. This is me making a new connection, reaching out to Gung Gung through numerals. A dulling calm washes over me. Actually, fifty-two feels *right*. Every colour I paint, I have to do a minimum of fifty-two brushstrokes. It's just an urge, something I can still fight, but why should I? Bring on the baby ritual—I need the numbness it offers. When I count like

A Drop in the Ocean 181

this, the numbers take up all the space in my head. One, two, three, four, five, one, two fills the bottomless pit of grief I was falling through. Mom takes my silence as a hint, and we both stay quiet. With the same thin brush that she used to make the branches of the cherry blossom tree, she now dabs on the flowers themselves, a soft cotton candy pink. I channel that exact level of patience and care into painting the fifty-two with black paint. I have to get the line thickness *right*, with no one part of the five or two stockier or lankier than the rest.

"Mira, are you almost done?" Mom asks.

I grunt.

"Time to put the glaze on," she says a while later, when I'm touching up the top curve of my two.

I ignore her.

Some time after that, her phone alarm blares, telling us our session is up. "Okay, put any more paint on the five and you'll ruin it. Throw some glaze on before they kick us out." Her voice has a bite to it. I look up and see the clerk in a paint-splotched apron walking toward our table, wheeling a cart of cleaning supplies.

"Coming," I say in a huff.

When I put the glaze on with a thick, stiff brush, I paint over my tile in fifty-two strokes. Mom apologizes to the clerk for our lateness while I count the last of them out loud. "Forty-nine, fifty, fifty-one, fifty-two. Fifty-two. Fifty-two."

♦

Fifty-two keeps creeping into my life. Well, specifically my rituals, which are most of my life. When I go on the stepper during rec, I go as fast as I can for intervals of 152, twice every ten minutes. At the very end, I climb fifty-two steps as hard as I can. I have to push myself until my body spasms, sweat streaming from me as I heave in air like someone being tortured and trying not to scream. When it comes to my cool-down, sit-ups are too basic. I do jackknives instead, bumping up my reps from thirty-nine to fifty-two. Any resting or collapsing means starting from scratch.

Other rituals are new, like my bathroom routine. If I floss each of my thirty teeth once and then the top row of fourteen again, plus my eight centre-bottom-row teeth, I can reach fifty-two. When I brush them, I scrub each tooth in a clockwise circle and then a counterclockwise circle, counting: one, circle, two, circle … all the way to fifty-two, which gets me to the halfway point of my sixteen bottom-row teeth. Then I repeat fifty-two, circle, for the last eight right-side-bottom-row teeth and that feels *right*. Funny, *right* used to be brushing my teeth for as long or as little as I wanted until a few days ago. Now that kind of freedom is absurd. Guess how many times I run the comb through my hair? Yup, fifty-two. Fifty-two strokes left to right, then fifty-two the other way.

Even boredom gets fifty-two-ed up. During social studies Donna lets us watch *Gladiator* because Nick and some other kids are studying ancient Rome. I've seen it before, but Nick hasn't, so he's too enraptured to chat. I make my own fun by clenching my abs as hard as I can and counting to fifty-two before letting go. I do the same thing when I wait in Dr. Grant's office for therapization.

"Why fifty-two? And why now?" I groan as I recount my new crop of baby rituals. How they've sprouted and spread like noxious weeds through the dirt of my brain. Dr. Grant says that the thing about intrusive thoughts like this fifty-two kick is that they have no point. Everybody gets them, the *did I really turn off the stove?* second-guesses and the *what if I just drove through these pedestrians at 150 kilometres*

A Drop in the Ocean

per hour? urges. Most people are able to let these thoughts go without paying any attention to them. They know how ridiculous they are and move on to more important thoughts. But people with OCD don't. They give intrusive thoughts unearned importance and have thoughts about the thoughts that are almost always negative appraisals. Things like *thinking this makes me a bad person,* or *thinking this will make it come true.* Or, in my case, with fifty-two, a just-right appraisal, where I need to repeat an action fifty-two times for existence to be *right.*

By now I know how *right* works for my rituals. The repetition is always there, while the actions and numbers change. Fifty-two just happens to be my new number du jour. When I bang my head, I add nine reps of the fifty-second bang to the 111 bangs I do per session. Along with my nine reps of the thirty-ninth bang, and nine reps of the ninety-ninth bang, and obviously nine final reps of the 111th. All in all, 147 bangs per session. That's my new *right.*

◆

I stifle a yawn as I rub sleep crust from the corners of my eyes. Lunch was mac and cheese, and all those carbs are a better sedative than Ativan. The spot on the wall where I bang my head still hasn't fully dried from when I scrubbed it with Lysol this morning. Too bad. I pull my bangs back to either side, exposing the scab, breathing in as deeply as I can. By the time my forehead meets brick, all my airholes are closed. My teeth ache as I clamp them down over my urge to yawn at bang twenty-eight. Blood is trickling into my eyebrows as I make the half squelch point. Half squelch is when there are still parts of my scab that haven't cracked. Damn, this is taking a while. I bang past forty, waiting for the chemicals in my brain to fire *rightness* to the rest of me. As painful as it is, even banging your head gets boring when you do it enough. I'm at full squelch by sixty-one. Shit, sixty-one.

What about fifty-two?

FUCK!

Fifty-two needs nine reps, and I'm eight ahead. *Wrongness* explodes through every cell in my body. Electrocutes me. I need to start ALL OVER AGAIN. To punish myself, I keep holding my breath. No breaks in between this failure and its retributive redo. One, I bang as hard as I can, like the brick is an opponent I'm trying to knock out with a headbutt. Two, I bang just as hard. Three, bang. Four, five …

Dizziness overtakes the *wrongness*; I quake as if actually jolted by thunder. Bang, bang, bang, nineteen, twenty, twenty-one. The shakes reverberate through my skull. I'm buckling. I smash quickly, thirty-five, bang, bang, bang, bang, bang, bang … knowing what's coming. Brain cells dying, lungs screaming, I'm screaming, except it's a grunt because I can't breathe. Not allowed, need to bang, bang, bang, forty-seven, forty-eight, forty-nine, fif—

Bang.

Body meets floor.

CHAPTER SEVENTEEN

I wake up in an even dinkier bed than I'm used to. A slab of a mattress on a gurney at Burnaby General Hospital. The nurses there wind gauze around my head, mummy style. Bandages droop into my field of vision, making a woven roof over everything I see. The only reason I tolerate it is because they've slathered enough EMLA on my forehead that I don't feel a thing. That, plus the non-negotiable five milligrams of Ativan, which zombifies me. Speaking of zombies, the nurses give me the flesh-eating disease talk. The doctor gives me the flesh-eating disease talk too. I scowl straight back at her. No, I'm not suicidal. Yes, I'm sure I'm not. Can I leave? Nope. She won't discharge me until I get scans checking for brain damage.

I doze during the CT scan. But the MRI is God's punishment for me screwing up. There must be a special part of hell for people who hate noise that's just row upon row of coffinlike MRIs you're strapped into. What keeps me from busting out or moving at all is knowing if I do, they'll just dope me up with more Ativan, maybe this time with a needle, and make me lie there again.

As soon as I can, I get the hell up and out. Ignore the new nurse waiting for me behind an empty wheelchair. The world tilts as I stagger a little from the Ativan fuzzing my every thought and move. It takes more effort than expected to reach my room on foot. I don't bother stifling my yawn—time for a nap. Except when I open the door, there's Dr. Grant with his arms crossed over his chest.

"Do you have any idea how lucky you are?" he bursts out before I take my first step to the bed.

185

I drag the chair from the corner of my room over to him. Stay standing until he sighs and sits down, then I allow my own butt to rest on the mattress, the only other seat available.

"Not very, because I'm guessing you're gonna lecture me before I can fall asleep."

"Sleep," he scoffs. "Sleep? You almost went to sleep and never woke up!"

"Guess it's true what they say, no rest for the wicked." I'm joking, but I'm not. This whole fainting thing just reinforces what I already know. Bad people deserve bad things, especially when they screw up their acts of penance.

Dr. Grant's eyes bulge. "Seriously, Mira, you're trying to be glib? You're a smart girl, what don't you get about death? Or if death doesn't scare you, how about paralysis? Damaging your brain at the base of the skull, maybe as you fall after fainting. Land hard enough on your upper spinal cord and you'll lose all motor function. You'll wake up only to never move again, not even to breathe on your own."

Okay, he wins, no more witty banter. "If that happens, pull my plug."

Now his fury is toned down by disappointment. "Is your life really so awful that you'd give it up? Can't you see how much of a disservice this is to your gung gung's memory? What do you think he'd say if he could see you right now?"

"None of this would've happened if you'd allowed me to go to his funeral."

"So you knocking yourself unconscious during your rituals is my fault?"

A Drop in the Ocean

"Uh, duh. If you'd let me mourn Gung Gung properly, I never would've gotten fixated on his race car's number, fifty-two, which is the rep I got stuck on when I was head banging and fainted."

"That is one whopper of a cognitive distortion. I know exactly which sheets we'll go through next session. As for now, let me repeat: you're a smart girl, you know as well as I do that if it hadn't been fifty-two, it would have been twelve or seventy-seven for any number of reasons. This is what your OCD does when you don't fight back. It grows and grows until nothing else is left."

There he goes again with his sheets and his therapist version of Ned Flanders. The last thing I need right now is Dr. Grant telling me how much OCD is ruining my life. I pick on the other thing he always does, which is to be way too freaking sunshine and rainbows. "What happened to Mr. Good-Mood-Or-Go-Home? If I'd known this was all I needed to do for you to take me seriously, I would've fainted way sooner."

My distraction tactic works. "What's wrong with my mood?" he asks.

"Your pathological cheerfulness is annoying as fuck, so it's actually refreshing that you're pissed off today."

He hunches a little, eyes downcast. "Sure, I'm an optimist, but with life full of so much suffering, isn't it better than the alternative? If what I concentrated on was all the bad in the world, I'd never get out of bed."

"Positivity's your coping mechanism?"

Dr. Grant shrugs. "You could call it that."

"What's so wrong with *your* life that's got you suffering?" Bitterness makes my voice harsh. "You have a really good job and an even better family."

"What about your family? Your parents, your poh poh and late gung gung, they love you to pieces. Having a loving family doesn't make life perfect. If it did, we wouldn't be here."

Well, that shuts me up.

It gets worse. After Dr. Grant leaves, I barely get fifteen minutes of shut-eye before someone else taps on my door.

"Come the fuck on," I moan, as I prop myself up. The door opens before I can get to it, setting off my OCD *wrongness*. I snap, "Can't you wait a second and not barge in?" to whoever's decided they have to see me.

It's Mom.

She's pale, haggard like she spent all night crying. Eyes swollen with bags under them, no makeup to cover her fine lines or accentuate her lashes. Not even any lip gloss.

"Next time, remember to let me open the door, okay?"

She looks at me with hurt stamped all over her face. "After what just happened, you're still doing everything OCD says?"

"All I did was faint for a few minutes, it's no big deal." All right, more like hours, but she doesn't need to know that.

"Stop defending it. You could've killed yourself. If that doesn't frighten you enough to change, I don't know what will. It's barely been a week since my father died. Do you think I'd survive if I lost my daughter right after?"

I pick sleep dust out of my eyes and fiddle with my head bandage. "Honestly, Mom?"

She looks at me like I'm crazy, which I guess I am. "Obviously honestly."

A Drop in the Ocean

"It would break your heart at first, but in the end, you'd be better off without me. Lawrence would be happier, you two would fight less. Maybe even have a baby together. You'd move on, just like how Poh Poh's replaced me with Rachel."

Mom's mouth opens in mute shock, then her jaws clench as she shakes her head. "Is that really what you believe? Are these new obsessions?" Her pupils shine as the water in them threatens to spill out. I can't hold her gaze.

"No. They're just the truth. The way things are."

"What that hateful illness wants you to believe is your truth. But not mine."

"What part of your truth did I leave out? You're going to say you'd miss me, but you can't deny that your life would be way less complicated with me gone. You'd be free."

"Don't you dare tell me what my truth is. You hurt yourself every day and you say it's to save me. But really, truly, it's killing me, kid." Her voice quavers. "Every time I look at your face and see that raw wound a few layers from your brain, a piece of my soul dies. And one day—her quaver turns to a keen—"there won't be any pieces left!"

I rush to hug her. Do anything I can to throw my arms around the pain, the pain I caused, and shoulder some of it. She won't let me. She flails and shoves me away.

"Don't touch me."

"Why?"

"Because I'm too upset at you!" she shouts. When I recoil, her voice drops to normal volume. "I should go now, I just came to make sure you're okay."

"No, stay, I'll stop being so negative." I try to sound light, as optimistic as Dr. Grant. My lips writhe into what probably counts as a grin. "We can play a game together."

Mom's already taken a step toward the door. Her teary eyes have turned steely, and she says in a firm voice, "I have to leave."

"How come?" I follow her to the threshold.

She grabs the handle and swings it open. "Same reason as before, I'm too upset at you."

It swings shut behind her.

I stand there, staring at the door but not seeing it. For one minute or five, I'm not sure. All I can think is damn. Mom's never just up and left me like that. No kiss or hug or even goodbye. Really, it was me trying to touch her that sent her off the edge. I feel it, that edge, feel how it's gone. How even though she's the one who pushed me away, it's because I pushed both of us off it in the first place.

CHAPTER EIGHTEEN

Everyone at the Residency knows. And everyone's making a bigger deal out of it than it needs to be. It didn't help that freaking Janelle, who was doing room checks when she found me on the floor, overreacted and called the ambulance. According to the scans, my brain has minimal bruising, and there's no coup or contrecoup lesions. A good thing, Dr. Grant assures me. I tell that to anyone who scolds me, and the science words shut them up. It doesn't work so good on kids, though.

"Almost pissed myself when I first heard those sirens. I was like shit, they found my stash, my ass is headed to juvie," Jorge told me. "Then when I saw you on the stretcher, I thought your ass was headed to the morgue."

Right now, my ass is freezing. The cold makes me cross my legs and press them tight against each other for the barest bit of additional warmth as I wait for Nick on the Ward 1 bench. There's grit under my nails. I chomp them down to the quick and spit the rinds out. It helps a little, but not much. Whatever Nick has to say, I doubt it's gonna be that he gets it.

"Nick!" I bolt up from the bench and spring toward him before he's finished closing the unit door.

He catches me in a loose hug that stays loose even when my arms squeeze tight around him. "Hey." His voice is strained, curt, and his eyes dart away from meeting mine. My smile sags into the same grim line that his lips are making. No, he definitely doesn't get it.

When we sit, he scoots to the right so there's space between us.

191

"I guess you're not thrilled about me fainting yesterday. I didn't mean to." I try one last thing and put my hands out for him to warm.

"But you did." He reaches into his pocket for a smoke, ignoring my trembling fingers. "I can't keep pretending things are okay when they're not."

I pull my hands back, sit on them to keep them still. "What, you mean between us?"

"Yes." He takes the biggest drag I've ever seen.

By now, my gut is in free fall, plunging the way it did when Elsie ushered me out of science for the phone call. "I'm sorry. I know it must feel like I cheat on you with OCD sometimes because of how much it's part of my life—"

"It *is* your life." Nick pounds his fist on the bench. The suddenness and force of it startle me enough to jolt, but I don't cry out. I don't move away from him either. He's the one who moves, standing up and turning his back to me as he puts a few paces between us. His shoulders rise and fall as he takes deep, ragged breaths. They even out by the time he comes back, his hands shoved in his pockets. "It almost took your life and you're still defending it. That's the real relationship. You cheating on *it* with me."

"But I hate it, I don't love it. I love you."

"I love you too. That's why I can't do this anymore. I can't watch someone I love fuck themselves up the way you do and make like everything's fine. The other stuff is what it is, I can live with it. But I can't be with you if you're going to keep banging your head."

I laugh—what else is there to do? A few chuckles turn into me holding back sobs. "I have to. You know that. It's all I have. Sweets left, Gung Gung died, you'll leave—if I don't have it, then I'll have nothing."

A Drop in the Ocean

The rage drains from Nick's face, leaving him pale and as sad as I am. "You'll have yourself."

I let the sobs come. "That's even worse."

He's about to cry, I can hear it in how his breath catches when he asks, "Will you stop?"

"I can't."

"Then I can't be with you."

◆

Oh my God, oh my God, Oh my God. It's the cheesiest thing I've ever written. But love makes desperate weirdo poets of us all. And, dammit, I'm taking Viktor Frankl's advice to live my life with meaning. Nick gives me meaning. He makes me want to be the best version of myself, which is why I'm wearing my lucky push-up bra and Baby Phat bustier to English again. And why a copy of *Man's Search for Meaning* lies on his spot at the table with this piece of crap, uh, I mean, this poem inside:

We met when our lives matched your eyes,
struggling to float in a storm at sea.
You were the lifeboat I didn't know I needed,
the fire that brought hope to me.

You warmed my hands and kindness kindled
a joyful spark straight to my heart.
You kissed my scars, confirming what I knew:
that I was in love with you.

I know I hurt you, but I'm asking again,
please see the girl behind the pain.

Usually, I like to write free-verse poems. This one rhymes because it's a reply to the one Nick wrote me, and his rhymed. My last two lines are a twist on his. Yes, there's pain—now let's move beyond it.

I started *Man's Search for Meaning* hoping for a guilt trip. I mean, what else would you expect from a Jewish psychiatrist's memoir of Auschwitz? Turns out it's inspiring and empowering. When he had nothing left to live for and was being tortured by Nazis, Frankl still found a way to keep his power and his shit together. He quotes Nietzsche: "He who has a why to live can bear through almost any how." I've decided my why is this: writing. Next, I'm gonna write an elegy for Gung Gung. Donna says he's not really gone. He's probably reincarnating as we speak, on to the next few steps of his spiral dance. According to my man Frankl, I'll always have him. "For in the past, nothing is irretrievably lost but everything irrevocably stored."

From my hiding spot, I see Nick come in. Yes, hiding spot. I'm hiding behind the computer desk so I don't actually have to talk to him when he reads my poem. Tension eases out of his posture when he sees my chair is empty. His sweatpants swish, swish together as he makes his way to his spot. His eyebrows furrow when he sees the book there. He picks it up and starts reading the back with the synopsis before sprawling in his seat. A few seconds later, he finds my poem. I can see his lips moving as he reads it to himself. When he's done, he looks around the room. For me, maybe? I duck, cover my face with my binder. Scrunch to make myself as small as possible while I count, one Mississippi, two Mississippi, all the way to nine. When my quivering hands put the binder down again, Nick's gone.

◆

A Drop in the Ocean

Gung Gung Poem Super-Rough Draft

Gung Gung, there were
whole selves to you I never knew. Reflections
frozen in ~~black and white~~ greyscale photographs.
Sepia blooming to colour as decades fly by
with the turn
of a page.
Each image captures someone new. [*should "new" be on its
own line?*]

Plump bundle of baby boy
precious zoeng zi, full lips a mirror
of his mother's. She holds you [*should "you" be capitalized?*]
in her arms, wrist bent so your tiny
hand can clutch her fingers.

You hold them on your shoulders, [*is it clear what "them"
refers to?*]
base of a human pyramid, proud tween
goh goh whose acrobat costume
matches his siblings'. In another you balance,
back straight as bamboo, atop a unicycle,
smile gleaming like the sequins
on your uniform.

That same smile in a grown
man's face, your fingers trace [*slant rhyme good or too obvious?*]
the hood of the race car you built

from spare parts. Your heart
was on the track, fast and furious [*lol like the movies*]
as your courting of Daisy. [*Daisy = Poh Poh*]

Newly wedded husband becomes
father of one, two children
balanced on your kneeling lap
sun in your eyes as you tilt
your head and smile. Three, four, then two more
pose on the porch of the house
you remodelled to a home.

Flip the page and your grown children's
own children surround you. Compete for the prize
of who gets to sit next to the gung gung
I recognize. Except now he's more.
Remodelled [*repetition necessary?*] from one role to many.
Each self
nested into another.

From baby to boy
what were your dreams? From teen to man
how did they change? Transforming
as your shoulders broadened
to take on new burdens. [*is "broad shoulders" too clichéd?*]
Business replacing racing.
Genetics pasting your gleaming
grin on six young faces who beget
a similar smile to eleven grandchildren.

One of them you hold
on your lap, in your arms
plump bundle of precious zoeng neoi.
You bend your wrist so my tiny
hand can clutch your fingers. [*Is "my" enough of a clue that
the baby Gung Gung's holding here is me? Is the ending too
cheesy? I kinda like it!*]

◆

Death surrounds us here at Forest Lawn Cemetery, three hundred acres of graves. I'm freezing, and the sky is one giant cotton ball of varying shades of grey. Poh Poh coughs. A tortured, hacking wheeze, so deep that I hear the fluid in her lungs. It blasts through the silence like gunfire after the last lines of my elegy.

"You're gurgling again," Mom snaps at her. It's a very me thing to do, getting angry at the symptom—Poh Poh coughing—instead of the source—Poh Poh's old age leading inevitably to death.

My Jell-O legs feel so far from the ground as I linger by Gung Gung's grave. I fold my poem into quarters to fit in my coat pocket, then crouch down and trace my hands along the gravestone, a plaque of antiqued bronze. "KONG," it says, embossed in raised letters. My fingertips glide over the simple Times New Roman typeface spelling "Wilson Michael" and the smaller "1923–2006" below. At the very top, in even smaller font, it says, "in loving memory," with dogwood flowers etched on either side. At the bottom: "FOREVER IN OUR HEARTS." Beneath my feet is yellowing grass. Beneath the roots of that grass and the lid of a coffin is Gung Gung. Well, his body, or "earth suit," as Donna would say.

This is it. We've all said our eulogies, and Mom and Poh Poh have walked a few paces away to give me space.

"Hey Gung Gung, it's Mira again. I'm so sorry I couldn't come earlier, my therapist was being a jerk. At least I get to be here now. I hope you liked my poem, it was even cheesier before I edited it. Anyway, I just want you to know how much you mean to me. You were the first dad I ever had. I saw you more than I saw Dad, and Lawrence wasn't around until later. You bottle-fed me and oatmeal raced me, taught me some of my first words in both English and Cantonese. You taught me about responsibility, about working hard at school and chores so that I could play hard later with you at the park. When I was old enough to appreciate them, you told me stories about the hard times, like growing up poor. Those stories made me grateful for the life I had because of the foundation you'd built. There's so much I'm grateful to you for. You made me feel safe, and special, and loved. So loved, at peace in our quiet." I take a moment to blow my nose and wipe my streaming eyes. Take another just to breathe before continuing.

"Some things are beyond words or language, like that quiet. Nothing can take it away, even if you're not physically here anymore." That chokes me up, Kleenex time again. "I still can't believe you're gone. But you're not, are you? If I'm quiet enough, I can sense you, warm and shining in my heart. You're with me. I hope wherever you are, I'm with you too. I love you, Gung Gung. I always will." I place a kiss on my fingertips and press them down onto the bronze's textured surface. Then I get up.

Poh Poh ends the ceremony with a prayer. "Dear Lord Jesus, we came here to honour your son, Wilson Kong, who rests with you. May we find peace by recognizing the peace he now has by your side. We want to thank you for blessing Wilson with a long life that saw

A Drop in the Ocean

him as my husband for fifty-six years, a father to Sarah for forty-three, and a grandfather to Mira for sixteen. He was a steadfast provider for our family whose heart you softened into a deeply loving gung gung. Lord, we ask that you send our love, prayers, and gratitude to Wilson in heaven so that he knows how dearly missed he is by his family here on Earth. Amen."

Throughout the prayer I clasp my hands, close my eyes, and bow my head the way I'm supposed to, but I stay stiff. A small, bitter part of me wants to yawn, to place my hands on my hips or roll my eyes. Fuck God—he condemned me with rituals, he took Gung Gung from us, and he hardened Nick's heart against me. How many times, head exploding with pain, have I screamed about hating him, about wanting Jesus dead? Of course I felt like shit for saying so afterward. And if I really, truly did believe in an omniscient, omnipotent being, wouldn't that being have better things to do than to make me suffer? At least that's what every therapist, religious leader (another kind of therapist), and Mom and Poh Poh seem to think.

I half open my eyes to peek at Poh Poh from under my lashes. See how her face glows as she speaks, no longer taut with grief because she knows her husband has returned to something bigger and stronger and truer than his earth suit. In every crease and line of care on her face, I see God. Gung Gung is energy now, and energy can't be destroyed. That's Thermodynamics 101, bitch. He's back home with the source of all the energy, all the life in the universe. Something less old man in the sky and more pool of endless light. The name Poh Poh uses is God, the name Donna uses is Mother Goddess. Other people call it nirvana, Brahma, or the Tao. Maybe somebody out there calls it Spot. They can call it whatever they like, I'm not here to judge. Spot is bigger than judgments, bigger than any names. Ever since Poh Poh's attempt to exorcise me three years ago there's been a rift between us. I've been angry at the version of God I used to believe in and at her for ganging up on me with dogma. Now I have to let her know that I've grown out of my Christian cocoon.

As we walk back to Mom's car, I hold out the crook of my arm for Poh Poh to lean on. We walk so slowly that I can read each gravestone as we pass it.

"What colour do you think God's eyes are?" I ask her.

"Huh?"

"Everybody always talks about God as a man. So if he's a man, he must have eyes, right?" Whatever colour she says, I'm going to say that I don't think God has eyes or a face or even a body in the first place.

Poh Poh's own eyes seek mine. "God is an It," she says.

"Huh?" Now I'm the one who's shocked. Is she … basically agreeing with me?

"The Bible talks about God as a father, but God isn't human. We just call it a Him to make things easier. What God really is, is love. The Bible says that too."

For one small, golden moment I lay my cheek on Poh Poh's shoulder while squeezing her hand in mine. In that moment I decide not to get into how much Christianity has harmed me. I choose this new and improved version of God instead. Because I choose God, I say, "I love that."

CHAPTER NINETEEN

Never have I ever had a shrink give me homework ... until I met Dr. Grant. My usual chair, with its perfect cushion-to-frame ratio, is not in its usual place. Instead of being two feet away from the desk and facing Dr. Grant, it's next to him. On the desk itself are a few loose-leaf sheets of paper, a pencil, and a stapled handout titled Cognitive Distortions.

"This is the sheet you threatened me with at the hospital, isn't it?" I raise my bushy-ass eyebrows at him. "CBT must kill forests of trees."

"So does writing," he replies, but in a friendly banter versus confrontational kind of way. Our fight at the hospital, if not forgotten, is at least forgiven. "And we can always do an exposure instead." Since I did missing the football on purpose, we've been doing exposures every other session.

"Touché." I grab the handout and take a read.

"These are more ways that people with OCD think wrong, aren't they? Like negative appraisals?"

"You know, that statement itself has more than one cognitive distortion. Go on, read the list, see if you can find them."

If this is how excited he gets over work, I don't even wanna picture him partying. Or maybe this is his version of partying. Listening to delinquents complain, rock on! I stifle a sigh and get back to reading. Magnification and minimization. I do that, but not in what I just said. Catastrophization, I do that too. Overgeneralization, that's another thing I do. Jumping to conclusions. Okay, yeah, reading the name of a list and jumping to the conclusion that it's about how people like me are wrong, that's one of them. Personalization too, I guess, as in "people like me," meaning me. Meaning I looked at a sheet and decided it was about how I was a fuck-up. For every new example I read—emotional reasoning, mind reading, fortune-telling—I can think of a bunch of times I've thought in those ways.

"Before what I said was jumping to conclusions and personalization."

Dr. Grant nods. "Good observations, and ..."

"That's just it, I do all these things all the time. Like every thought I have might be wrong."

"There's another one."

"What?"

"All-or-nothing thinking."

I read the definition—"thinking in absolutes such as always, never, or every"—then shrug. "Add that one to the list of ways my thoughts suck."

Dr. Grant's therapy high just plateaued. He continues with 25 percent less enthusiasm. "Not every thought you have is wrong. Besides, the fact is that thoughts aren't wrong or right, they're thoughts. Nobody is ever wrong all the time. Just like no one is ever always right. You're seeing the world in binary black and white when really, it's every shade of colour imaginable." And on those last six words, he's back to excited glee. "Can you think of any times recently when you've challenged that kind of thinking?"

My mind double-speed rewinds through the past few days up to an image of Gung Gung's gravestone. I remember Poh Poh balancing on my arm, our convo as we walked back to the car. "I think my views on God are broader than they used to be. Poh Poh and I had a talk about God being bigger than gender, and she totally got it. She and Mom are as close to God as you can get."

A Drop in the Ocean

"You know, the thing about all-or-nothing thinking is that it goes both ways. You seem to view yourself in the most negative way possible, but putting your loved ones on a pedestal is another kind of trap."

"What's wrong with thinking the best of my family?"

"The higher up you put someone, the harder they end up falling."

"But what if they never fall because they're just that good?"

"They're human, they'll fall. And when they do, you have to take responsibility for your part in denying them their humanity."

How could he ever think I'd not let the people I love be human? They're better than human to begin with. He knows how much I love Mom, what I do for her. "What the fuck do you mean?"

"It's not just the people we hate and demonize whose humanity we deny. When we pretend to ourselves that someone is perfect, we deny them their humanity by refusing them their right to make mistakes."

"I told you," I say, raising my voice, "Mom doesn't make mistakes. Not really."

"Then why were you yelling at her on her last visit?"

And now I'm yelling again. "Because she screwed up my rituals. She opened the car door too soon."

"Isn't that a lot to expect of someone?" There is no blame in Dr. Grant's tone, only calm questioning. "For them to perform the compulsions of your OCD, which they don't have, exactly right? Especially when those compulsions change so much that you can barely manage them?"

Shame floods me. It was there under the anger all along. I deflate, my hung head staring down but my eyes seeing nothing. "Yeah, yeah, it's a lot to expect."

"Who else do you put on a pedestal?"

I lick my lips and think about Nick's. How much I miss their cigarette-scented presence on mine. "Nick, maybe? I kind of see only the good about him and ignore that stuff's tough for him too. Not that it matters anymore, he's still not talking to me."

Since therapists aren't allowed to hug patients, Dr. Grant does the psychiatrist's equivalent, an awkward shoulder pat. "Love is tough in all of its forms. What I admire about you is that you have so much of it. Here's some advice: one of the greatest gifts and most basic decencies you can give someone is the chance to be human. Let your mom be human. Let Nick be human. Let yourself be human."

◆

Nick doesn't look good. I mean, he always looks good, but right now I can tell by the way he's breathing that he's barely keeping it together. He keeps clenching and unclenching his fists, cracking his knuckles like he can't wait to smash them into someone's face. We've been in English for half an hour and he hasn't even bothered to open his textbook. Donna's busy grading tests, either oblivious or, more likely, smart enough to know that he needs space. Too bad I'm not gonna give it to him. Seeing him like this is more than I can bear. I get up from the chair near the computer, where I've been sitting since our breakup, and move back to my old spot next to him.

"Hey, what can I do to help?"

He doesn't look at me, intent on clamping his left hand, squeezing each finger individually, then, smack, punching his open right palm. "Nothing. Unless you've got a private jet that can fly me home."

"How come? Did your mom's rheumatoid flare up again? Did your dad lose the roofing contract?"

"They're fine. Emma's not."

A Drop in the Ocean 205

Emma, his little sis. Super goofy and into anime. She's two years younger than Nick, who's one year younger than me, which puts her in grade seven. "What's wrong?"

"Some stupid little shits keep stealing from her, threatening to beat her up if she tells."

"Like her lunch money?"

Nick switches to clamping his right hand, one finger at a time. "Might've started that way, but the thieves pulled a knife on her, slashed her hand up 'til she gave them the emerald ring she inherited from Nan. She called me crying cuz Ma told her not to wear it, and now she doesn't know how to tell our folks it's gone."

I suck my teeth, wincing in sympathy. "Aw fuck, I'm sorry. It's awful Em had to go through that."

"She wouldn't have if I was there. I'd beat the shit out of anyone if they tried. That's why they did it now, when I'm here." At the last few words, Nick's voice rises enough to scare me and get Donna's attention. She comes over to redirect us back to work. I return to my seat and my essay on Canadian autonomy, straining my ears to hear the convo between her and Nick. Something about mindfulness, meditation, or returning to Ward 1 for a cool-down. Donna sits in my old spot and stays with Nick for the rest of class. Whatever they're doing, it's working. Nick deep breathes, grunting as he exhales, letting his shoulders slump and his back loosen into an almost relaxed posture. Even though it wasn't my help that got him there, I settle for just being happy he's okay. That's why when the bell rings and I pack up for rec, I'm kinda startled when he asks if I'll go to art therapy with him.

Let's see, sit on my ass barely moving, or do the only exercise I'll get today? It's not even a choice. Except Nick. He's the make-or-break factor here. After I inhale, my shoulders slump more from shame than from eased tension.

"Art therapy for the win," I say.

The clack of hockey sticks slapping against each other makes its way through the cracks of the art room's closed door. So much for the hallway and the billiards room between us and the gym. I bite my lip and set my jiggling knee to turbo speed. Small freaking measures of comfort to combat the anxious guilty energy that has my every molecule vibrating. It keeps me on edge, unable to draw a straight line because I want to leap from my seat and barge into the game, making up for all the exercise I've missed. But that isn't what I want. Not really.

What I want is a who. He sits beside me, filling in his Choice Point sheet with exquisite sketches. The triggering situation he's chosen is, yup, you guessed it, the news from Emma. To the right are Toward Moves, actions that move him toward his ideal life and self, which he's listed and illustrated, while to the left are Away from Moves, actions and things that move him away from them. He's colouring a left-side drawing of his fist clobbering one of the thieves' cheeks, spit, blood, and a tooth flying out. I'm being meta and doing this exact moment as my Choice Point.

"I showed you mine, now you show me yours," Nick says.

"Hell no." My sheet wrinkles as I hug it to my chest, hiding my drawing of the life I want, where we're a couple again. Now is so not the right moment for that. He uses some of his strength to pry my hands away, not counting on how much power embarrassment gives me. Soon he switches tactics, opting for tickles. Damn him! Giggles burst out of me as I squirm under his fingers. The sheet falls to the table. He keeps tickling me, even though the object of our playfight is right there for the taking. Maybe this moment isn't so bad after all.

A Drop in the Ocean

This is the closest I've been to him in ten whole days. I savour every second. His strong, warm fingers on my arms, his specific Nick scent that's somehow sun-warmed hay, olives, pine nuts, sweat, and pheromones all smushed together wafting through my nostrils. I breathe in deeply, not for calm but for pleasure, and our eyes catch.

His are crinkled and smiling, just like mine. They widen, taking me in, then lower. I press in closer to him, lifting my face to his. His lips are centimetres from mine. We breathe in each other's breath. I stay where I am, heart pounding, barely daring to breathe as I wait for him to make the next move. As bad as I want this, the rest is up to him. His hands cup my head, pulling me in until our mouths meet. He must've missed me too, because this kiss is hungry. Not just our faces, but our entire bodies surging with its rhythm. I pant as I pull away.

"What?" he groans, frustrated.

"I need to know that this isn't it. That there will be more kisses after." Both of us know the question under the question: are we back together?

His eyes lose their edge, and his voice softens. "Yes, there will be. But eventually, the time will come for a last one, when I'm discharged."

My turn to groan. "I won't let you leave. I'll lock you in the storage closet and feed you at night."

"That's the nicest thing anyone's ever said to me."

$$\blacklozenge$$

Dinah never joined our smoke huddles. Like me, she isn't smoke or toke dependent. Unlike me, she's left the Residency.

Jorge passes Nick what's left of the joint, which is basically all cherry.

"Shotgun?" I ask him.

Nick hunches down while I tiptoe up until we're kissing. Beneath the ash and stronger than the herby chronic is the taste of him, my drug of choice. The smoke hits the back of my throat, and I use my coughs as an excuse to fall into his arms.

Jorge is more patient with Nick and me making out than Sweets was. He pulls out a Player's and takes a thoughtful drag. "So, how many alternate worlds do you think there are? And would there be ones where time is all sped up and shit, the way it was in *Hypercube*?" At this thought he grimaces, probably picturing the decomposing bodies scene, like I am when I pull away from Nick. We toss around ideas on the nature of existence, quantum mechanics, life after death, that kind of stuff.

"Infinity, bro, there are an infinite number of worlds. Like in one world, Mira didn't do shotgun with me, and in another world, we're still doing shotgun, and in another one, you've never blazed in your life."

My favourite thing about this theory is that it means Gung Gung is still alive in a million other worlds. In a bunch of those other worlds, I don't have mental illness. Somewhere out there is an un-fucked-up Mira eating guilt-free McDonald's with her Gung Gung after another day of normal high school. If that's not science fiction, then I don't know what is. My Archetype Chronicles take place in a multiverse where there are as many worlds as there are in your standard space opera. The collective name for all these different worlds is the Realms Beyond. The second-last book will be set in a high-tech dystopian realm where elves are slaves. Science fantasy.

"That means there must be millions of worlds where Dinah doesn't go to Riverview," I say. This, even more than decomposing bodies, kills the mood. "So what if she was eighteen and aged out? Why couldn't they just let her stay? She doesn't deserve to go to that hellhole."

"No one does," replies Nick.

*A Drop in the Ocean*209

For a moment we all just stand there, lost in our thoughts. I'm thinking about how lucky I am to be here instead of there. Wondering if there is where I'll end up in two years anyway, when I age out. Aging out is what happens when you're no longer a youth and you have to go to adult care. In BC that almost always means Riverview. It's been around since 1913, when it used to be called Essondale. When Poh Poh's sister went there, she got nonconsensual electroshock therapy, which they did there a lot. Elsie told me she was lucky they didn't forcibly sterilize her, because they did that there too. Even though it's not like that anymore, Riverview's still scary, because once you're an adult, that's it. If you're severe enough, i.e., too fucked up, that's where you'll be for the rest of your life.

Mostly though, I'm thinking about Dinah. How we were friendly but not exactly friends. We'd do group activities together—play poker, build puzzles, or laugh our asses off at Monty Python because we'd both pick the BBC when we got channel choosing privileges. But we won't stay in contact the way Sweets and I do. That's kind of how it is with most people you meet in treatment. You learn to get along. Like how I learned to save my berry-flavoured yogurts from morning snack for Dinah because they were her fave. Or how we'd give each other manicures and she never complained about how I'd just bite her hard work away within a few days.

At her transfer—not discharge—party a few hours ago, I did my best nail painting yet. The same pastel-purple base for both her hands and feet, speckled with tiny flowers I dabbed on with a toothpick. Five orange dots for the petals, a tiny yellow one for the centre. They looked almost pro except for her left pinky toenail, where one of the flowers got smushed. It was because we were watching *Monty Python and the Holy Grail,* and the killer bunny scene was on. I should've known better than to try and power through our giggles. To preserve her mani-pedi I put on two layers of topcoat. How long will they last? Will she try and protect this last trace of the Residency during her first weeks at Riverview? Will seeing it on her fingers and toes make her smile?

Mani-pedis aside, it still feels like we ~~disappointed~~ failed her. The Residency and me. Neither of us put in as much effort helping her as we should've. See, Dinah never went to the Quiet Room. Never hurt herself or anyone else. She'd say shit, that was all. Terrifying shit that was just plain bonkers about her delusions. (Though no more bonkers than my patricidal prince obsessions.) Some I've mentioned before—she was a mermaid raped by a shark, she had a dead baby— and some new ones: Paris Hilton was in league with the Taliban, and they were gonna bomb Vancouver International Airport. But it was only ever talk. We weren't supposed to engage with her when she was in those states, so I didn't. I got very good at not engaging with Dinah. Too good at it. Now she's gone.

CHAPTER TWENTY

*I*nhale for the Christmas Pass. SLAM. Exhale for the Christmas Pass. SLAM, SLAM. Inhale, SLAM, think: home visit overnight. SLAM, exhale, imagine: waking up in my actual bed. SLAM. My heart beats so fast that my head aches. A few slams later, the dizziness transforms into bile rushing up my throat. I choke back a dry heave and force myself to inhale. Every atom of every molecule in my body vibrates with panic/pain energy, neurons screaming *wrong, wrong, WRONG* almost as loudly as Dr. Grant's car door crashing back into its frame. Exhale. Out of my throat comes a dying rabbit noise.

"What are your SUDS at?" Dr. Grant yells over slamming the door. This exposure is what he calls a triple whammy. 1) I have to breathe with the car door constantly opening and shutting. 2) I'm sitting down in the car while he's standing. 3) It's loud banging noises.

"A million, my SUDS are at a million." We've been making our way up from the bottom of my OCD fear ladder and have done exposures of each thing, one at a time. Him opening the door for me, a walk past a construction site, me sitting in Dr. Grant's car with all the doors open. Breathing. Wouldn't the logical jump be to go from one trigger to two triggers at a time? Not motherfucking three all at once. Every exposure is the hardest thing I've ever had to do. They drain me for days. Now triple that. As Dr. Grant slams the driver's side door, I put my hand on the passenger's side door handle. He sees me about to open it, shifting in my seat to leave, and stops.

"Mira, wait. Tell me five things you see." He runs around the hood and opens my door for me. Great, now he's exercising even more than me.

"I see myself getting the fuck out of here."

"What about your Christmas pass?"

I let out an irritated huff while I plop my butt back down from hovering above the seat.

"Just humour me and tell me the first five things you see. Describe them without any judgment."

"Fine-nuh." I roll my eyes. "I see your stubble and some of it is grey, I see the frost you didn't scrape off the bottom of the front window, I see the blue-and-white-checkered BMW logo on the steering wheel, I see our breath coming out as fog, I see sunlight gleaming on the car's black hood."

"Okay, describe four things you're touching."

"Um, I feel the soft liner of my pockets that my hands are jammed into because I forgot to bring gloves, I feel the freaking freezing cold air stamping goosebumps on whatever part of me isn't covered, I feel my skin-tight jeans squeezing my legs, I feel my back sinking into the leather cushions of this seat."

"Three things you hear."

By now I'm getting into it. "I just heard you speak, I hear the wind battering against my ears, I hear my heartbeat slowing down."

"What about two things you smell?"

"My gross anxiety sweat and your crisp, woodsy cologne, which is way better than that overly sweet Axe trash you had on before."

"I think that counts as a judgment, but I'll take the compliment anyway. And, lastly, one thing you taste."

"I taste traces of Splenda and coffee from the two cups I had at breakfast."

He doesn't give me the lecture Elsie does about how Splenda is bad for my liver. Instead, he says, "Now what are your SUDs at?"

My suds, I'd forgotten about them. My sweating's stopped, and I no longer feel my pulse pounding through my skin. I'm breathing evenly. "Um, an eighty."

"Down from a million to eighty," Dr. Grant says, then whistles. "Not bad, not bad at all. That was a grounding technique called Five, Four, Three, Two, One Senses. Super-original name, right? Anytime you feel intense distress, you can use it to refocus your mind."

"You know what my mind's refocusing on as we speak?"

"The Christmas Pass?'

"Yes, the Christmas Pass."

He shrugs his shoulders, like it's not the most important thing coming up in my life. "All in good time."

What's that supposed to mean? "Did you not just see what I did? Christmas is less than two weeks from now."

"You were Eowyn slaying the Witch King, and it's going to pay off. I'll schedule a meeting where you, me, your mom, and Lawrence can discuss realistic expectations along with a safety plan. In the meantime, give yourself a break. Your homework is to do some self-care."

Self-care? Ugh, that's for people who deserve good things. That's almost as bad as doing exposures.

◆

Nick winks while waving me forward. "Go on, gorgeous." I lean deeper into my skates and push, speeding past him and a blur of other bodies. There is a delicious whoosh of air from how fast I'm going that cools the heat from my heart and muscles working. It's also delicious because the wind in my ears drowns out some of the Christmas carols on blast. There's only so much "Rudolph the Red-Nosed Reindeer" a girl can take. My hair beneath the helmet fans out in the air. I'm not Kristi Yamaguchi good, but I remember enough of my lessons to twirl around on one foot and do awkward little hops from forward to backward. There's a jolt as I land back on the ice. Momentum bends my ankle too far, shit, and I have to thrust out my arms for balance. Thank God I tied my laces so tight. If my foot had slipped, I'd have wiped out for sure. Not like that hasn't happened a few times already.

Nick's only fallen once. He glides with one foot, then the other, lifting his whole skate off the ice with each stroke. He's as slow as the little kids who hold hands with their parents. I wouldn't mind that, holding his hand. Except it means I'd have to go at his snail's pace, and then everyone would pass us. *Slow = lazy!* my OCD snaps.

On the left side of the rink is a stack of skating aids that look like oversized shopping cart handles without the carts. Maybe if Nick uses one, he'll be more confident. Then he can go just old people slow, not preschooler slow, when we hold hands. The coolness of the metal bites through my thin-ass dollar store gloves as I push the skating aid ahead of me, then catch up to it so I can push it again. I don't use the skating aid properly, because that would also make me lazy. People look at me weird. A group of tweens I pass erupts in giggles. They were laughing at me, weren't they? Little bitches.

Nick shakes his head to both. No, he doubts they were paying attention to me, and no, he doesn't want a baby's skating aid. *There are babies going faster than you,* I want to say, but I settle for a question.

"What time is it?" An hour, I have to skate for an hour, and then I can be. Just be. Exist while skating as slowly as I want.

His blue-grey eyes widen as he winces. He looks at me like I've just run over a kitten. "You're asking again?"

"Guess that means it hasn't been very long?"

"Four and a half minutes."

I breathe deeply. More long-suffering and seething than DBT soothing, but at least I gave it a try. His slowness, though, I just can't. "Okay, I think I'm gonna ..."

"Do your thing," he says.

To make time go by faster, I count. Thirty-nine scalloped strokes backward. Next, thirty-nine lunge strokes as fast as I can without banging into anyone. Then nine reps of the thirty-ninth lunge. *What about fifty-two?* asks my OCD. I picture Gung Gung on the respirator and force myself into a sharp turn.

No.

I'll do thirty-nine more backward lunges instead. On my third time around the rink backward, I see someone really good gliding with their right leg in the air over their head. The closest I get to copying them is my left leg up around butt height. For seven glorious seconds I hold the glide, then wipe out. Nick speeds up infinitesimally and stretches his hand out for me to grab.

I ignore it. Offer encouragement—"Babe, you're getting better so fast"—as an apology. I don't ask him what time it is until five carols pass. One of them is a Mariah Carey song, and I sing along. Another is "Baby It's Cold Outside." I've never paid attention to its lyrics before. Turns out they're creepy. If Nick were like that dude, I tell him, I'd kick his ass.

"If I were like that dude I'd kick my own ass," he says.

How can I not give him a smooch? The hour is finally up. I slow down with minimal guilt. While we skate, Nick warms my hands with his. There are a few times when he starts to lose balance and places his full weight on my arms. The strain makes me shake, but neither of us falls. Lots of people pass us, though. My heart rate quickens when the little kids from before end up in front of us. We lumber past the length of one wall, and they pass us again. I clench my jaw, going quiet through Nick's story about cold weather power outages in his hometown.

"When we did go down to the basement a few days later, we found the mouse's body there. It had frozen from the cold."

"Gross! I still can't believe you think I'd like this place."

"It's gorgeous. Nothing like the city, and … well, now I know when I'm going back." He says the last part softly, clenching my hand harder as my own grip goes limp.

"Your discharge date, they gave it to you?"

Nick nods, holding back a smile. I know the only reason he doesn't have a shit-eating grin is because he's worried about me. I want to be the reason he beams, not someone he has to hide his feelings from.

"Go on then, spill." My voice barely trembles.

"January tenth." He hears my sharp inhale and rushes on. "So it's still, like, a month away. We have time, lots of it."

"Yeah, we do." I nod my head hard to show him it's fine. That I'm happy for him, because I am. Even though it means he's leaving. He gets to go home, where it's gorgeous. He's gorgeous, he deserves to be somewhere gorgeous. With someone gorgeous, but instead he chose me. "And you better promise me that we'll spend it all together."

"Of course."

Because I don't want to let go of Nick's hand, I use my teeth to pull the glove off my free one. Then hold out my naked pinky.

"Pinky swear?"

"Double pinky swear." We skid to a full stop at the edge of the rink, where we toss off our gloves. That spark of us touching isn't as sharp as when he first warmed my hands months—that feel like forever—ago. It's softened as my feelings have deepened from a shallow crush to

A Drop in the Ocean

actual can't-touch-the-bottom-with-my-feet-deep love. His pinkies are so big, with wiry blond hair on their knuckles. They hold mine snug. When I start to let go, he pulls my hands to his lips. "I wish I could take you with me."

I try to imagine life outside the Residency. How would that even work? My brain goes blank. Fuzzes out like a TV channel with no signal. I shiver, but not from the cold. "I wish we could just stay here like this forever."

But we can't.

We pick up our gloves, step up off the rink onto the solid rubber floor, hobble to the bench, and take off our skates. The magic of the moment fades as I realize that I've gotten blisters on my toes, my feet stink, and I really, really need to pee.

♦

Five more days 'til Christmas! The whole Residency is becoming a ghost town as more and more kids leave for holiday passes. Jorge's gone, and Franco didn't want to help, so I ended up decorating the unit by myself. Oh, and I guess Elsie helped a tiny bit in the beginning. She wouldn't let me carry the fake Christmas tree out of storage by myself because, "Ce'Nedra, Ce'Nedra, don't you know it'll be my ass on the line if you break your back lifting that thing?"

Dr. Grant's office is sparse in its holiday spirit, but even he has a row of Christmas cards lined up neatly on his filing cabinet. The place where his personal records of us patients live. Shit, why didn't I get him a Christmas card?

He presses the last few digits of Mom and Lawrence's phone number, then we wait as it rings. Conference call time, bitches. The way the phone rests in the middle of the desk and I'm chomping at my fingernails like they're popcorn, you'd think this was a hostage negotiation. It kind of is.

"Hello," a confident male voice booms. Lawrence. A second later, Mom chimes in with extra cheer. "Hi Mira-babe, hi Dr. Grant. How are you both doing?"

Why does she have to call me Mira-babe? Why not just my actual name? "We're doing good, Mom," I answer.

The small talk goes on a bit longer until Lawrence clears his throat in a *let's get down to business* kind of way. I can see him in my imagination, shoulders back and squared, clean-shaven chin tilted up. "As excited as we all are for Mira to sleep over, we need to have some guidelines in place."

"Yes, a safety plan," Dr. Grant says. "Mira and I have discussed it already. It's short, sweet, and simple while still covering all the bases like emergency calm-down PRNs and de-escalating techniques."

"Okay, then, what are the parameters of this safety plan?" Lawrence asks. "How badly do things have to go before we call you? If things are really bad but you're busy, do we call 911? What about property damage?"

"I'm gonna do my rituals outside, on the garage's cement wall, so there won't be any dents, duh." Sounding pissy right before spending twenty-four hours under "his roof" probably isn't the best call. Too bad. Dr. Grant catches my eye and mimes a deep breath. God how I hate breathing, hate even him at this moment. I roll my eyes and inhale.

"And the blood? Your mother shouldn't have to see that."

I sigh, suddenly grateful for every time Elsie's made me scrub the unit walls. "I'll clean it up myself. But everybody has to leave me alone, I can't have any interruptions."

Mom barges in. "What if there's an emergency? What if you faint?"

"I won't."

"You could. We're not going to just leave you there for hours."

"You won't need to."

Dr. Grant cuts through before things get heated. "That's a good point, Sarah, one we hadn't thought of. Mira, how about we put a time cap on how long you have outside the garage? Let's say ten minutes, and if you're not inside by then, your parents can check on you?"

"Twenty, and they can't touch me or speak to me."

"Godverdomme," my stepdad swears under his breath in Dutch. Then, louder: "How about fifteen? And if you've fainted, we are definitely getting you medical attention."

You want this, Mira, I tell myself. *You want to have Christmas with your family, in your own house, like a human being.* After being denied it and deciding to hate it instead, it's weird to even think that the place where it all started—the hours of jumping jacks and sit-ups, and arranging things and checking them—is actually still my home. Even if it doesn't feel like it. It never will feel like it unless I spend time there again. I suck my teeth, scowling. "'Kay."

They'd better have some amazing Christmas presents for me.

We go over my other rituals. Lawrence will drive us to Uncle Ken and Auntie Lydia's for Christmas dinner, and he'll park in their driveway, which means I'll be able to touch their front door and breathe in under thirty seconds. I can help with food prep and dishes as long as Mom monitors me to make sure I don't get obsessive. By now my nails are all bitten down to the quick and I've made a pile of their rinds. I fiddle with each rind, breaking it into slivers.

Once the rinds are slivers of slivers, we've moved on to my medications. They're in a blister pack: morning, afternoon, bedtime.

Everything so clearly labelled it's unfuckuppable. My PRNs, five milligrams of Ativan, are in a separate vial. If I get agitated and my DBT skills aren't working, Mom and Lawrence can suggest a PRN. If I am screaming or physical, then I have to take one or they'll drive me back here. If all goes well, my pass will last twenty-five and a half hours. Mom will pick me up from Ward 2 on Christmas around 10 a.m. and drop me back off on Boxing Day at 11:30 a.m. More than a full day of normalcy. Holy shit.

"What do you think, team, happy with the plan?" asks Dr. Grant.

"Sounds great," Mom says, before Lawrence's "It'll have to do."

"Mira, how do you feel?" Dr. Grant looks straight at me.

I feel like this will be a fuck ton of work. One long day of exposure after exposure. Dr. Grant as lifeguard up on the beach while I thrash in the open ocean. Sink or swim, motherfucker, sink or swim. "Let's do this," I say.

CHAPTER TWENTY-ONE

Joy to the world, for Mira goes home. It's Christmas! I swish around the asymmetrical hem of my dress as I wait at Ward 2's front door for Mom. It's a Baby Phat red-and-gold halter that looks great with my high-heeled ankle boots. Not the most practical shoes to do running and jumping rituals in, but goddammit, it's Christmas, and I get to go home. Obviously I'm gonna dress fancy. The heels make the most gorgeous click clack as I stride to the nurses' station again to check the time: 9:58 a.m. and twelve seconds. I know, I know, I'm early. I pivot and click clack down the girls' wing to the bathroom, where my stuff has free rein over the entire counter. Sweets has been gone for so long, and now that Dinah's left, I can take up as much space as I want. A small perk that does little to fill the void of their absence. Uh-uh, now is not the time to be bummed. I wrench my drifting thoughts back to the present, gather all my lipsticks and glosses together so I can deliberate over which to put on. By the time I'm swabbing the chosen gloss over my Cupid's bow, Alan's yelling at me to hurry up and not keep my family waiting.

Family? Shit, is Lawrence with Mom? He always complains about my breath holding and running. Even though I've had these car door rituals for years, it's a gamble whether he'll remember that I have to get in and out of the car first. Anxcitement (anxiety/excitement) has me at a slight tremble as I make my way to the front door.

"Merry Christmas, sweetheart." Mom throws her arms around me. Beneath her floral perfume is the scent of vanilla shea butter, and beneath that, the tangy sweetness of eau de her.

221

When she and I break away, Lawrence says "Good to see you" like he means it. We exchange a stiff hug. He doesn't make a sound, doesn't even roll his eyes, as I take one last deep inhale before my breathless bolt to his dark-green Volkswagen. My heels sink into the slushy remnants of snow from two days ago, kicking up clumps of grey sludge as I veer past some ice. I slow down as I reach his car. My hand brushes its hood with the gentlest of touches, breaking the ritual's spell. I breathe. He's too far behind me to appreciate me babying his ride, but I do it as a gesture of goodwill. After a few deep breaths, my head stops pounding. Lawrence clicks the car alarm on his keys, unlocking the door for me.

"Thanks," I call out and climb in.

The drive home doesn't take too long, which I'm grateful for. We talk about school, the weather, what TV shows we're watching. All of us on our best behaviour; Lawrence doesn't complain when I admit I only got a B in math, and I pretend to care about the latest episode of *House Hunters International*. As we drive to our house at the end of the cul-de-sac, I go over what I need Mom and Lawrence to do. He heaves a long-suffering sigh before reassuring me that he will wait in the car for me to finish and not enter the house until Mom and I've settled.

My heartbeat's trot skips from canter straight to gallop as I throw myself out of the back seat, heels skidding on a rogue patch of ice. I squeal, mouth closed, jogging carefully up the path to the front door that bisects the yard. Lawrence did a decent job shovelling, so I don't slip again. Mom tails me from a few footsteps away, staying silent because I can't be distracted. Her hand shakes as she pushes the key in the lock, missing the first two times, which shoots my heart past horse gallop to cheetah sprint. Once she unlocks it, she steps back

A Drop in the Ocean   223

as I tap the side of my head nine times against the white wooden door. The side, not the front, and a soft thud, not a slam, the first two exposures of many more to come. Still holding my breath, I open the door for us, almost shutting it on her coat because I close it so quickly. As I cross the threshold, I ignore the enormity of the moment, powering through my ritual. Keep ignoring it as I jump twenty-one times, spikes of pain jolting up my legs whenever my heels pound the floor. It's not until I bend over to take off my boots that my knees buckle. Less from exhaustion than from the weight of the knowledge that I'm back. Home for the first time since the summer I turned fourteen.

◆

Being in my room is the weirdest. The walls are the same robin's egg blue that I chose when I was twelve, shortly after we moved here. There's the close-up pic of the lime-green and tangelo-orange frog on my left; my giant, jam-packed bookshelf and the window overlooking hedges on my right; and the greyscale grove landscape shot in front of me, right above the head of my bed. My bed, my glorious bed, is a freaking queen. Mom's old one from before Lawrence moved in. Not the piece of shit single that I sleep on at the Residency. Mom's made it IKEA catalogue perfect with my favourite duvet, floral but under-stated fluffed pillows, and some of the stuffies I've accumulated since childhood. I collapse onto it and starfish sprawl my limbs, not caring that this short-ass dress rides up and my underwear is out for all to see.

There's no one here but me to see it anyway. Mom and Lawrence are lingering in the living room after our gift exchange. Him checking out a new camera and her gathering the nicest bags and wrapping paper to reuse. I'll have to haul my loot in here. A pair of

True Religion jeans with jewels on the pockets; Tamora Pierce's latest Tortall book, *Terrier*; another book called *The Orphan's Tales: In the Night Garden*; and a box of Purdys caramels that I didn't want because then I'll eat them but that Lawrence got me because it's a Christmas tradition. My fave gift, I'm already wearing: a beautiful white-gold oval locket with a star made from tiny diamonds on its front. Inside, there's a picture smaller than my thumbnail of young Mom cuddling baby me. It dangles from my neck, brushing the carpet as I wiggle on my belly, reaching below my bed.

I stretch my arm, grasping this way, then that, until my fingers close around a box. My journal box. This is where my seven most recent journals live, documenting my life from my stay in Remuda Ranch all the way up to now. Older ones are in the drawers of my nightstand, easily accessible. They're mostly full of drawings or non-sense scribbles. The eldest has baby cherubs on the cover. Yes, baby cherubs, and one of those dinky locks that girly diaries always seem to have, because three-year-old me had zero taste. It's full of Mom's elegant handwriting. Transcriptions of *Mr. Dressup* or Disney fanfic stories that I'd dictate to her. When I was a preteen is when shit got serious. Around twelve I stopped caring about switching my coloured gel pens every paragraph and just wrote to cope.

I flip through the hippie angel diary with an account of my first-ever trip to the psych ward. A week's stay at CAPE in Vancouver Children's Hospital. Dried tears splat my scrawled complaints across from an angsty poem about how death would bring me peace. Damn, I was a stupid, whiny bitch. Wait up, I still am. The only reason I don't rip the poem out and tear it to shreds is this vague, ridiculous hope that one day, maybe, I'll be a Tolkien-level famous writer. People will make a biopic about my life, and they'll need evidence of my earliest

A Drop in the Ocean 225

attempts at writing. And the only reason I'm still around for a hypothetical biopic is because of these journals. Shitty and illegible as they are, writing the words inside them kept me going. Knowing that one day what I'd been through would make one hell of a story.

Like when I was hard-core anorexic and terrified my PRNs would make me gain weight because they tasted like sugar, wouldn't even brush my teeth because toothpaste did too. One of the nurses caught me spitting my meds out and, BAM, she's yelling at her co-workers and then two of them are slamming me to the ground as she preps a syringe. I don't get a second chance to take the meds, just a hollow needle full of haloperidol jammed into my ass.

Except it was so much worse than anything at the Residency, because it was my first. You never forget your first. Especially when it's a violation. I wasn't hurting myself or anybody else. My forehead at fourteen was as smooth as my left butt cheek, which they stabbed full of booty juice. So why the tackling? Why the shot?

Around that same time, another girl on the unit, Eileen, cried almost as hard over having her tube taken away. During our five months at the fatten-up farm, we ate three meals and three snacks a day, plus got pumped full of liquid calories at night. Yellow rivers of nutrition dripped down from medical bags, up through our noses, and then down again into our shrunken stomachs. We'd spend every minute of the thirty we got to finish a meal racing to eat the slowest, because that meant we had self-control. She hated me because I needed a tube for longer, and I hated her because everyone else seemed to love her.

Now, Eileen's face is a blur in my mind. What makes the story epic isn't the her-versus-me way I used to think about it. It's how we were the same. Lonely. Both pushing and shoving each other deeper into hell when we could've walked through it together, holding hands. Here in my leather-bound journal is the Tinker Bell she drew me on her last day of treatment. Tinker Bell's arm is extended, her dainty fingers outstretched. It reminds me of this graffiti I saw in a Denny's bathroom that said "The world is full of other yous." Just like all these other journals piled next to my current one, other mes surround me. Kids like Eileen, or Sweets, or Jorge, or Nick. We can make hell better for each other or we can make it worse. How many other mes did I meet in all those places? Over a hundred, easily.

Maybe, after my fantasy series gets published, I'll write a memoir. A psych ward survival guide for the mes who aren't fucked up yet, who might not even be born. I'll let them in on a secret: it's okay, I'm fucked up too. So is everybody else. Give them some tips: Get the shrink to explain your meds to you. Take them. Get off them if the side effects are scary. Get the staff to be your allies, not your enemies. Get friendly with the other kids but stay on guard until they earn your trust. Get a journal, it will help.

◆

It's been years since I visited Uncle Ken and Auntie Lydia's house, which is also how long it's been since I've seen them, Thomas, or Tim. Wish I could've run into one of them at the hospital and not Rachel. I do the car door ritual as fast as I can and take off running as casually as I can while holding my breath, and carrying presents, to get to their door. Before they … shit. Auntie Lydia's opened it. What do I do? Why didn't Mom warn her that I need to open the door on my own? Why do I "need" to open the door in the first place? *Right* comes to me with a rush of relief: I'll close the door, then open and shut it again. Christmas miracle or improvised compulsion? It doesn't matter,

A Drop in the Ocean

because now I'm being squished between Auntie Lydia's arms. I wrap one arm around her and keep my other hand on the door, where it has to stay until I shut it twice. She hangs on tight to me for close to a minute, long enough for Uncle Ken and my cousins to show up behind her as Mom and Lawrence wait patiently behind me.

Or maybe not that patiently. Lawrence's hand creeps toward the door but Mom bats it away. "It's part of her ritual," she hisses at him. If Uncle Ken, whose arms around me are as hard as Auntie Lydia's are soft, hears them, he's tactful enough to ignore it. I get cursory hugs from Thomas and Tim. And something in between her parents' and brothers' embraces from perfect Rachel. She must've gotten the okay from Jesus to touch me. Or, more likely, Mom complained to Uncle Ken. The pearls she's wearing dent my skin, missing my locket by inches. Good, because if her fifties housewife jewellery scratched my pendant, I'd flip shit.

"My turn next," says a crackly voice I'd recognize anywhere.

"Poh Poh!" Hoping nobody notices, I do this foot thing so that I'm touching the door with my right foot while stretching and bending down to give Poh Poh a proper two-armed hug. If I weren't sixteen or if it were just us, I'd lay my head in the flesh between her neck and shoulder. Except there isn't flesh there, only skin stretched over protruding tendon and bone. The last time I saw Uncle Ken and Auntie Lydia, I'd looked like that too. A feeding tube trailing through my throat instead of a dainty locket clasped around it. This time, I get to taste what goes into me. After I shut the door twice and stow away my boots, I rush to the kitchen to see what Auntie Lydia needs help with.

The kitchen is crowded with us females the way it always is at family gatherings. It's a stereotypical gender thing, but it's also where we get to bond. Poh Poh and Rachel are busy making a salad. God, even the way Rachel cuts celery is perfect. I turn away, practise the DBT skill of the half smile to keep from rolling my eyes. Auntie Lydia buys it. She motions for me to come help her unload the fridge full of premade dishes. The premade dish Mom brought was Schwartzie potatoes, also known as artery cloggers. They're in a tie with Poh Poh's no mai, also known as Chinese sticky rice, for my favourite holiday food. I help Auntie Lydia stuff the glutinous rice full of dung gu, lap cheong, dried shrimp, garlic, and green onions into the hole right between the turkey's legs. If Nick or Sweets or any of the Residency kids were here, they'd make some gross joke about fisting.

We pack the no mai loosely so that all of it can get thoroughly cooked. The bird is a giant among poultry, and I can't help grabbing the metal tray it's on to do a quick bicep curl. Oof, twenty pounds, enough for lots of leftovers. Besides timing the turkey perfectly so it's all cooked but still moist and tender, we need to whip up gravy and bake the other dishes like the Schwartzie, artichoke dip, Brussels sprouts, and marshmallow yams. Once that's done, the table needs setting. After the last dessert fork's been laid, everyone needs drinks. Wine for the adults, punch for us kids.

"You know I'm in my first year of uni, right?" Thomas raises an eyebrow at me as I hand him some punch. "Can you spike this for me, please?"

"Mine too," Tim echoes.

"Want yours dirty, Rache?" I ask.

She blushes. "Oh no, I'm too young for that. Just punch, thanks." I can't make any comment about her being a prude because all I'm drinking is ice water. I know better than to drink excess calories when I'm going to be stuffing my face with carbs and dessert. Yes, dessert,

A Drop in the Ocean

because Auntie Lydia is Martha Stewart on 'roids and made a slew of options.

I come back with two spiked punches, one just punch, and one ice water, to find everybody holding hands, waiting to say grace. Once I drop off the drinks, I beeline for Mom and Lawrence. Protection. Mom lets go of Lawrence's hand and squeezes mine, her sparkly red nail polish glinting in the dining room's chandelier light. Sure, conversation will be awkward, but at least it won't be a play-by-play of Thomas's frosh life at Sauder or Tim's and Rachel's latest Christian school achievements. Or a barrage of questions about why I missed all these family events, what kind of grades I'm getting, and, worst of all, more heartfelt congratulations on how "healthy" I look. Instead, I'll get to hear Lawrence complain about accounting clients. A safe kind of boredom.

That's exactly how it goes down. Me able to savour the so-bad-for-me goodness of cream sauce oozing through hash browns topped with melted cheese, and the slightly-less-bad-for-me goodness of no mai with chunks of deliciously addictive lap cheong. Once everyone's done, we slouch back in our chairs. I'm so stuffed I can't move. The giant, bloated bulge of my stomach stretches against my dress's clingy fabric. I groan. Mom catches my eye and mimes wiping her mouth. My cheeks heat up as I rush a napkin to my lips, which comes back smeared with hollandaise sauce and lip gloss. With the last mouthful of water in my glass, I do a quick swirl. Its coldness is a refreshing shock to my gums, swishing away anything stuck between my teeth. Another trick of Mom's, whose plate I stack above my own as I get up from the table to start cleaning.

The clearing of the table is a joint effort. I cringe, wishing it weren't when Thomas takes away a bunch of the plates I'd wanted to lift. He stole my exercise. My consolation prize is getting to lift what's left of the turkey platter all on my own by reaching in front of Tim. Saying "I'm fine, thanks," a little too quickly to be polite and a little too quietly to be yelling when he asks if I want help. People let me clear the rest of the table alone after that. My luck ends with one of the last chores left: dish duty. Anything too big or too fragile for the dishwasher needs to be hand washed. I gear myself up with gloves and various scouring pads, turning the tap as hot as it will go while waiting for the water to come out steaming. Rachel sets herself next to me at the drying rack with two thick towels. She rolls up the sleeves of her cardigan, then tosses her hair behind her shoulders.

"You know, it was Jessie's twentieth last Friday. All of us cousins threw her a surprise bash at Double One. We missed you."

"Oh." I stir the dishwashing liquid with both my hands. As a layer of bubbles froths above the surface, I clench them into fists, thinking about what to say. What excuse will she respect? "I'm sorry I couldn't make it. You know how it is. School. Finals. I just had a bunch of stuff on my plate." Both of us are smiling. Except my smile is more a baring of teeth. I can feel the heat of the water through my gloves and the crust of hardened artichoke dip baked onto the casserole dish. When I finish scraping the thing clean with steel wool, Rachel grabs it from me before I can place it on the rack.

"Even God took a break on the seventh day," she says, wiping the dish dry with precise, circular motions. "School isn't everything."

That's another reason I can't stand Rachel. It's always God this, Jesus that. God doesn't dole out vengeance to her, only blessings. And maybe what I hate about her most is that blessings are all she deserves. Other than not hugging me that time, she is an actual good person.

A Drop in the Ocean • 231

"Oh well, you're only in grade eight, right? I'm in grade ten, so my transcript's gotta be perfect if I want a scholarship."

"Ooh, a scholarship, what are you doing for extracurriculars? Did you do any volunteer work in the summer? That would look good on your records."

"Not this summer."

She frowns, her lips forming a Disney princess moué. "What about your scholarship? If you weren't busy, why weren't you around?"

"Oh, I was busy. I was at …" And I can't say treatment. Or, if I did admit to treatment, then I definitely can't say the Residency, where criminals go. "Camp."

"Camp, huh? That sounds cool, what kind of camp?"

"Just, uh, a wellness camp, I guess you could call it. Like overall focused on health." I'm washing the carving tools now. As I scrub the tines of the giant fork, part of me wants to push my thumb down, down, until it pierces through the rubber gloves and even more easily through my skin. "What about you, what did you do this summer?"

But Rachel won't let it go. "Good health is so important, it's one of the things I pray for every night."

I know that line. It's the last part of the prayer Poh Poh would say before putting me to bed on our sleepovers. *And Dear Jesus, please continue to keep Mira safe, healthy, and happy. Amen.* When my face twists into a grimace, it's more like one of a Disney villain about to cry. I DBT the shit out of my expression and return to some semblance of a half smile. Even do the willing hands part of the technique with open palms under the salad bowl I'm washing. By then Rachel's had to repeat herself.

"I was just wondering whether camp was effective. Is it somewhere you'd recommend?"

That turns my smile into something more genuine. I stifle a snort. "No, you don't need it. And it wouldn't be your thing."

She dries the carving utensils, taking care to avoid the sharp edges I'd reached for. "But it's yours?"

"Yeah, I have OCD. You don't."

"What's that supposed to mean?"

"Trust me, it's not something you want." I give her a CliffsNotes version of my diagnosis. Explain the anxiety part and mention my less weird compulsions.

"Oh, you know what, I think I might have that too. But instead of having to repeat stuff, my clothes *have* to be organized by colour and season. Like, no pink turtlenecks next to my jean shorts. If someone messed with my closet, I'd flip out."

She's trying to make me feel better. Is back to her cheery grin and pleasant voice. I know that if I told her the truth, I'd become the villain for real. Go from being crazy in a cute way like the Mad Hatter—*she needs to do things over and over, aw*—to full-on bad-guy bonkers like the Queen of Hearts—*off with her head!* Except instead of a guillotine, old school blunt force. I wiggle my forehead beneath my bangs. The scab is as hard and crusty as the dip I scraped off the casserole dish. I'm lucky it hasn't cracked. "It's a bit more complicated than that," I say. Before Rachel can open her mouth to ask me how, I add, "But that's enough about me. How 'bout you? What's school like? Are you popular?"

She casts her eyes down demurely, takes her time drying the last few items as I drain the sink and peel off my borrowed gloves.

"That means yes, doesn't it? You don't have to be modest." The air felt amazing against my clammy hands a moment ago. Now it just

A Drop in the Ocean

feels like air. She's great at everything else, of course she'd be great at friends.

"I'm not popular," she says.

"Sure you are."

"No, really I'm not."

So maybe she's not at the top of the social pyramid. Probably because she's too virtuous to talk shit about her peers the way queen bees always do. "I bet you don't realize it because you're so nice."

"Too nice," she mutters. And the way she says it, her voice so small and resigned, lets me know to keep quiet. Makes me think of her, for the first time in maybe years, as something other than perfect.

I wipe up the counter with the towel she isn't using, stay silent until she continues.

"Everyone calls me a goody-goody."

Shit, this story sounds just like mine. First it's goody two-shoes, then it's nerd, and nerd becomes teacher's pet, which spirals into she must want to screw the teacher.

"And the people who call you that—"

"Everybody, even my friends."

"Fine, everybody, what do you say back to them?"

Rachel shrugs. "I don't. I try to ignore it or change the subject. And I try not to draw attention to myself."

With effort, I keep my face blank and my voice light, curious. Like we're discussing her favourite flavour of tea. "What does that mean?"

"Like, I won't answer the teachers' questions anymore unless they ask me something directly, by name. And when they do ask me stuff, sometimes I'll pretend not to know, or say the wrong thing on purpose."

Yes, this sounds eerily familiar. The same kind of shit I did in grade seven before I turned crazy. I guess, Christian or not, all schools have their bullies. It's the Christian part of Rachel that she values most, so I speak Christ to her. "Didn't Jesus say not to hide your light under a bushel?"

"Jesus also said to turn the other cheek."

"What about those who hunger and thirst for righteousness? They're blessed, right?"

"Yeah, but the meek inherit the earth."

I grunt in frustration. There's no way I can out-Bible this chick. Time to switch tactics. "Fuck being meek!" It must come out pretty loud, because Poh Poh, Mom, and Auntie Lydia look up from arranging the desserts, craning their necks in unison toward us.

Rachel shrinks. "Mira, there's no need to swear," she says in a strained whisper. She wrings the towels with fierce intensity, then walks away from me to hang them up on the oven handle to dry.

I follow her, speeding my pace to match hers as she shuffles into the hallway that leads to the bathroom and the study. "Yes, there is. You're trying to change who you are so that small-minded douchebags won't be douchey to you, but that's not going to work. You have to stick up for yourself or they'll keep talking smack about you forever."

"What if standing up for myself just makes it worse?" We're at the end of the hall, away from everyone else, yet her voice is still so small.

"It might." I can't lie to her. "Especially with bullies. But your friends aren't your friends if they keep razzing you when you tell them to stop. And they won't know to stop unless you tell them."

"Thanks for the advice." She wants to leave, body angled toward the bathroom door, hand stretched toward it.

"One more thing, then I'll let you pee in peace."

A Drop in the Ocean

She sighs. "Go ahead."

I hold out my arms. "Gimme a hug."

♦

The next round of hugs happens when we say goodbye around 11:30 p.m., after watching the Claymation Rudolph movie, exchanging presents, and having dessert. By the time I'm shoving the eight meds I should've taken at 10 p.m. into my mouth, it's 12:17 a.m. I swallow them all in one big gulp. In my room, I peel off my dress and change into the monkey pyjamas I got during my stay in UCLA.

"Don't worry, I'll be back," I tell my beautiful queen of a bed, stroking her fluffy duvet cover. Then, legs quaking, I march down-stairs, out the door to the garage's cement wall. For a few moments I just stand there, procrastinating. Mom left Lysol, paper towels, and a sponge at the basement door, making cleaning up both easier and inevitable. The porch light turns off, leaving me in darkness except for the distant pinpricks of stars and the pale pearl glow of the waxing moon. My heartbeat spikes. Our safety plan didn't cover this bullshit.

Yeah, Mira, how dare it be dark at night? My inner Sweets gives me a reality check. Inner Elsie says to slow down, take it step by step. Find out how much you can see. Almost nothing. I can barely make out my hand when I wave it in front of me, let alone the boxes of recycling and old junk my parents have lying around. They all appear as slightly darker shades of grey in an already dark-grey and midnight-blue world. I reach both my arms out in front of me toward the wall. Hopefully my hands will make contact with anything first before I trip on it. My fingertips smack the concrete wall. Good. I sigh with relief. The next sigh I heave is of anxitipation (anxiety/anticipation). Time to get this over with.

It hurts more than the walls at the Residency, because this concrete is porous and coarser. I can't see my blood, but by squelch time, seven bangs in, I know that it must be soaking into the tiny holes like a sponge. Fifty bangs in and my head slips on its own slickness every now and then. Still, it throws me off enough that I let out a shrill, breathless "hrrrrrmm" that gurgles off into several sobs.

A door's thrown open, and heavy footsteps plod down the kitchen porch stairs. Next thing I know, a flashlight beams on me, so bright in the dark that it's violent. I squeeze my eyes shut, still banging, and try to keep count—seventy-nine, eighty, eighty-one—while Lawrence yells, "Mira, are you okay?" When I don't answer he plods closer. I can tell because his voice is louder. "Hello, what's wrong? Do you need help? Answer me."

Why the fuck is he here?! Didn't I say in our family meeting not to interrupt me? To leave me the fuck alone? The airless grunts, "EEERRRR, URRRR," are me begging him to shut up, shut up, God, please shut up. I bang harder. Hoping the intensity will scare him away.

"You do? Is that what you're saying? Nod if you mean yes."

Shit, he's getting closer, ruining everything. He's doing this on purpose, isn't he? He wants me to fail, or else why would he do this to me? If I can just get through this, just finish the ritual, then I'm home free. I bang faster. Faster and harder now, racing. 105, 106, 107. I'm almost done. I concentrate on the numbers and only the numbers. And finally, at 111, for the last nine reps, I do nine more as hard as I can, screaming, "FUUUCK, LAAAWREEENCE!" I put all my righteous rage, all my sudden hate into the three syllables, making my throat rasp. Bash my head so hard those last few times that I see flashes of white.

The flashlight retracts as I sob. Blood drips down my bangs. Caught in my eyelashes, it gives everything a red roof as I turn to look at this

A Drop in the Ocean 237

man who prides himself so much on intelligence but couldn't even follow the simplest of rules. His hazel eyes are wide, his auburn-brown eyebrows raised so high he could be a cartoon. His mouth an open scowl. He shakes his head. "I came down because I heard you and I was worried. Now the whole neighborhood has heard you too."

"Go"—I heave in breath, then exhale—"away."

He does. Turns his back on me, the light turning with him. Both disappear as he plods up the kitchen porch stairs.

Alone, again, in the dark, again, I allow myself to cry. I wipe my snotty nose with the back of my hand and wipe that against the wall, because I don't want to ruin my pyjamas. Enough things have been ruined today. All I can think is fuck fuck fuck fuck.

The litany of fucks continues as I push off the wall, trailing my snotty left hand against it. I make my way to the light, then to the door where the cleaning supplies wait. My only thought as I wet paper towels, squirt Lysol on the wall, and wipe away the stickier, thicker wetness is fuck fuck fuck fuck ... all the way up the stairs, through me dressing my wound, until I crawl into bed. Queen or single, it doesn't matter, I'm still fuck fuck fuck fucked.

◆

I can't sleep. That's why I'm writing. I've gone from best-case scenario—Lawrence apologizes for interrupting my rituals, as if—to worst-case scenario—Lawrence breaks up with Mom because I'm not even his real daughter, so why should he stay? What he did wasn't right. We'd talked about leaving me alone when I bang my head. What I did, though, might not have been the most constructive thing either. There's enough oxygen circulating in my brain for me to recognize that he didn't come downstairs to fuck with me. He broke the rules because he was worried about me being in distress. Because he cares about me. And how did I thank him? By screeching hatred at the top of my lungs. Why couldn't he just leave me alone? Damn, it's hot in here. I yank my duvet off and shift from sleeping on my back to my left side. Maybe that will help.

It's been either thirty seconds or thirty minutes, and I'm still conscious. Now shivering because my PJs are damp with chilled sweat. As much as Lawrence ruined things, I know that no one else (Mom, Dr. Grant, Elsie, the other treatment team members, all the neighbours I woke up) will see it that way. I'm less and less sure that screaming was the right thing to do. It certainly was dumb, even if it was justified. I could've still banged my head really hard and then confronted Lawrence with a gruff, raised voice instead. Could've used the DBT "when you ... I feel ..." language to make him understand why I was so upset. Although come on, when I'm doing my rituals, just leave me alone. Or at least wait fifteen minutes, which was the number he'd come up with, before doing a *silent* checkup. How hard is that? In the morning, I'll talk to him. I'll explain (again) how I can't be interrupted because it could make me lose count, and I'll see if he says sorry. Maybe, if he really does seem sincere about it, I'll apologize back.

Fuck it, I'm up. The fact that I slept at all is kind of astonishing. Also astonishing that, after how much I gorged last night, I'm hungry. Way back when Lawrence was still just Mom's boyfriend, we used to have this special occasion tradition of pancake breakfasts. Birthdays and every other Hallmark holiday, I'd wake up to the sizzle of batter on the frying pan, Lawrence pouring out hearts for Mom and Mickey Mouse heads for me. The heat of the stove and the yeasty, sweet scent wafting

A Drop in the Ocean 239

through the bottom of my door. If we had any, he'd add blueberries or chocolate chips to the Aunt Jemima's mix, substituting the milk for cream and insisting on butter, not margarine, to make the pancakes richer. On my thirteenth birthday, the last one I'd had at home, he'd made them with skim milk and margarine because that was the only way I'd eat them. The kitchen is next to my bedroom, so I'm footsteps away from the perfect apology gesture. Pancake breakfast in bed. I put on Mom's pink-checkered apron and get to work.

Since Elsie's been teaching me a bit of cooking and baking, I know what sifting means when the recipe asks for it. In terms of ingredients, I settle for a compromise. Regular milk instead of cream, and fucking actual butter to appease Lawrence, because the whole point of these pancakes is appeasement through grand gesture. A little after 6 a.m. I knuckle out the rhythm of "Jingle Bells" on Mom and Lawrence's bedroom door with my right hand. My left hand sags under the weight of Lawrence's TV tray with its stack of four pancakes slathered in more butter and maple syrup. I even made him a fancy espresso with the coffee machine he brought back from his last trip to Europe. Mom's tray waits on the kitchen counter with three pancakes, not four, and orange pekoe tea instead of coffee.

I hear her yawn become a groan.

I knock louder, no Christmas carols this time. "Can I come in?"

There's some terse whispering I can't make out before Lawrence answers, "What do you want?" in a not-quite snap.

Appeasement, pancake penance, I remind myself, so I don't reply with the same pissy tone. "Just dropping off some apology breakfast in bed." I make my words ooze, singsong them as sweet as the syrup I just poured.

"Ohhh, lecker lecker," he says when I come in and present the food with some *Wheel of Fortune* prize flourishes.

Mom lets out a soft, appreciative noise. "Mmm. Those smell delicious, babe."

While I transfer the tray to Lawrence, I stumble through an apology.

He sighs and makes a brushing-away gesture with his hand. "Yeah, yeah, yeah, I know that it took you by surprise and you wanted to be left alone. Listen, let's just move on, we don't need to mention it anymore."

"What about Dr. Grant—he's gonna want to know how it went." Without the tray to hold, my hands don't know what to do, so they open and close, open and close. "What will you tell him?"

Lawrence takes a whiff of the coffee, but before his first sip, says, "I'll leave that up to you."

Operation Flapjack was a success.

CHAPTER TWENTY-TWO

So, guess who encouraged me to go AWOL? Hint: it wasn't one of the other Residency kids or anyone from the real world.

Give up yet?

It was Vikas, the hard-ass! He said that over all the time I've been at the Residency I'm the only patient with outside pass privileges who's never broken curfew. When I told him it's because I don't want to get in trouble, he chuckled and said, "You're a teenager, getting into a little trouble is part of growing up. But don't tell anyone I said that, because I like my job."

Tonight, I'm taking his advice. Nick and I are both okay being stuck on unit the next few days, which is probably the worst-case scenario, punishment wise. While everyone else is in bed by lights out at 10:30 p.m., we're snuggled on a bench in a secluded part of Stanley Park at 11. His feet stink even worse than mine as I knead his toes, one at a time. A few of them poke out from the holes of his disintegrating socks. We walked along the Seawall for about two hours, mostly on the beaches themselves instead of the actual path, to avoid any late-night joggers. He bore through me dragging him at a clipped pace whenever I noticed the reflectors of bikes speeding from behind and then beyond us. It only happened like four, okay, maybe five times. His heavy panting always shamed me into slowing down a few metres later. Oh, and the beachcombing. He'd stroll far ahead of me (even at his super-slow pace) while I crouched down, oohing and aahing at the tide's scattered treasures. My purse's outer pocket is bulging with rough quartz pebbles, indigo mussel shells, pearlescent fragments, and

241

spiral shells. Nick helped me wrap them in napkins so they'll make the journey back to the Residency intact. His pockets have my surplus.

Now, he makes me groan with pleasure as he presses his thumbs down hard on the inner arch of my foot. Just like how I avoid his blisters, he gives a wide berth to my newly forming scabs from where I cut myself walking barefoot in the surf.

"Damn, Mira." He leans closer, murmuring something.

The Nine O'Clock Gun, which we were standing way too close to when it fired, fucked with my hearing, so I go, "What?" By the way his voice is all deep and serious, I know it's something heartfelt or a sex thing, or both. I'm glad that it's too dark for him to see me blush. Then again, he always likes when I flush furious red after he says something dirty.

"I said, I love the little noises that come out of you."

On the bench, I get up from sitting with my right foot in his lap to crawling on my hands and knees until my lips are close enough to his for a soft, lingering kiss. He bites my bottom lip with his teeth. I yelp, not in pain but surprise. Dart my head left and right to make sure no one heard. Nope, still nobody around but us and the sea and the trees. Of course I have to nibble his lips to settle the score. The only reason we stop is because we're both laughing so hard that we're shaking and can't hold still enough to kiss. Once we're calm and have our shoes back on, Nick pulls me down so our bodies press together. Between my legs, his boner pokes out at me. So that's why they call it a boner, because it literally is hard as bone. I've seen it before, tenting his baggy jeans or raggedy sweats, but never felt it. Blood rushes to different parts of me, and my pulse throbs like his.

"You know what my favourite thing to do is?" he asks.

"Uh, kiss me?" My voice rises up in a question.

A Drop in the Ocean 243

"Close. It's making girls come."

I stiffen. "Excuse me? Girls as in girls who aren't me?"

His grin goes from sexy to sheepish. "Okay, just one. My ex, who isn't even my friend anymore. She said it made her feel like a goddess, and I want you to feel that way, the way I see you."

"Cheesy, but good save." I lean my cheek against his shoulder. I'm still tense, thinking about having that thing inside of me, how big it is, how much it would hurt versus how good it could feel. How this is probably the last chance we'll have to screw in private unless we have a quickie in the bushes at the Residency. How, unlike for him, this would be my first time. They say your first time always hurts, and as romantic as it is in a hot, risky way to fuck under the stars, it's also really damn cold. The goosebumps on every inch of my skin are half from being turned on and half from being outside with only my puffer jacket and Nick's body heat to keep me from freezing. Like my goosebumps, my shiver is only partially from the cold.

He takes off his coat and spreads it on top of us. "We don't need to do anything you're not ready for. Let's just Lay Lady Lung."

"What the hell's that? Code for oral?"

"No." He smirks. "Haven't you ever heard that Bob Dylan song?"

Again, I don't know what he's talking about. "Isn't he that old country dude your dad likes?"

"Oh, well there goes my erection."

"Wait, what did I do wrong? Is it my boobs, are they too small?" There seems to be a Residency-wide consensus that my flat chest makes me a butterbody. Yet as much as I'm not ready to go all the way, I don't want to turn him off. I love that I can do to him and his body what he does to me and mine.

"Naw, babe, I love your ping-pong titties." To prove his point, he grabs them lightly over my shirt. "It's just that there's nothing like bringing up parents to kill the mood. Anyways, Bob Dylan wrote this song called 'Lay Lady Lay,' and since one of your last names is Lung, I can sing it about you."

In a deep, husky baritone, he hums the tune, singing about me, Lady Lung, lying across his big brass bed. With my ear against his chest, I hear his heart's steady thud through his sweatshirt. I slide my hands under it and grasp the fuzz of his chest while he murmurs about how cold my fingertips are. His hands pass beneath my bra and later, beneath my jeans as he whistles at the curves of my ass, its dimples, the ridge of my hips, and the way my panties are soaked.

We lie like that, at second base, dozing and stroking and making out. Looking up for only a moment as fireworks erupt in bright jewel tones across the night sky. It's New Year's, and the whole point of going AWOL was for us to do the countdown together, but we're too engrossed in being together to notice anything else.

◆

"Do a cake face!" Jorge tells Nick. Everyone at the discharge party takes up the chant. "Cake face! Cake face!" Except not Elsie and me, because we were the ones who made this double chocolate masterpiece. I even put peanut M&M's, Nick's favourite candy, in a border around the top and spelled his name with them. The M&M's forming the C stick to his lower-right cheek and chin, chocolate icing acting as glue where he smushes the bottom part of his face into the cake. People laugh and clap when he lifts up his icing-smeared head. He swipes the icing, along with the M&M's, in a goopy handful, licking it clean.

"Mmm, thanks for making this, babe, it's delicious."

A Drop in the Ocean 245

"Wait 'til you try an actual bite," I say. Then, because I can and because I'll use any excuse to get my hands on him while I still have the chance, I lick the last few traces of icing off his cheek. Elsie rolls her eyes at our PDA as she cuts the cake into slices, saving a small one for me and a jumbo one for him. She and Alice went easy on us when we came back late: only twenty-four hours of Residency grounds confinement, because they know our time together is finite as fuck.

Screw the calories, I'm glad to have forkfuls of something sweet to shove into my mouth to keep me from crying. I mean, I'm gonna hold on for as long as I can because this is Nick's discharge party, dammit. He deserves to enjoy it. But that hasn't stopped my insides from falling since I woke up this morning and realized what day it is. It's that feeling you get right after you've jumped off the highest diving board, when you've already begun to plunge but your internal organs are just catching up. This might be the last time I see him.

Ever.

Because unlike Sweets, Nick isn't a forty-minute drive away. It takes a plane to get to his island, then a ferry from the airport to reach his hometown. We won't be able to call each other either, because it's long distance and the Residency is too cheap to keep our love alive. I hunch down so nobody can see my face contort as I wrestle my sorrow into a DBT half smile. Fuck this, I need cake. But there's none left, because I've taken giant, greedy, eating-my-emotions bites. Even the crumbs are gone. I settle for scraping at the smears of icing left on my plate. At this point the overload of sugar isn't masking the bitterness of reality the way I need it to.

People keep coming up to Nick, telling him how much they'll miss him and how much of a stand-up guy he is. Everyone, including Noor and the other pretty girls from Wards 1 and 3, want to give him hugs.

Watching me watching him, he gives them all one-armed big-brother pats, and I am appeased. One hug goes on for a while. He lifts tiny Margaret, his primary, up off the floor with the strength of his embrace. She's old enough to be one of Poh Poh's sisters, which means even someone as insecure as me can't be jealous of her. The rec staff are in line behind her and move in to give Nick high-fives. As Margaret walks off, I see her lift her wire-rimmed glasses to wipe away tears. Oh shit, you think you're sad, Margaret? Try being the girl who has to watch the love of her life leave. Nick must notice my scowl, because he looks over at me, blond brows raised in concern.

I shake my head, whisper, "It's nothing."

He squeezes my shoulder anyway, and I nuzzle his hand with my cheek.

At some point we move to Ward 1's living room, where Nick gets to open his going-away gifts. I say gifts and not gift because, besides the chess set that the Residency got for him, I got Nick presents too. A set of artist's drawing pencils that come in their own tin and a spiral-bound sketchbook with heavyweight, off-white paper. I spent my last four art therapy sessions painstakingly collaging its front and back cover with *National Geographic* photos of things he likes. Everything from spiral galaxies to ancient Celtic ruins to steaks frying on a barbecue to gorillas using tools. He tears through the tissue paper to unearth the sketchbook and pencils. Then he's fully belly laughing, except no one besides him gets the joke.

"What's up? What's so funny?"

"Great minds really do think alike."

"Huh?"

He grabs the last present on the couch, suspiciously book-shaped and wrapped in newspaper, and hands it to me.

A Drop in the Ocean

"Open it."

I put my hands on my hips. "It's *your* discharge party and you got *me* a gift? That's not how these things work."

"If you don't want it, I'll take it back." He calls my bluff, holding the present out of my reach.

"Of course I want it." I snatch it from him. Peel back the tape carefully when really, I want to rip last week's news to shreds and see what he got me. My fingertips grasp fabric—a book with a satin cover? It's red-wine burgundy embroidered with delicate flowers and gold leaves. Suspended in the middle by thick strings hangs the Chinese character 福 (fuk), for prosperity, carved in polished wood. I flip inside, pleading with the universe for the paper to be …

"It's lined!" I shout in triumph, already launching myself at Nick in a full-scale bear hug. "Thanks, babe, this journal is exquisite!"

"See what I mean about thinking alike? We both got each other works of art to hold our works of art."

I wrinkle my nose at that. "I don't know if I'd call my journal rantings works of art."

Nick gives me a noogie. "You're not allowed to talk shit about my girlfriend's writing. Besides, the only way a writer gets better at writing is by doing it. Put in your ten thousand hours, that's how you get good."

We pass around our presents, along with a watermelon blunt, at Nick's last toke circle. Jorge flips through the first few pages.

"To Mira Meilin Anne Coralie Lung Kong Durand … Holy shit, girl, you have enough names for like, five people."

"Hey, no reading that," Nick wrestles my journal out of Jorge's grasp. "It's private, man." He turns to me. "Promise me you won't read this 'til you're done your old journal?"

The thought that he won't be here by the time I get to his message, that he'll be GONE, makes me gulp. I nod and croak out, "Okay, fine." Pretend that the frog in my throat is from the fat toke I take. Hold the weed in so long I scorch myself and cough.

"What's the first thing you're gonna do when you get home?" Noor asks. She throws her head back, shapes her mouth into a perfect *O* and blows out smoke rings.

Nick takes a deep drag before answering. "Easy, I'm gonna go to the dump."

"That sounds ... fun?"

"It's where the bears are," Nick says. "My earliest memory's being like, two, and my dad driving me to the dump. I'd sit in the back seat, and black bears would get so close to our car I could see their breath fog the window glass."

The more I've thought about it, the more and more down I've gotten with the idea of going to his hometown. Especially now, when he'll be leaving in less than an hour. I clasp my hands like I'm praying. "Please, please take me with you."

"Sure thing," he says. "There's still room in my suitcase, you just need to scrunch up in a tiny ball, and I'll leave the zipper undone so you can breathe." That turns the convo quickly into contraband stories where we all list off rumours of the weirdest ways Residency kids have snuck in forbidden items. From there the talk quickly progresses to cavity searches at juvie, which derails into sex jokes. Typical Residency shit. By the time my cheeks are crimson after learning what a "strawberry cheesecake" is, the blunt's a glowing cherry burning our fingertips.

♦

A Drop in the Ocean

Half an hour after the cherry's put out, it's just Nick and me. We don't bother pretending to be cheerful as we Lay Lady Lung on the Ward 1 bench for the last time.

"What will you miss most about us?" I ask.

"This," he says. "Just holding you."

"Promise you won't forget me?"

"I couldn't even if I tried."

We hold each other until the end. Barely stirring when Margaret comes out wheeling his suitcase. Both groaning when a Dodge pickup pulls into the parking lot and honks. We keep holding each other as we make our slow way to it. Nick does everything one-handed—introduces me to his parents, John and Lorraine, loads the cargo bed with his suitcase, gets into the back seat, puts his seat belt on, all while I grip his right arm with as much of my body as I can. I won't let go of him until I have to. Each time we kiss, I think *This is the last*, then, *No, this is the last, okay, this will be the last. No, this one*, until he pulls back. He looks at me, eyes drowning.

"Goodbye, Mira."

But how can saying bye to him ever be good?

CHAPTER TWENTY-THREE

D r. Grant can't even let me be heartbroken in peace. Nope, Nick leaving is yet another reason I should be working harder on exposures.

"You know, Nick said that his island has over a hundred hikes. There's even a blowhole on his fave beach walk that goes up a hill," I say as we do slow motion laps around the parking lot. I'm talking Poh Poh with a broken hip level slow. So slow that my heart beats five times to every one step we take. It wouldn't be so bad if we were walking at the same pace, but noooo, then the exposure would be too easy. Dr. Grant is two steps ahead of me. Exercising harder, faster, than I am. Getting me to slow down whenever I start to close the distance between us.

"How about we walk a few laps without talking?" he replies. "The goal of exposures is to sit, or in this case to slowly stroll, with the anxiety. Feeling its intensity and knowing that's okay. That it will pass. Even sadness can be a distraction from facing distress."

"As in I'm choosing to be sad over choosing to be anxious? I don't want to be either, they both suck."

"Remember, distress tolerance is a muscle that you have to build. You need to exercise it regularly to see results."

All the muscle and exercise talk give me an idea. Isometrics. I clench my abs. Get a good burn going as soon as I squeeze. Suddenly, it doesn't matter that he's ahead of me or that a snail could beat us if we were racing. I'm exercising in a better way. My legs start to tremble a little from the intensity of how hard I'm squeezing my stomach. Uh-oh, can Dr. Grant see how I'm straining? He calls these

250

A Drop in the Ocean 251

replacement behaviours "fixes." A fix renders the exposure obsolete. It wastes both of our time. Do I really want to be doing this for nothing? I heave out a sigh and let my stomach go. It's a disgusting pooch of post-Christmas paunch. That whole session, I wait for the "results," for my anxiety to drop down after it's peaked.

It doesn't.

♦

Finally, another girl on Ward 2! Woot, woot. Her name's Sharon and she's only twelve, which is as young as they get at the Residency. No wonder she's crying her eyes out. Her banshee wailing on the big couch drove Jorge and even Franco away from the TV to their respective rooms. As soon as Jorge put "Locked Up" on blast to drown out her sobs, the wails got louder. The bass and swear words in full-out war with Sharon's wordless keening. I make my way to the living room, where Elsie's got her set up with a box of Kleenex on her lap and a garbage can by her feet. An ever-growing mountain of used tissues piles up in it.

"Hey," I say with a smile. My first instinct is to tell her that it gets better, that there are worse places to be than Ward 2. Then I think about how pissed I was when people told me that during my first trip to CAPE. How it felt like they weren't taking my desperation seriously. How at that time, I was Sharon's same age, not even in high school. I change tactics. "I'm sorry things are so tough. What can I do to help?"

Sharon looks up at me, her round face even puffier from crying, especially her red-rimmed, bloodshot eyes. Every other word, she hiccups and gasps, trying to catch her breath. "Will-hic-you-hic-be-hic-my-hic-friend?"

"Of freakin' course I will." But before the words are fully out of my mouth, she's thrust herself against me and collapsed in a sobby, smushy hug. She sniffles, sucking in snot against my chest, clutching me as tightly as I did Nick a few days ago. It makes me squeamish, this tween leaking tears on my shirt, but this is my chance to pay it forward. I can be Sharon's Sweets equivalent, a Residency big sis. We talk basics: diagnoses and why we're here, where we'd rather be. She has tics and some developmental disabilities, she's had them for as long as she can remember. She'd rather be home, duh. Her tics are pretty subtle, a tongue click, eye twitch, and sniffle. They're easy to ignore, barely breaking the flow of our conversation. I warn her about my rituals. Ask her to please not slam doors if she can help it because banging noises freak me out.

"But why, though?" she asks.

I shrug. "They trigger my anxiety. People with concussions can be extra sensitive to loud noise, so maybe that's got something to do with it. If I'm really stressed, I have to run away from them. That's what I'm working on with Dr. Grant."

Sharon jolts as soon as I say Dr. Grant. Her eyes flash and narrow, twitching rapidly. "How do you know my boyfriend?"

I'm stunned for a moment—is she for real? "What do you mean? He's my psychiatrist," I tell her. "Almost everyone on Ward 2 sees him for meds and therapy and stuff."

"Well back off, he's mine!" she snarls. It's like someone flipped a switch, and sad, cuddly Sharon's vanished completely. The air between us crackles with electricity as Mad Sharon twitches, sniffles, and gets up in my grill. "You better not come between us."

I scoot away from her laser glare. "Chill out, he's so not my type. Besides, he's like, a staff member, and he's got a wife and kid. My actual boyfriend left four days ago." I tell her how just seeing Ward 1 makes me miserable, but I still can't help sitting on the porch bench, imagining being with Nick. I cling to the sadness because it connects us.

"So," she sniffles, "you promise to leave my Granty alone?"

"Umm, sure, I just see him for therapy, that's it."

"Good," she declares.

And all I can say is "Yeah."

After a super tense silence, I do my twenty questions routine. Asking everybody a ton of questions about what they like best (favourite school subject, favourite book, what animal they'd be if they could be any animal, mythical or real) is my go-to strategy for small talk, and it works. The electricity in the air fizzles out as her expression calms and her tics get less frequent. There's this show called *Teen Titans* that she goes on about for, I shit you not, an hour and a half. She grabs DVDs of it from her room, which used to be Sweets's, and jams one into the player. I try to tell her that she's put the disc in upside down, but she won't listen. The thing doesn't play, which prompts another bout of tears and twitches from her until Alan does what I said to do in the first place, and then Episode 1 introduces us to a cartoon superhero world.

"Tomorrow, when we play *Teen Titans*, I have to be Raven, okay? Dr. Grant's Robin. And I'll let you be Starfire," she tells me.

◆

SLAM. I moan as banging noises erupt through my subconscious. SLAM. SLAM. My eyes stay closed as I grasp my pillow, using it to shield my ears. My brain is too sleepy to flood my body with adrenalin and stress from whatever bullshit's going on. Then a series of loud knocks pounds against my door, and Sharon's yelling at me.

"Mira, Miiiraaa, come play with me or I'll slam the door more. We're supposed to play *Teen Titans*, remember? Hurry up or I'll slam."

Is this a nightmare? I open my eyes a crack to see what time my alarm clock says—6:12 a.m. Meds are at 8:00, which is when my alarm rings. Getting up now means missing basically two hours of shut-eye.

I moan again. "Sharon, let me sleep."

"You're up, play with me." The pounding continues, panic blazing through me with each separate knock. Anxiety gives me the fight or flight energy I need to scramble up. Through the Plexiglas window, I see the top of Sharon's head craning to peek at me. Her knocks get faster, go from knuckle raps to fists booms. She needs to stop. How do I get her to stop?

"I'll play with you, I promise. Just not right now."

"No, now. You're awake. Do you want me to slam?"

Motherfucking motherfucker! She's blackmailing me. Forget little sis, she's a little shit, using my OCD like a loaded gun. "Why are you doing this? What's wrong with you?" I hate how whiney my yell is.

"You're the one who's wrong!" Sharon shrieks at me. "You're mean." She stomps a few steps away. Thank God, she's fucking off. Then I hear the loudest slam yet.

SLAM, SLAM, SLAM, SLAM.

To make something other than the noise echo through my skull, I bash it. First with my knuckles, but it doesn't hurt enough. As Sharon continues to slam, I smash the back of my head against the wall, sparing my forehead for later. "Elsie!" I yell. Then, when no one responds, "Nurse! Nurse! Make her stop."

Twenty bangs later, Janelle opens my door, shutting it quickly and rushing over when she sees what I'm doing. "I'm so sorry, but there's nothing I can do."

A Drop in the Ocean

"Please."

"She was going to slam your door earlier, when you were still asleep. We told her off for that, but right now she's slamming her own door, not yours. As frustrating as it is, and believe me, I'm frustrated too, I'm not allowed to restrain her unless she's doing bodily harm to you or herself." Janelle reaches out like she wants to give me a hug, but draws her hand back when I don't stop thumping the back of my head. "I wish I could help you more." Anything else she says I can't hear as dizziness fills my rattling brain like fog.

"Miiiraaa, I'll stop if you play with me," I hear Sharon say. She giggles, and it takes everything in me to swallow the stream of swears I want to scream at her. They'll just make things worse.

Instead, I say, "Okay, okay, I'm coming."

◆

Subject: It's HELL Here!!!!!!
Date: Sat 20 Jan 2007

Sweets, I dunno what to do.

You're gone, Nick's gone, and Sharon the new girl's taken over my life. All she has to do to get what she wants from me is slam the doors til I cave. She thinks we're friends when it's really a fucking hostage situation. I do whatever she tells me to. Play Teen Titans or Poké-mon, colour stupid little kid's colouring sheets, purposefully let her win Go Fish or Yahtzee or any other game she wants to play. Do her homework for her. Do her makeup for her. Do everything she wants. My only escapes r school, therapy, and outings b/c she doesn't have off-unit privileges yet. She's 12 but she acts like she's 4 and I know its cuz of her mental stuff, but it's hard to feel sorry for her when she's making my life HELL.

Guess what she did when Mom came to pick me up? She went into my room and came out holding Stella Bear. Then, when Mom and I were at the front door, steps away from freedom, she threw Stella Bear on the ground, yelled, "This is your mother!" and stomped on Stella Bear's neck. Even Mom was scared because, hello, that was a DEATH THREAT. The little bitch is lucky I didn't stomp on her neck. Instead (I don't get why everybody's proud of me for this) I just bolted, like a fucking coward, to Mom's car. Kept holding my breath past when Mom got in and started driving. Didn't stop til everything turned blurry and grey, but at least we were away from the Residency. Wished Mom and I could just drive away forever. Pick u up, pick Nick up, then spend the rest of our lives on the road. The best I got was an extra hour out.

Back on unit Elsie helped me fix Stella Bear's burst stitches and put in extra stuffing so her neck wasn't flattened anymore. Working with the needle reminded me of our tats. My star/ankh is the best! One day when you're the next Amy Lee, I'll show it to ppl and be like, yeah I knew Sweets b4 she was famous.

Hope your life is going better than mine. Missing the shit outta you.

HUGZ,
Mira

CHAPTER TWENTY-FOUR

My throat bobs as I gulp, jumping off the stepper, which makes Sharon clap in delight.

"Yay, my turn." Since the whole stomping on Stella Bear incident, she's gotten a bit better. Even cried to me about how sorry she was because her "boyfriend" (Dr. Grant) had a talk with her about inappropriate behaviour. It's too late, I'm trained. Still her dancing ~~playmate~~ puppet while she jerks the strings. If my baseline SUDs are a thirty, since Nick's discharge two and a half weeks / an eternity ago, they've gone up to forty, and being in any kind of exercise space raises them to a fifty. I don't need Sharon making banging noises to spike them even higher. Easier to give her what she wants. The stepper that Sharon clamours on and gets Alan to help her reset is my happy place, the safe cardio machine. It's old, so it doesn't have the calories-burned counter that the stationary bikes and the treadmill have. I climb myself to exhaustion at resistance level eleven, maybe count my steps if I'm really anxious like when I was going through my fifty-two phase. That's it. No obsessions over the calories and speed compelling me to push past my brink, because there are no stats to look at in the first place.

I walk toward the other cardio machines, wipe sweat off my forehead with the bottom of my shirt. The bike is not an option, doesn't burn enough calories, so I'm left with my old nemesis, the treadmill. It looms in the corner with its incline option, colourful buttons, and large stats screen. Back on Ward 1, I was banned from using this torture contraption because I kept putting it on the highest speed, twenty kilometres per hour, and freaking out when I couldn't run that fast.

Time to play exercise Russian roulette. Will the numbers take over? Will I tweak? Will my body fail me first, or my mind? Or will I find some miraculous state of balance? Only one way to find out. My legs tremble as I lift them onto the sleek black runway, right index finger pushing the up-arrow incline button. Maybe, just maybe, it'll be okay.

Epic rap music plays in the background, Jorge's weightlifting mix. He's at the bench press machine, where Vikas spots him. Vikas sees my walk pick up to a jog, then a sprint, as I push the speed button to my favourite number, nine. He yells to me over Eminem rapping about how great he is.

"How about you put something over the screen to hide the numbers?"

It's a good suggestion. If it was the start of our rec hour and not twenty minutes in, maybe I'd take his advice. But I've already wasted enough time standing still, being lazy, as I deliberated over my inevitable choice.

"Sorry, I've already started," I yell back, beginning to pant when I'm not even one minute in. To prove to myself that I can fight the OCD, I look everywhere but the screen. Stare at my feet, where my purple Skechers blur against the even blurrier whirring black deck. Ooof, the motion makes me dizzy, which makes me pukey. I look to the left instead. There's Sharon marching on my stepper. She plods along, stifling a yawn. When she notices me watching, she picks up her pace and waves. My arms are pumping in rhythm along with my steps, helping maintain my speed. I break out of the motion to fling her a quick wave back and lose momentum. God, I hate that girl. But I hate myself even more, because I caught a glimpse of the screen. Calories burned: less than ten.

A Drop in the Ocean

Time to go into turbo mode. I press the speed up to eleven. It's where I'll stay for the next five minutes. If I look at the screen before they're up, I have to punish myself by going to thirteen speed for not having enough willpower to just endure it. Sweat streams from my bangs and my hairline, plopping onto the deck. It soaks my exercise tank even though the material is supposed to be Climawear something. Shoulda bought that sports bra from Lululemon, but I didn't like how it showed so much skin. That makes me think of my abs, which makes me want to clench them. I do, counting to ten in every language I can to distract myself: English, Cantonese, Mandarin, Japanese, French, and Spanish, where I make up what I think seven, eight, and nine sound like because I don't know them for sure. Jorge would know. I look to my right, where he's moved on to doing lunges while holding dumbbells. Even farther to my right, Franco holds a plank while Alan pushes down on his back to make it harder. I zero in on their routine, watch Franco's expression turn from a grin to a grimace as Alan gets him to lift up one leg. He wobbles, grunting with the strain of balancing, exercising harder than me. *Lazy!* screams my OCD. *Hurry up. Harder.* And because I'm clenching my abs already, I push my speed higher without looking at it. I keep staring at them until Franco's done his plank routine. When I look at the screen again, seven minutes have passed. Good.

By now my sweat's pooled at my feet, and every step I take squeaks. I cry out as my Skechers lose their grip on the slippery deck. My heart pounds, just as heavy against my chest as my feet are before they slide. For the first two times, everyone ignores me. I've gone from panting to wheezing. Hoovering in as much air as I can through my open mouth, where it scrapes against my throat the whole way down to my lungs. Still barely enough to keep me going. Little whimpers won't stop coming out of me. When I stumble a third time and the whimper becomes a wail, Alan has to get his two cents in.

"Remember what I said about pushing yourself hard versus pushing yourself smart?"

How does he expect me to talk? "You're not my trainer," I wheeze.

That shuts him up for a little while as I stagger, step, squeak, stagger, step, squeak, back at measly level nine speed. I replace my shame at one number with other, newer numbers. Count in French to 239 to keep my mind occupied with anything other than my exhaustion. A lurching semblance of rhythm keeps me going. Once I'm back to counting to ten in every language I can, Alan announces to all of us, "Last ten minutes." This is it, the home stretch. I've almost made it. No one can tell, but the noise I make is a furious woo-hoo of relief. Ten more minutes, then I'm done.

Meanwhile, Sharon's already done. She's freaking abandoned my stepper. The machine that she knows is my one safe cardio space, that she wanted to use so badly, with ten whole minutes left. Was this her plan? Was the only reason she wanted the stepper in the first place to keep it from me? In my mind's eye, I see her stomping on Stella Bear's neck, dirty sneakers squashing my favourite stuffie's face, yelling, "This is your mother!" Fucking hateful bitch. Of course she wanted the stepper to screw with me. Rage gives me an extra burst of energy. My index finger throbs as I jab the speed up, up to thirteen.

We're back to the beginning of Jorge's playlist, Eminem's "Till I Collapse." It fits my mood perfectly. What was it some famous dead author dude said? Art imitating life. Yes. It's that. I match my sprint with each thump of the chorus's beat, going extra hard every third step when the resounding CLAP kicks in. As the lyrics blast about his legs giving out, my own legs are beyond burning. They pound and

A Drop in the Ocean 261

slide on the sweat-slick runway. Seconds take forever as my world narrows down to the beat and the rhythm of running, of forcing my body beyond its brink. Nothing matters except the next frenzied foot stomp, and the next. And the next stomp. And the next. And then I slip, falling in my sweat pool as my legs do exactly what Eminem raps: give out. There's the boom of me landing on the floor. Pain. The force of it vibrating through me, but I barely hear the thump I make because a much louder shriek tears through my throat while my OCD screeches, *WRONG, WRONG, WRONG! FAILURE. PUNISH. HURT. RAGE.*

So I do.

Sharon's theatrics have nothing on mine. I smash my head on the corner of the treadmill, welcoming the explosive ache. It's not as sharp as the corner of the wall, but any hard surface will get the job done. Eighteen bangs in and Alan is between me and the machine. His body blocks my head, his raw, reddened hands clamp my shoulders, and he scowls with contamination OCD *wrongness* as he makes contact with my sweat. I try to jerk out of his grip. The sweat from my hair splashes his arms, making him shudder, but he holds fast.

My foot's free, and if I can't hurt myself then at least I can hurt the treadmill. I kick it with as much force as I can. Vikas, who's running toward us from the other side of the gym, is on his cell. "Needle," I hear him shout, "at the gym in the rec building. Now!" And I know what that means—booty juice. They're going to restrain me, jab me in the ass with a sedative shot, and lock me in the Quiet Room.

"Nooooo," I cry, busting out of Alan's grip. The threat of the shot gives me enough energy to propel through the door and escape. I stagger past Sharon, who backs away from me, a tic attack making her face twitch.

"Run, Forrest, run," cheers Jorge, while Franco watches mutely. Head reeling, huffing and wheezing, the brightness of the hallway lights burns even more dizziness into my brain. I look at the floor—less light, better—while bolting down the hall, as Alan and Vikas close in. Alan's hands are his weakness, scrubbed raw from overwashing. I'm not above fighting dirty, and when those same hands reach out to pin my arms, my bitten fingernails grasp through the air, ready to claw him.

I grunt as he flinches and warn both of them, "Don't touch me."

"We have to," Vikas says. "Unless you promise to calm down." They're both close enough to spit at. But I'm not that Mira anymore. I haven't had a PRN butt needle in months.

"Calm down? Y-you mean if I calm down you won't restrain me?" It takes a different kind of energy to stay still. Mental energy. Me fighting against the reptile part of my brain that wants to lash out or flee. I sway as I stay in one spot. The light isn't fucking with my vision so much anymore, it's really the tears I won't let myself cry blurring everything.

Seeing that I'm still, Vikas backs up and holds his hands out like Jesus on the cross. They're spread too far apart to grab me, and something tells me they won't unless I make a break for it. He motions for Alan to do the same. Nods eagerly when Alan takes a step back too. I wait, keep holding myself stiff until Alan's hands are up and away from me.

"Isn't this better? Now we can talk like rational beings," Vikas says.

Around the same time that I say, "I wish I were dead."

Alan flinches as if I've just spit at him. He wipes his nose against his shoulder, avoiding the sensitive skin on his hands. "Do you really mean that?"

"Yes," I say out of reflex. Then, "No," blinking back tears. Then, "I don't know." I take a deep, shuddering breath. "I'm just tired. So,

A Drop in the Ocean

so tired." There's nothing left in me. After the treadmill disaster and being Sharon's puppet, and even before that, since Nick's been gone, everything's felt flattened. Things have gone from bad to worse.

Meanwhile, a nurse from Ward 3 walks slowly toward us. She has the PRN booty juice needle in her gloved hands. Great. Things just went from worse to worst. I can't help it, I whimper.

Before she gets any closer, Alan goes over to talk to the nurse. My ears strain to hear snippets over the pounding of my heart.

"... safely de-escalated ..."

"... have to administer the sedative, but ..."

After their murmurs end, the two of them nod at Vikas. He's inches away from me, hands spread up and out. The mass of wrinkles on his forehead softens as his frown lifts into the smallest of smiles.

"Mira," he asks, "how would you feel about getting the shot in your arm?"

And the kindness of that hits me harder than when I fell from the treadmill. Knocks me clear off my soul's feet. No one's ever given me a choice before. I bury my face in my hands and let the tears free.

CHAPTER TWENTY-FIVE

The Christmas cards are all gone from Dr. Grant's office, which is fine, because this isn't a Christmas-gift-giving occasion. Staff and patients aren't allowed to exchange gifts, so we're just doing a perfectly rule-abiding trade of the exact same thing. I take out the tissue paper from a candy-cane-striped bag to reveal a hardcover copy of *Parable of the Sower.* My first ever sci-fi recommendation from Dr. Grant, who swears I'll love it because the protag, Lauren Olamina, is an empath just like Evvy from my series. His idea to trade copies means neither of us will get in trouble with the rule sticklers of the Residency's higher-ups.

He rips snowman wrapping paper with no regard for its cuteness, uncovering the same blurred sepia photo-collage cover with a full moon in the foreground. Identical copies. Except when I flip to the title page of the one that's now mine, there's the elegant but still-legible scrawl of Octavia E. Butler's signature, making it monetarily much more valuable than the one I traded with him. His own inscription and signature on the following page make it sentimentally priceless.

"One day," I tell him, "You'll be reading hardcover copies of my fantasy series. And I'll pay you back with tons of praise in the acknowledgments section."

He chuckles. "First things first. You gotta write it."

"First things first, I gotta get outta here so I can go to uni. Get good enough to write that debut novel."

His grin falls into something much more serious. "On the subject of getting out of here, you can't be having episodes like the one

A Drop in the Ocean

you had on Friday. What about all those distress tolerance skills I taught you?"

"When I screw up like that it's too late. Five, Four, Three, Two, One Senses doesn't do shit once my SUDs hit ninety. It just pisses me off more when staff tell me to stop, or calm down, or take a deep breath."

"Ah, so now we're back to the singular entity, the amorphous blob of staff?"

I look down and to the left, at the bruise on my shoulder where the needle went in. Shift in my seat, moving my ass, where it should have been injected. "No, it was Alan and Vikas and a nurse from Ward 3. They were all really nice to me."

"You don't need me to tell you that you were lucky."

It's hard, but I stop my eyes midroll. "No, I don't. But since you read the incident report, you must've read about how I de-escalated. That's good, isn't it?"

"Mira, you were smashing your head and trying to destroy a 275-pound machine. One of our first forays into exposure was a pros and cons list about not head banging outside of your designated times. What happened to fighting the OCD instead of reinforcing the cycle?"

"I had to! It wasn't a small screw-up, I fell."

"And how is that taking your power back? You're the boss of you, not the OCD. Not unless you let it control you."

"Don't you get it, the OCD *is* me."

Dr. Grant's giving me that same stricken look that Alan did. Like I just admitted to killing his family. "What do you think Nick would say about that? Or Taryn?"

"Well, they're not here, are they? So what does it matter? What's the point of even trying to fight when everyone I care about's just going to leave me anyway?"

Now he's slowly shaking his head, his wounded look replaced by something sharper. "That's bullshit and you know it."

"How so? Nick leaves and a few days later who shows up? Freaking Sharon with her slamming doors until I do what she wants."

"Let's put a pin in Sharon," he says. "We'll talk about her in a bit. As for people who care about you, what about your mother and the rest of your family? What about me and your treatment team?"

"As if any of you are gonna stay in touch with me when I finally leave. And in the end, everybody dies. Gung Gung did, Poh Poh's next. Eventually, so will Lawrence and even Mom, no matter how many times I bang my head."

Dr. Grant's voice rises, not enough to be yelling, but enough for me to pay his words extra attention. "You're right. Everybody you know will die someday. But you know who you have to spend the rest of your life with? Yourself." His eyes glint as he says those last words with the finality of a judge hitting their gavel. In a quieter voice, he continues. "Vikas wrote in the report that you said you wished you were dead. Is there any part of you that still feels that way?"

"No." I slump in my seat and stare at the carpet, keep my head bowed. "You don't have to put me on suicide watch, I don't wanna kill myself. I just … hate me … so much. The only way I can make up for my mistakes is through the OCD, even though a lot of the time it's the OCD, or screwing up on it, that makes me lash out."

He goes for the therapy classic. "How does that make you feel?"

I snort, a mirthless, hollow noise. "Like I'm damned if I do, damned if I don't. I can either hate myself for not following every single OCD urge, or I can hate myself for giving in to the urge but not doing the ritual good enough. No matter what I do, it's never good enough. *I'm* never good enough."

A Drop in the Ocean

He keeps his face neutral, no deep gazes of pity or cutting me off as I spill my latest woe-is-Mira sob story. With that same neutrality in his tone, he asks, "And is there any version of your life where you don't hate yourself?"

"I guess if I did everything right?"

"But perfection is impossible."

"Yeah, duh." It's so obvious that I don't know why we have to rehash it. "That's why I hate myself."

Dr. Grant takes a deep breath. "Look at me, Mira."

"What?"

I can feel his eyes boring into my downturned face. "I need you to look at me and really focus on what I'm saying."

His gravitas is infectious. I bite my lip, feel it scrape against my teeth as I raise my head level with his. "Fine." My shit-brown irises look deep into his green ones.

"Self-hatred is not a virtue. Hating yourself harder because of your mistakes doesn't make up for them. Think of it this way. If worthiness is water and hatred is poison, then it doesn't matter how much poison you pour into yourself in retaliation for not having water. Poison on top of poison isn't going to alchemize into something you can actually drink."

He's got a point there. "Then if I'm full of all this poison, how does it ever become something I can live off of, like water? What if the only thing I'm good at is making poison?"

"That's the thing." He rubs his hands together and leans in across the desk. "You don't have to be good at change to do it. It's hard, really hard, which is why so many people don't change. However, change is key. Changed behaviour is what shows progress, where the transmutation of toxic to life-sustaining takes place. And the hard work of real change requires compassion, for both yourself and others."

"Shouldn't you have to earn compassion?" I raise my hand to my lips, about to nibble on a nail. Stop myself midbite. "Why be nice to someone unless they deserve it?"

"Here's another secret. By virtue of your very existence, you deserve compassion. Take Sharon, for example. She hasn't done anything to earn your kindness."

The nail I was about to bite digs into my palm along with the others as I clench my hands into fists. "She's done the opposite, actually."

"Exactly. But how do you think you'd feel about her if you just, out of the goodness of your heart, gave her some compassion?"

"I let her have her way."

"That's not the same thing as having empathy for her. What's something about her that you can relate to?"

"Um, she's lonely. Really, really lonely, which is why she blackmails me into spending time with her."

"Okay, and who besides you spends time with her?"

"Not Jorge or Franco. And the kids from the other units pretty much avoid her. She usually hangs out with her primary, Janelle, or Elsie."

"So the only people who she regularly interacts with are you or people who are paid to work with her. And what about her family?"

"She talks about them sometimes, but no one is allowed to visit her yet. I guess that's why she went apeshit when Mom came by. Not like that makes it okay or anything."

"What if your roles were reversed? What if your mom never visited and you watched Sharon go off with her parents all the time when you weren't allowed to leave the unit?"

I know where this is going, and I hate to say it, but it's working. "Yeah, yeah, I'd be angry and resentful of her too." After a moment of silence, I sigh and spill even more. "You know, when she first came on unit, crying her eyes out, I thought it'd be cool to be her big sister. Help her out the way Sweets helped me."

"As in paying it forward?"

"Yeah, except less cheesy than the movie. And she did apologize to me for the whole Stella Bear thing. Whatever you said to her really worked." And now my fists unclench as I make air quotes—"Robin."

Dr. Grant's face contorts into a half wince, half grimace—a wimace. "Ugh, no *Teen Titans*, please, I've had enough of them for a lifetime." We both complain about the show for a little while before he steers the convo back to being a big sis. "What would your first order of business be, to continue this legacy of sisterhood? What would or could you do to help Sharon?"

"Hmmmm." I tilt my head to the side and think about it. "Well, I know I couldn't have survived without my journal. Thanks again for rescuing it from the dumpster all those months ago. It's almost full now."

"Of course. It was … not quite a pleasure to retrieve, but I'd do it again in an instant. You take that thing with you everywhere. Even when it stank, you toted it along."

"I guess I do bring it around a lot. And I guess I could always buy Sharon a journal too with my allowance. I was planning on getting this new eyeshadow, but MAC will still be around two weeks from now."

He laughs. "It most definitely will."

♦

☺♡☆♡☺ Damn, that gel ink comes out smoooooth! This purple is freaking gorgeous.

It's the same grape Kool-Aid shade as Sweets's new faux-hawk. The upward spikes of her pompadour give her extra height, as do her Converse wedge high-tops, so her hair at its highest reaches the tip of my nose. The Residency's ridiculous three months with no visiting rule is finally up. We're celebrating. We stride through the candy aisle of Dollarama on our way to its tiny stationery section. As we pass the gum, she swipes a package of Hubba Bubba. Still walking, she opens it casually, popping a cube in her mouth.

"Want some?" She tries to shove the package into my hand. I shove it back, making the Winners bag threaded through my arm sway. It's semi heavy, weighed down by curly hair shampoo and conditioner. That, along with carrying *Parable of the Sower* in my purse and the four or so hours of shopping we've been doing, has me tired out. Park Royal's got about the same amount of shops as Metro but spread across an outdoor and indoor mall. Shopping the full circuit may as well be a marathon. Sweets says next time we visit I can go to her house, a fifteen-minute walk from here. That made the two transfers and the hour-long bitch of a bus ride to West Van worth it.

She throws her arm around me as I refuse her shoplifted gum a second time. "You might be a prude, but you're my prude."

I elbow her—a gentle poke, not a fighting one—and roll up my sleeve so she can see her handiwork on my right wrist. "Would a prude have a prison tat like this?"

We do a quick peek through the shitty-quality makeup section, spend a few minutes riffling through greeting cards to find the funniest (a groaner of a birthday card that says "Happy Birthday, You Bad Ass" next to a picture of a biker donkey), and sniff a bunch of

A Drop in the Ocean

candles before finally discovering the journals. There's a surprisingly decent variety: some notebooks with floral prints or cute animals, black journals that could pass as Moleskines for a quarter of the price, sketch-books (though the one I got Nick had way better paper), day planners, address books, and finally, cartoon cover journals. No *Teen Titans*, that coincidence would be too freaky. Nor am I about to blow my budget custom ordering something Raven themed. Sure I want to help Sharon, but I don't like her enough to drop fifty bucks on a journal.

"Would she like this?" Sweets crouches down to a bottom shelf, where there are *Cars* and *Naruto* spiral-bound notebooks. I grab one and take a quick flip through.

"Naw, they're blank. We need something with lines." My knees creak as I join Sweets in a crouch to look at other cartoon options.

"The second-last email you sent me was all about how you hated this chick's guts. What happened?"

"A lot." I explain my change of heart to Sweets, go over the talk I had with Dr. Grant about paying it forward. "So now, since you were so awesome to me back when I was new, I'm going to be her you."

She blows a bubble, and after it pops, says, "You know, at first I wasn't super thrilled with you either."

"Really?"

"Yeah. Before Elsie made you, you didn't clean up after you head banged, so there would be these, like, horror movie smears on the walls. Your jumping was super loud and annoying, and all you did besides OCD stuff was write. I was sure it was all judgy shit about the rest of us. That's why I never told you about overhearing Elsie's nick-name for you."

"Oh my God, what was it?"

"Cunt-Faced Bitch." Sweets snorts as she watches my expression change from shock to admiration.

"That's *so* much better than Bitch Douche Bag!"

Both of us have a long laugh.

Once I get my breath back, I ask, "then why did you end up friends with this cunt face?"

"Hearing your life story. The way you explained how your obsessions tie in to your compulsions helped me get why you did all that crazy stuff. Like, hello, she loves her mother, of course she's going to do whatever it takes to keep her alive. And, don't kill me please, but I did peek in your journal."

"You *what*?" I chuck one of the smaller notebooks at her. "How could you?"

She blocks it with her arms so that it thumps harmlessly to the laminate floor. "Hey, I said don't kill me. It was just a quick glance."

"Still, you shouldn't read someone's private writing. Respect the journal code!" I aim another notebook at her, dropping it with a sigh when she ducks her head behind both arms. By now my outrage is overcome with curiosity. "So, are you gonna tell me what you read, then?"

"It was that stuff about not feeling good enough." She grabs the notebook from the floor, picks it up, and hands it to me with a rueful grin. "I get it, really get it. A lot." She waits for me to look at her before continuing. "In my depressive episodes, I'd drown in that feeling until I went numb. The cutting was how I knew I was still alive." Holy shit, Sweets almost never talks about her scars. This is new bestie territory for us. If what she was saying weren't so sad, I'd be smiling. Something in my face must give me away, because she clears her throat and says, "Anyways, I think everybody feels that way to some degree, it's part of being human. That's why we need friends."

A Drop in the Ocean

"To violate our privacy?" I use snark to lighten the mood.

It works. "No, smartass, to tell us we're awesome when we forget." In the end, we settle on a notebook with a kawaii bear sliding down a rainbow. It's not hardcover, but it's got 120 lined pages and, as Sweets says, "When in doubt, go for cute." She walks me to my bus, where we get in a last chat while waiting for it to pull up. I hug her with all my might before I get on the bus, then I run back to hug her a last time, even harder.

◆

At art therapy I find the perfect tissue paper to wrap Sharon's journal in, black and dark purple, the colours of Raven's superhero costume. That same black blazes on the TV screen as rays of psychic power Raven shoots from her hands. The *Teen Titans* fight scene has Sharon transfixed. At the edge of her seat on the couch, she crams a handful of Cheetos into her mouth, munching rhythmically, not noticing when some of them fall. I brush the Cheetos crumbs from the spot next to her, sit down with her gift in my lap, and ahem.

No response.

I wait thirty seconds for Beast Boy to take on the bad guy before ahemming louder. Sharon waves with one hand and shoves the bag of Cheetos at me with the other.

"Want some?"

"Actually, I have something for you."

Although she doesn't turn away from the screen, she does raise her eyebrows. "You got me a present?"

"Yup." With a small flourish I present it to her, butt the corner of it ever so gently against the Cheetos bag so it's inches from her face. "Tada!"

Finally, she looks my way, dropping the Cheetos bag so that she can place mine on her lap instead. She beams, still smiling through her tics, then giggles with delight as she tears through the tissue paper. I beam back, brace myself for the inevitable smush of Sharon's arms wrapped tight around me. When she gets to the journal, though, the smile as wide as an orange wedge freezes. It shrinks as she holds the journal up and flips through the pages. O-kay. Her forehead furrows as her flattened smile upends and her full lips jut into a pout. Not the reaction I was waiting or hoping for.

"It's your very own journal. Isn't that cool?" Desperation makes my voice high and squeaky.

"Yeah," Sharon says with zero enthusiasm, "cool."

"What's wrong?"

She shrugs, putting the journal down between us. "The bear on the cover is cute." At this point I'm not expecting heartfelt gratitude, but a thanks would be nice. I wait for some sort of acknowledgment as Sharon grabs the Cheetos bag from the floor and resumes munching. Her face smooths into placidity, attention absorbed by the Titans hanging out in their tower, victorious. Poor journal, it has orange Cheetos fingerprints on it now that stand out starkly against the white of the rainbow's clouds. When I try to wipe them off with spit and my sleeve, they end up smearing in deeper. Great.

I try one last thing. "Hey, Sharon, I'm gonna go write in my journal. We could write together, if you want?"

She keeps her eyes on the screen as she shakes her head no.

◆

At dinner Sharon says nothing about her new gift. I'm not about to bring it up, because that would be fishing for compliments, and it's

A Drop in the Ocean 275

not like I got Jorge or Franco anything. Jorge and I debate what the weekly unit outing should be. Franco suggests go-karting, which means even he speaks more than Sharon. Usually she's a chatterbox, talking with her mouth full. Tonight, she pushes peas around with her fork, eats about a third of her mashed potatoes and Salisbury steak. I don't know what's bugging me more, having to finish everything on my plate while most of her meal is left across from me, or her silence.

It bothers me into the night, messing with my head so that I read a paragraph of *Parable*'s seventeenth chapter four times without anything sinking in. My covers swoosh as I throw them off, lurching out of bed. Time to find Sharon and get to the bottom of this. She isn't in the day room working on our latest puzzle, isn't in the kitchen grabbing a snack, or in the living room, where Franco has a basketball game on. The girls' bathroom door's open, so she isn't there. Only place she can be is her room.

"What?" she yells when I knock the rhythm of the *Teen Titans* theme song on her door.

"Checking in on you," I say as I swing it open.

She's lying on her right side, spooning a Wish Bear stuffie, with her sheets tucked up to her chin. As I walk over to sit on her bed, I almost step on the journal. Except I don't know it's the journal until I have it in my hands, because the front cover's torn off.

I grit my teeth while gulping down the lump in my throat. "Why would you do this?" It still comes out croaky and strangled.

Sharon points to the wall across from her bed where the bear sliding on a rainbow cover has been taped, on a tilt, at about chest level. "'Cuz he's cute, duh. Now I can see him when I'm lying here."

She waits for me to say something. Congratulate her for her great idea, maybe. My jaw hurts now from being clenched for so long. She notices that I'm hugging the coverless remainder of her journal to my chest. "You can take the rest of the book back, I don't need it."

"You really don't want it?" It still hasn't sunk in yet. That she's so thoroughly shat on my big sister gesture.

"Nope. I can't use it."

My eyes bulge as I burst out, "Of course you can, you write in it, or draw."

Sharon's pout is back. She mutters, and I have to ask her to speak up. "Can't draw with all those lines. And I don't write good."

"You haven't even tried yet. I bet if you put in some effort you'd have fun."

"No, I wouldn't."

I meet her glare without looking away. "How do you know? You have to try it first."

She's twitching, her tics worsening like both our moods. "I just know, okay."

But I'm not letting it go. "Without even trying?"

"I don't wanna," she snaps. "Writing is hard. I don't like it and if you make me do it, I won't like you." She shoves me. Not enough to hurt me but enough for me to get the message. Me and the journal, we're not wanted.

My non-existent poker face gives me away when I go to the nurses' station for nighttime meds. Elsie takes one look at me and asks, "What happened?"

First comes business, the mandatory med taking and her check mark in my chart that, yes, I've swallowed them. Then I tell her everything. About my talk with Dr. Grant, how stoked I was to be a psych ward big sis, how Sharon didn't even thank me for the journal and ripped it up instead. How I didn't mean to make her feel bad.

A Drop in the Ocean

"Give it here," Elsie says, picking her pen back up. She takes the journal from me and starts to draw. A circle, two dots for eyes, a small hook for a nose, a sideways capital *D* for a smile. She adds some streaks of hair and then gets to work on the body. Arms outstretched in fists followed by a squiggly rectangle.

"What's that supposed to be?"

"A cape, obviously."

I get it, she's trying to salvage the journal. Maybe turn it into a sketchbook. "You know, Raven doesn't really look like that," I tell her.

"Good, because it's not Raven. It's Super Sharon, can't you tell?"

I roll my eyes. "She doesn't want anything to do with writing or me, and a drawing won't change her mind."

"Then your story better get her to."

There goes my free time before lights out. "Do I have to?"

Elsie pats my arm. "You'd know that better than me, now, wouldn't you?"

♦

Past lights out with a flashlight under my covers, I work on the epic narrative of Sharonelle, Raven's soul clone (who has all of Raven's powers and spiritual essence nested in Sharon's body and mind) from an alternate post-apocalyptic dimension. I end the first chapter on a cliffhanger. Something with life-and-death stakes that I hope Sharon won't be able to resist. Tomorrow morning I'll read it to her and ask what should happen next.

♦

Life skills! Life skills! Life skills! I've been waiting all day for my life skills surprise. Ignoring polynomials in math class, highlighting but not retaining any info on how the Italian Renaissance affected the rest of Europe, because the Mirenaissance at the Residency is about to begin. Except I have to keep it on the DL from the other kids. This is something new Elsie's trying out—I'm her lucky lab rat. What mysterious adult wisdom is she going to initiate me in? Is it cooking, I wonder during lunch, where I sub my barf-a-roni for a giant Caesar salad with canned tuna for protein. I'd love to learn how to actually make tuna or salmon after buying a slab of it raw. Ooh, what if she taught me how to make sushi out of it? That would be balls-to-the-wall awesome. Or, even better, what if it's part-time-job related? I could work at Chapters or the library. Getting paid to talk about books? Fuck yes.

Speaking of books, Sharon's journal smacks against my back as she hugs me goodbye, about to go to an art therapy session. The Sharonelle Adventures are a thing. We come up with them together every Monday, Wednesday, and Friday evening. Sharon talks way faster than I can write, which means I might have to develop some shorthand soon.

When she and the others leave, I settle down with *Parable*'s sequel. I don't read much before Elsie pops out of the nurses' station. I spring to my feet. If I'm really lucky, maybe we'll do something like driving lessons. Getting my *L*? 'Ell yes! God, I can't believe I made that pun. If Nick had been here, he would've laughed at it just to make me smile. Remembering his absence wilts me, until I DBT my frown upside down before Elsie can ask what's wrong.

"Follow me, Miss Ce'Nedra," she says.

So I do. Except, instead of going outside of Ward 2, she leads me farther into it. We head down the girls' wing, where I drop off my book in my room. Do I need a change of clothes or something? Nope, she says. We continue, past Sharon's room and then the empty room that used to be Dinah's, finally stopping at the girls' bathroom.

A Drop in the Ocean

She opens the door, revealing the disaster zone I left there in the morning (after throwing on cover-up, liner, and mascara) utterly untouched. The bathroom counter has the same exact soap scum and toothpaste splatters, crumpled tissue, used Q-tips, and makeup smears as it did a few hours ago, before Rob or one of the other janitors should have cleaned this shit up. The garbage has been left overflowing, while inside the sink, there's still a clump of Sharon's hair from when she brushed it. Meanwhile, the towels piled next to the shower are drenched in water, because the plastic seal is eroding, so it always fucking leaks. The toilet lid, mercifully closed, is still gross, wet with grimy condensation. The roll of toilet paper hanging beside it has half a square left. The one thing that's different about the bathroom is the presence of a cleaning cart. It's stocked with a bucket of hot soapy water, mops, a toilet scrubber, Vim, other cleaning chemicals, gloves, sponges, etc., and a giant garbage bag hangs at its edge. Pretty damn easy to put two and two together.

"So much for Ce'Nedra, you're straight-up turning me into Cinderella." I resist the urge to shake my finger at Elsie, grabbing one of the sponges instead and dipping it into the bucket. The water's so hot that it burns my fingertips. "I already know how to clean. How is doing the janitor's job for him going to help me live on my own?"

"Uh, uh, uh, first of all you need to put on gloves." Elsie slides a pair on, stretching them and then letting them go so they snap against her wrist for extra emphasis. "Secondly, everybody cleans. Unless you're making enough money to employ your own janitor, that is. And cleaning a bathroom is harder than it looks. I assume you'll have one of those in the home that you live in after here."

"Assuming makes an ass out of you and me." Wow, I'm on a wordplay roll. "But yes, my house has bathrooms in it. I just thought we'd be doing something cooler than this, I guess." The plastic gloves flop loosely on my hands. Better than nothing, though, especially with bleach.

Elsie starts picking up the Q-tips and tissues on the counter. I follow her lead, but leave the sink with its Sharon hair for her.

"After these basics we'll move on to more exciting things like budgeting and home repair."

"Uh, you mean home repair as in hammering? Those are banging noises."

"You'll be the one making them."

I think about that for a moment. Pretend to concentrate hard on wiping up spilled liquid liner. Exposure therapy around construction sites has forced me to develop a tolerance for banging noises. While it still bothers the shit out of me, I'm able to stand next to construction for up to a minute without even knocking my knuckles to my forehead. Realizing I could be the one in control of the banging, able to stop whenever I want, gives me a dizzying rush of ... what's this strange, heart-beating-fast-but-with-more-than-just-terror feeling? Empowerment? Yes, empowerment. Scary? Hell yes. A challenge? Duh. Exciting? Maybe? And if it gets too excruciating, I can stop. "I guess I could make a bookshelf," I say, "but then I also want driving lessons. Or for you to help me with my resumé."

We've moved on to scrubbing the sink and counter with sponges. Elsie flicks soapy bubbles at me. "I'll do you one better. You know that long hallway we pass in the administrative building to get to Dr. Grant's office?"

"Yeah."

"It leads to an empty unit where we used to have a day patient program. Now, you're not quite independent enough for day patient, but Dr. Grant and I have been discussing it, and we think you're ready

A Drop in the Ocean   281

for a halfway step. Since none exist, we're hoping to put one together with what we have. A unit with minimal staff supervision, where you'd do your own cooking and cleaning and get to go on longer passes."

My heart hammers with hope. "Like spending weekends at home?"

Elsie nods as she squirts Windex on the mirror with her left hand. "We'd work up to that. First, we'd get you that job you're so dead set on, so you might be off unit in the evenings for your shifts."

The girl reflected in the mirror wipes a shine onto it with a smile that beams equally bright. Her dimples pop out as she cheers. "Don't worry, Elsie, as soon as I land that job at Chapters, I'll get you a friends and family discount."

Elsie chuckles. "You better." Her voice echoes, bouncing off the tiled walls of the shower as she spritzes them with Vim, explaining how life on the new unit would work. It would be a progression, from a trial run with two staff and still getting cafeteria food brought up to just one staff member and a weekly food and outing fund. Each week I'd have to work out a meal and activity plan that staff would approve. Budget for both, then go grocery shopping for what I need.

"Would I have to clean this hard-core every day?" I ask her. We're busting our asses, starting to sweat with the effort of scrubbing soap scum off the tile grout.

"Twice a week you'd do a comprehensive clean of the entire unit, which would include things like mopping the floors and taking out the garbage. Some things, like wiping up any makeup spills or food messes and loading and unloading the dishwasher, you'd do daily."

"What about the toilet?" Despite knowing that I have gloves on, I still cringe as I lift up the lid and the seat. Some of the fluff under the seat is dust and some of it is pubes and specks of pee. Right where the water ends, there's a ring of yellow-brown that stains the bottom of the bowl too. Acid reflux burns up my throat as I clamp my lips closed on a gag.

"Every day," Elsie says, no mercy in the firmness of her voice. She pours vinegar in the bowl and sprinkles a generous helping of baking soda, which fizzes in the filthy water.

I sigh, even though it's the answer I expected. "Shit."

"Literally."

It's amazing how well the baking soda works after we give it a few minutes before attacking the stain with the toilet scrubber.

"Would you believe this is the first time I've ever used one of these things?" I ask her, perfectionism kicking in as I scrape away the stain until the bowl gleams white.

"Okay, that's good enough." She scoots me away from toilet, closing the seat and the lid with a clank. The banging noise makes me want to wince, but I don't. "Soon you'll be a pro at this, if the plan gets approved."

And that's the thing, *if* ... Even though Dr. Grant, my parents, and the rest of my treatment team are down to let me try this new unit thing out, they still have to present the idea to the Residency higher-ups, who won't even let psychiatrists and patients exchange gifts. The muckety-mucks, as Elsie calls them, are a board of directors who will have to be okay with the cost of running a new mini unit. The last thing Elsie and I do is mop the floor—a piece of cake after the grossness of the toilet. The whole time, she's warning me not to get my hopes up, because this is all pending approval. It's too late, though, I can't unhear what she's just told me. A brand-spanking-new unit all to myself. Minimal staff, a job, weekend passes home. Damn, my world just grew bigger than I could have hoped. The Mirenaissance is happening. It's happening!

CHAPTER TWENTY-SIX

*G*ung hei fat choy! Screw the Mirenaissance board meeting being postponed—Lunar New Year is legit. The wind strokes cool fingers through my hair and makes the lei si in Poh Poh's outstretched hand flap. The serpentine dragons on the bright-red envelope undulate in the seaside breeze.

"Just something small," she says as I grab the envelope, then enfold her in a gentle hug. As I tuck the lei si into the inner pocket of my purse, I open it and take a quick peek. Two neatly folded twenties. Nice. When Mom's driving, I'll find a way to sneak the money into her wallet to pay her back for our dim sum brunch. It's year of the pig, and that's exactly what we did, pig out on our favourite dishes at Pink Pearl. If I close my eyes and concentrate, I can still taste the buttery crust and rich egg custard of the dan tat we ordered for dessert. My memory of its sweetness is cut starkly by the brine and salt that whooshes up my nostrils. The ocean laps at a small rocky beach to our right, and joggers pass us on the field to our left. Out of reflex, I quicken my pace to catch up. Speedwalk for a few steps before realizing that Mom and Poh Poh are behind me now. With a deep, frustrated breath, I force myself to turn around and march back to my family.

Poh Poh holds on to Mom's arm, panting with the effort of trying to hobble along faster. Pushing her body because it took me so long to push my mind against my urge. Shame weighs down my head as I meet them on the path. I walk over to Poh Poh's right side and hold out my left elbow for her to hook on to. She smiles, nodding her thanks as her twig-like arm loops through mine. We three generations walk as one, matching each other's steps. Poh Poh in the middle, with Mom and I supporting her. It feels right. Not the OCD *right*, but something deeper. Truer. The two women who came from this one woman help her move across the Earth she ushered them onto.

"Mom," I say, "will you and Lawrence be at the board meeting that decides my fate?"

"Don't be so melodramatic, honey. Even if you don't get to move units, there are plenty of ways you can be more independent on Ward 2."

"What's this about moving units?" Poh Poh asks.

I fill her in on Elsie's vision for me, talk to her about the life skills I've been learning.

"It's taken you sixteen years to learn how to clean a toilet bowl?" She shakes her head in bewilderment. "I taught your mother that when she was half your age. And my mah mah had me cleaning every room in the house when I was four."

"Every room?" I ask. "Weren't there like, eleven of you?"

"Yes," Poh Poh says. "We'd be put in pairs. Me and your great auntie Joyce would do chores together like washing all of the windows or waxing and polishing the wood floors."

"Tell Mira about how you used to sleep," Mom says, raising her eyebrows and grinning.

"Head to toe," Poh Poh declares. "We sisters would alternate, three or four of us to a bed. One's head by the other's feet. From as early I can remember, I had Auntie Joyce's big toes in my face until I moved out."

I mentally rehash all the complaining I've done about the bed that I have to myself on Ward 2. Some more people pass us and I barely even register them, too busy asking about logistics. "How did you all fit on the bed? What if one of the aunties was a kicker or a blanket

A Drop in the Ocean 285

hogger? Who had it worse, the aunties at the edges who could fall off, or the one in the middle who got squished by the others?"

Our next slow steps take us past the park to where the path melds from dirt to sand. The ground sinks beneath our feet, and logs block our way. Poh Poh falters. Mom and I stop, waiting for her to regain her footing. We pause every few steps to plan our route through the natural obstacle course. A couple, hand in hand, balance and hop from one log to another. They leap ahead of us, continuing their game until they reach the edge of the water, where they stop to passionately kiss. I sigh, thinking of Nick. How his lips fit perfectly pressed against mine. How sometimes now I'll bum a puff of a joint or even a cigarette just to remember the way he tasted. Except the best part of tasting him was always him, not what he smoked.

"What's wrong?" Mom asks, concern creasing wrinkles on her brow where none normally exist. "Are you triggered? You can walk ahead of us if you want."

I shake my head. "It's not that so much as missing Nick. The last time I was at the beach was with him." My cheeks heat as I realize I'm talking about the boyfriend Poh Poh insists I'm too young to have.

Poh Poh pats my arm and squeezes it. "Your mother was telling me about this Nick of yours. I'm glad you're still together, he seems like a nice young man." Hold up, did Poh Poh just give me her blessing?! I resist my urge to fist pump and settle for squeezing her back. "He really is. But enough about Nick. What was Gung Gung like when you first went out? What kinds of dates did you go on?"

"Hmm." Poh Poh takes a moment to think. "That was so long ago. I'm pretty sure our first date was roller skating. I'd never gone before, so your gung gung teaching me how was a great excuse to hold hands."

"That's so G!"

Both Poh Poh and Mom look at me, puzzled. Shit, there's no way I'm telling them that G means gangster, they wouldn't get it. "Gentleman," I say. "Gung Gung was such a gentleman." To switch the focus, I ask, "Mom, you and Lawrence's first date was sushi, right?"

"Yes it was, a dinner date. And we talked for so long that by the time we went back to our cars, his was towed."

"Well, that takes the cake for most romantic parking misdemeanour. Did you guys kiss?"

Mom's magenta-glossed lips spread into a smirk. "No, we didn't kiss until our third date. Although I don't think that's any of your business."

"What about you, Poh Poh?" I've never asked her anything like this before, so I have no idea how she'll react. How far she'll let me in to discuss the other hers who aren't just my grandma, like the her who was a young lover.

She looks down, clears her throat with a modest ahem. "Back when I dated, we had chaperones. Couples rarely spent any time alone together." When she does look up, her eyes twinkle as they meet mine. "But if you must know, your gung gung was a good kisser."

Mom looks over at Poh Poh with playful shock. "Mum, how is this is the first time I'm hearing about this?"

Poh Poh shrugs. "Well, he was." That makes all three of us giggle.

Our stroll comes to a stop by one of the logs closest to the shoreline. Poh Poh sits on it while Mom hunts for shells. Meanwhile I'm yanking off my sneakers and socks, rolling up my jeans to my knees so I can go wading. The shock of the sea against my feet is deliciously cold. I step in farther, swaying in tandem with the waves, sighing as I listen to them crash against the shore and burst into so much froth and droplets on my legs. The part of me that's not submerged is blasted

A Drop in the Ocean

by a gust of wind that floods my nose with brine. The women who raised me are metres away, and I'll join them soon. After they drop me off, I'll go back to Ward 2 and finish the last few pages of my current journal by writing about today. Then, who knows how I'll fill the rest of the afternoon. But for now, for this one moment, I savour how it's just me and the ever-shifting sea.

I surrender to its sway. Bending down, turning my hands into cups, then spilling the ocean water in my upturned palms over my face. If my makeup runs, I can always put more on, plus my mascara is waterproof. The splash drenches me in radiant wetness. Donna lent me this book of Rumi poetry, and my favourite bit so far is this: "You are not a drop in the ocean; you are the entire ocean in a drop." As in, you are not a tiny part of existence within the whole, you are the whole. The bad (patricidal, Gollum pathetic), the good (empathic soul-magic goddess), and every degree of achingly human in between. All of it, just as you are.

Yes.

Yes, I am.

◆

Nick's Note

To Mira Meilin Anne Coralie Lung Kong Durand van Kraft,

I never know what to say in these things. By the time you
read this, it will be a few weeks or more since I went up
north. Being apart will be hard as hell. Just know I'm the
luckiest guy alive to have someone who cares for me the way
you do. Our lives are changing, not for the first time and not
for the last, but I will always love you. I love you the way I

see colours, the way the best bud always stinks, but you kiss
me anyway. God, I'll miss kissing you. And I'll keep missing you 'til the day your cold, trembly hands are back being
warmed up in mine. It'll happen sooner than you think.

That's right, I'm psychic 😊

EPILOGUE

The Mirenaissance starts with a bang after I take my morning meds. I pack up my shit in the suitcase that I came to Ward 1 with over eight months ago and a garbage bag full of the extra books, clothes, and makeup I've gotten since being on Ward 2. The garbage bag gives me hard-core déjà vu, except this time there's no dumpster diving as I move units.

I let Elsie carry the garbage bag for me, powering through my OCD guilt about being lazy as I wheel my suitcase down the girls' wing and through the dining room area all the way to the door. The staff give me fist bumps and high-fives. They'll all be rotating shifts in pairs, and then as my one-on-ones, so it's not like a huge deal. The other kids, though, my fellow locked-up inmates, I won't be living with anymore. Franco gives me a goodbye pat on the back. Jorge, who's getting discharged two weeks from now, clasps me in a tight hug. Sharon's hug is even tighter; she straight-up lifts me in the air for a second, squeezing the breath out of me.

"Don't worry, you can be the first one to visit me on Ward 4," I say, wiping a tear off her plump cheek.

Then it's out of the door and across the parking lot, my suitcase bumping and rattling against the uneven pavement. In the chilly administrative building, we run into Dr. Grant. He comes out of his office as we pass it, accompanying us the rest of the way to the old day patient ward, now all mine. We stop at the door, which isn't steel bolted, so Elsie can sort through the keys on her carabiner to find the right one.

Ward 4 is small, which makes sense. All of the windows are bare, no chicken wire obscuring their views. Its nurses' station also serves as the shift change and staff room. The dining room table has actual chairs, six, instead of the long banquet benches that seat fourteen on Ward 2. That means I could throw a dinner party one day like a fucking adult. There's a living room with only one couch, but it's a nice couch, plush green with soft cushions that I sink into as I test it out. The TV sits on a stand with an Xbox console hooked up underneath it. I touch it just because I can. Next to the living room is the kitchen. It's basically the same as Ward 2's kitchen, with all the equipment I need to keep learning how to cook, except everything's shrunken in half. The bathroom's shrunken the same way. Not a problem, since I won't have to share it.

Lastly, there's my bedroom, which used to be Ward 4's Quiet Room. It's also smaller than my old room, but only by a bit. Since this isn't a designated patient's room, there's no bed frame built into it. Instead, the single mattress has been set up on a box spring that Elsie brought from her own home. "I just couldn't bear the thought of you sleeping on a mattress on the floor," she whispers in my ear, as I give her a thank-you hug. She sets my garbage bag down gently by the dresser, then leaves me to get settled in and unpack. The first things I get out are my new journal and a gel pen.

The blank, black lines on the cream page unfurl millimetres below the nib of my pen. Keep flowing across all however many hundred or so pages there are in this book. Each line crackles with fresh promise, the infinite potential of the new. What will I fill them with? Ranting? Profundity? Poems? CBT homework? Grocery lists? Who knows? I guess it depends on what life throws my way. And life depends on what I make of it. I'm the writer here, I give it meaning, choose whether to build upon the beauty or the pain. Word by word, moment by moment, whatever happens next, I hope I write it into art.

Author's Note

Hello again, dear reader,

Mira isn't me anymore, but at sixteen, I was her. All her intersectionalities and character traits, including her obsessions, compulsions, depression, and anorexia were my adolescent OCD symptoms and comorbidities. Likewise, her journey in psychiatric care is a condensed version of my own. Other neurodiverse characters like Nick, Sweets, Jorge, and Sharon are fictionalized versions of wardmates I lived with during my six years of in-patient treatment. And yet, my depictions of OCD and other psychiatric conditions are idiosyncratic portrayals that may be unlike your own lived experience and/or knowledge. There are as many versions of mental health as there are individual minds. I have aimed to showcase nuance and dimensionality by spending time with characters at their best and worst, holding space for all that they are.

This novel captures a period of my life that would have resulted in its end, had I not been in the right place to meet the right people at the right time. And that's the thing, timing, because no matter how many resources are available to you, help isn't helpful until you are ready for it. Nonconsensual psychiatric treatment can often lead to trauma. Due to privilege, advocacy, and pure luck, mine ended when I finally met health care professionals who earned my respect and trust. It shouldn't be this way; safe, adequate mental health care is a universal human right, one covered by the Canada Health Act. At present, far too many people fall through the cracks. That's why I beg you to reach out for help if you need it, no matter what age you are.

I say no matter what age you are because mental health disorders are lifelong and require dedicated lifelong care. Despite ableist narratives in popular media, neurodivergence cannot be "fixed," and realistic treatment measures for most mental illnesses involve treating relapse as an expectation, not an exception. This part of your life (or a loved one's life) is not over just because you are no longer receiving in-patient treatment or experiencing symptoms. Maintenance is always necessary. It's infinitely better to have a safety net and never use it than to not have one when it's too late. That's what happened to my fiancé, the man Nick is based on. When he most needed help, he asked numerous doctors and programs for support but was put on months-long, even years-long wait-lists. It took him only seconds to end his life.

If you are experiencing suicidal ideation, call or text 988 at any time to reach the Suicide Crisis Helpline in Canada or the 988 Suicide & Crisis Lifeline in the US. Visit 988.ca (Canada) or 988lifeline.org (US) for more information.

If you are a youth in Canada, the Kids Help Phone can also support you. Call 1-800-668-6868 for 24-7 care or text CONNECT to 686868. Learn more at kidshelpphone.ca. If you are a youth in the US, call Kids in Crisis at 203-661-1911 or visit kidsincrisis.org.

Take good care,
Léa ☆♡☆

Acknowledgments

I am indebted to the hən̓q̓əmin̓əm̓- and Sḵwx̱wú7mesh-speaking peoples whose land I live and write on.

Wholehearted thanks to my editor, Catharine Chen. Your eye for detail and care in preserving Mira's voice as we deliberated word choices alchemized a third draft into a thoroughly polished publishable novel. Thank you to every member of Arsenal Pulp Press, including publishers Brian Lam and Robert Ballantyne, book designer Jazmin Welch for the amazing cover art, publicist Cynara Geissler, JC Cham, and Erin Chan. Thanks, as well, to meticulous proofreader Alison Strobel.

A joyous, giant thank you to my incredible agent, Ali McDonald, and to Darren Groth for generously introducing us.

For their professional expertise and heartwarming kindness, I offer my gratitude to Indigenous sensitivity reader Jenn Ashton and US-based sensitivity reader Grecia Magdaleno.

While the earliest versions of *A Drop in the Ocean* are journal entries I would rather burn than share, I owe particular thanks to JJ Lee, my non-fiction mentor at the Writer's Studio (TWS) in 2020. JJ, you saw the seed of potential within my short story and said, "This could be a novel." You've been with me ever since.

I am immensely grateful to my TWS 2020 speculative and YA fiction mentor, Claudia Casper, and to my cohort members: Danica Longair, Susan Taite, Erin Pettit, Jack Murphy, Emily Louise Chan, Stephanie Charette, Clare McNamee-Annett, Rob Weber, and Sofia Pezzente. Your thoughtful critiques and enthusiasm were crucially motivating.

Utmost thanks to my thesis supervisor, a.k.a. novel midwife, Annabel Lyon, and my second reader, Nancy Lee. Your enduring support, craft expertise, and faith in this story empowered me throughout every stage. From scene planning to developmental edits to sentence-level finessing to your exquisite blurbs, learning from you was as inspiring as it was humbling. Heartfelt gratitude as well to Amber Dawn for encouraging me to speak my truth.

Many appreciative hugs to dear friends who have served as beta readers, including Cecily Downs, Chelsey Anderson, Lenore Rattray, Jolène Savoie-Day, Michelle Willms, Cid V Brunet, Jasmine Ruff, Hailey Glennon, Avery Dow-Kenny, and Madelaine Longman. Your insights and advice helped transform this vision into a reality.

I am deeply grateful for the endorsements I received from Tanya Boteju and Susin Nielsen, both authors whose work I adore.

I also want to acknowledge the financial support provided to me by the Canada Council for the Arts.

A giant thank you to patients, like Angelika Ritchie, and staff, like Leslie Middleton, Dr. Mathias, and Crystal Ireland, of the Maples Adolescent Treatment Centre during 2006 to 2008.

Immeasurable thanks to my family, both found—like Sworn Sister Yilin Wang and Soul Siblings Alex Wetter, Miranda, Ren, Fawn, and Naia Neptune—and blood—like my mom, Brenda; and stepdad, Peter van Engelen; my French Taranto family; and my Baggaley in-laws.

Lastly, gratitude beyond words to those who have passed: Shaun Baggaley, Poh Poh, and Gung Gung.

Photo credit: Maria Koehn

LÉA TARANTO is a disabled Chinese Jewish Canadian writer who lives with OCD and comorbid disorders. An MFA graduate of the University of British Columbia, alum of the Writer's Studio at Simon Fraser University, and member of PRISM *international*'s poetry board, she resides on traditional, unceded Halkomelem and Squamish territories in BC. Her work has been published in the anthology *Upon a Midnight Clear: More Christmas Epiphanies* and in various Canadian literary journals. *A Drop in the Ocean* is her debut novel.

Find Léa online at her website, *leataranto.com*, or on Instagram *@leatarantowrites*.